They Shall Run and Not Be Weary

*The Story of an Eighteenth-Century
German Family's Voyage to the New Land*

KATHERINE
ALTHOFF
ALEXANDER

They Shall Run and Not Be Weary
by Katherine Althoff Alexander

Copyright © 2023
All rights reserved.

This is a work of fiction based on the lives of many immigrants to Philadelphia in 1742 along with certain historical figures and events of the time. Any resemblance to actual persons, living or dead, or to actual places or events of the time, are the product of the author's imagination or are used fictitiously.

Library of Congress Control Number: 2023947329
International Standard Book Number: 978-1-60126-881-5

Masthof Press
219 Mill Road | Morgantown, PA 19543-9516
www.Masthof.com

But they that wait upon the Lord
shall renew their strength;
they shall mount up with wings as eagles;
they shall run and not be weary;
and they shall walk and not faint.

ISAIAH 40:31

Table of Contents

Introduction

They Shall Run and Not Be Weary is the story of my 8th great-grand family who left the small village of Massenbach in the State of Wurttemburg to migrate to Philadelphia in the British Colony of North America. They were "German speaking" with their own dialect, culture, and customs. The Germany we know today had not yet been created out of the many small and large kingdoms, states, and duchys that would come together in 1871 to form the German Empire.

The family most likely left in 1742 because they were poor. The father, Jacob, had died in 1735, leaving his family to fend for themselves with the help of the church, village, friends, and relatives. But the town itself, technically owned by a baron, was impoverished, probably with not enough land to feed its population. The peasants of the village, some most likely free and others serfs, farmed narrow strips of land that they leased from their lord. These strips had been divided again and again through different forms of inheritance so that peasants could not grow enough food to keep the wolf away from the door. The peasants, depending on their status, owed the lord so many workdays each year for the privilege of living in the lord's domain. Other areas had been set aside for communal grazing. Most of their protein would have come from the swine they farmed and slaughtered in the fall along with the eggs produced by their chickens. But by early spring, the root cellar might have been almost empty, and the pork preserved for the winter had all but disappeared. The wheat may have been planted, but it would take months for it to grow.

But all the rest in and of the village confines—firewood, game in the forest, fish in the lake, even the ducks on the pond—would have belonged to the lord and could only be taken with his permission. In most areas, peasants could not cut trees, but only use the fallen timber. Villagers, therefore, lived a life of want, with a modest amount to eat, little firewood to keep them warm, and no hope of ever making their lives different. Immigration within Europe or across the Atlantic was the only solution.

The village council, under the direction of the lord's men, ruled over the people of the village with an iron fist. While members of the community participated in some decisions, strict rules and norms abounded. Peasants were required to attend church or face a consequence. Women with sharp tongues were punished. A young man could not marry until he could show he had the resources to support a family, and some never did. Premarital sex was forbidden with many punishments for breaking the rules. A peasant could not just up and move to the next village; he had to have permission from the lord to leave. Nor could someone move into the community without showing he would not be a drain on the village resources.

And so, the Fridberg family found themselves facing the daunting task of traveling up the rivers of the Rhine Valley to Rotterdam in the Netherlands, across the English Channel to Deal in England, and then sailing over the Atlantic Ocean to Philadelphia.

Riding the boats on the rivers and sleeping on the banks would have been extremely uncomfortable. But the trip across the ocean to their new home would have been terrible beyond imagination. Passengers were purposely packed into ships, which had brought trade goods to Europe and were then retrofitted as passenger vessels. The food they received was of poor quality, with little variety or nutritional value. Water for the trip was often putrid and downright undrinkable. Often the food and water would be gone or greatly diminished before the voyage ended.

Seasickness plagued everyone, even to the point of death for some passengers, especially children. Other diseases transported from the mainland took their toll. Mice and rats were everywhere, along with lice and other vermin. Boredom filled their days as they simply tried to stay alive until the voyage was over.

But life went on as they bobbed along to the coast of North America. People died, babies were born, and they experienced hunger and thirst just as they would have at home. Interestingly, their chance of survival was slightly higher if they emigrated than if they had stayed home. Simply by the fact that I exist, we do know they reached Philadelphia safely.

This book is based on facts, known traditions, and the contemporary history of the times. Much information on the Fridberg family is true, but physical characteristics, personalities, and the stories that happened along the way are fiction. All of what is known about them in their village comes from their births, death, marriages, and other information. But most important for our story, one night in the spring of 1742, while the Pastor sat sipping his wine in the candlelight and recording the day's events, he wrote, "The widow Fridbergen has gone to the New Land with her children." Little did he imagine that two hundred and eighty years later, this widow's 8th great-granddaughter, would wonder, as she sat sipping tea by the light of her computer, whatever happened to this family. She vowed to find out.

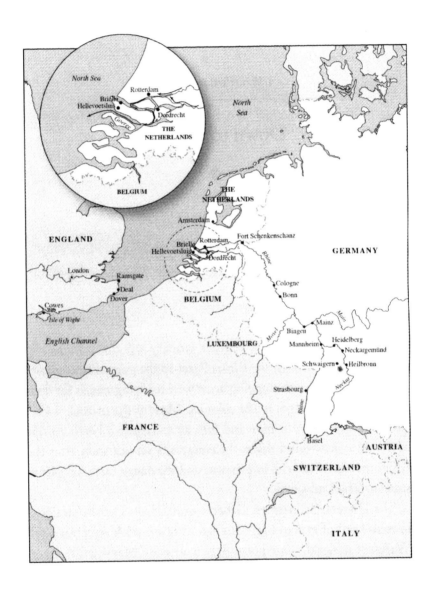

Main Characters

FAMILY

Maria Barbara Fridberg (41) – "Barbara" .... Main character

Ludwig Jacob Fridberg (19) – "Ludwig" .... Barbara's son

Bernhardina Dorothea Fridberg (15) – "Thea" .... Barbara's daughter

Carlina Fridberg (10) – "Carlie" .... Barbara's daughter

Christina Catharina Fridberg (6) – "Christina" .... Barbara's daughter

FRIENDS AND OTHERS

Johan Phillip Stephen Poppenmeier (21) – "Stephen" .... Co-traveler

Johannes Ludwig Schmaltzhafft (22) – "Hans" .... Co-traveler

Jurg Adam Muller (24) – "Adam" .... Co-traveler

Catharina Christina Stocker (20) – "Kitty" .... Adam's wife

Gabriel Kohler (27) – "Gabriel" .... Co-traveler

Anna Elisabetha Poppenmeier (25) – "Lisabeth" .... Gabriel's wife
and Stephen's sister

Anna Margaretha Kohler (1) – "Margaretha" .... Gabriel &
Elisabetha's daughter

Catharina Barbara Kohler (4) – "Barbara" .... Gabriel & Elisabetha's
daughter

*Johannes Hauck (51) – "Jan" .... Guest house owner

*Marta Hauck (52) – "Marta" .... Jan's wife

*Herr Franken (55) .... Reader onboard ship

Capt. George North (42) – "Capt. North" .... Master of Ship

*Gustav Merner (49) – "Gustav" .... Landlord in Philadelphia

*Maria Merner (47) – "Maria" .... Gustav's wife

Fictional Characters

CHAPTER 1

The Decision

Tuesday, 27 March 1742
The Village of Massenbach in the State of Wurttemberg
The Holy Roman Empire

Maria Barbara walked slowly toward Jacob's grave in the northeast corner of the small graveyard behind the church, holding back tears she knew would soon have their way. The ancient cemetery was filled with residents of Massenbach going back many hundreds of years. It reeked of the poverty and scarcity its village now possessed—scrubby grass, sunken graves, wilted bushes, and a twisted, cherry tree right in the middle that was fighting a losing battle to stay alive.

Misshapen wooden crosses of all description dotted the small landscape, some made of twigs lashed together, while others had been crafted to a higher quality. The only dots of color were bouquets of wildflowers, picked with love, and placed where they were needed to comfort a sorrowful heart.

The wooden cross Barbara had placed on Jacob's grave seven years before was still standing, although it seemed to list a bit to the right. The elements had almost destroyed the polished finish she had applied to the beautiful sticks of cherry wood with lard strained through a piece of linen. But, yes, it was still standing.

Kneeling down beside her husband's resting place, Barbara placed her hand softly on the top of tufts of new spring grass that grew sparingly in the depleted soil. She knew he lay below, his bones giving themselves to the soil of eternity. But his soul, the real Jacob, was far away in heaven, waiting for her and their five children to join him. She glanced over at the graves of Wilhelm and Carlina who had already passed into their father's arms. But she knew none of the bodies of the rest of the family, save one, would ever rest beside his in Massenbach.

Barbara had told him the family was going to the New Land, but not when. And now she had come to tell him it would be next week. On Sunday.

The previous November, the family had gone to the neighboring town of Schwaigern to declare their intent to emigrate to America in the early spring. Both Barbara and their son, Ludwig, applied for passports, while their three daughters presented birth certificates to show their ages. The passports declared the mother and son were in good health and showed their hometown was Massenbach. If they had been serfs, they would have had to pay another fee to gain their freedom, but the Fridbergs were free and would not have to bear the high costs of manumission. But at any rate, they intended to leave by the dark of night, not paying any of the fees they owed.

"We are going away on Sunday," she finally said, still attempting to staunch her tears. "We are going to the New Land, to Philadelphia in America, and we will not be coming back."

At this, she gave in to her sobs, knowing his family would be leaving Jacob forever.

The Fridbergs were not desperately poor, but nearly. The cold, the hunger, the lack of any comfort beyond lying in a field of warm clover on a sunny, summer day sapped each one of them of their strength and resilience. The backbreaking work Ludwig provided to Baron von Massenbach for the mere privilege of existing in this pathetic village had left him depleted. No opportunities existed for any of Jacob's children, not a trade for Ludwig or prosperous husbands for the four girls. Nothing beckoned to them from a distance to take their minds off their misery.

Their strength resided in their family, which Barbara knew could fall apart at any moment. Jacob's death had tried to break them once before, but had failed miserably. But by the grace of God, the six of them were still together, bound in His love, all still alive, at least as far as this day had come.

Fear gripped her, as it did almost every day since she and Ludwig had made the decision to emigrate. Would their hopes for success blossom like a mountain flower in the sunshine, or their downfall come from a black destitution they could never have imagined?

Barbara's resolve to leave their home waffled back and forth every few days, putting her in a constant state of flux. She tried to keep her feelings from Ludwig, but, just like his poppa, he often knew what she was thinking. On the other hand, Ludwig had been ready to leave Massenbach behind and climb on the next boat to North America as soon as he heard what the agent in Schwaigern had said.

"Land so cheap it is almost like stealing. Cherries grow to the size of pumpkins. Beautiful, plump women, ripe for the plucking." Ludwig wanted it all.

He often thought how hard life was here, so devoid of any wealth the crows did not even bother to peck at it. He knew he would not be able to marry here for a long time, if ever. Owning no land, nor having citizenship in the the village, nor possessing the assets to learn a trade, he was trapped in a life of want too extreme to support a family. The Village Council would never allow him to marry. His greatest fear was that he would die never knowing the touch of a woman's hand, which was only slightly worse than fathering a child out of wedlock.

Barbara soon left the dead behind and returned to the living. She trudged toward the small church, which had been a part of her life since she was born. Her baptism was recorded in the St. Georg's Lutheran Church Book:

> 8 June 1701, Maria Barbara, Parents: Johann Jacob Nellinger, schoolmaster, and his wife, Maria Sybilla. Witnesses: Maria Barbara von Schlegel, Jacob Bixeler and his wife Maria Ursula

Barbara felt drawn to the church, wanting to say goodbye as if it were an old friend. She walked around to the side where the ivy-covered wall held a thick, weathered, oak door. Tucked among the greenery to its right was a plaque that announced the door had been placed there in the year 1520.

Years before, Pastor Klein who served the church when she was a girl told her their church started as a small, wooden chapel, even before 1520. It was consecrated to St. Georg and still bore his name. The building had been added onto, taken away from, and otherwise modified into a structure of wood, stone, and plaster, which set one to thinking of the past.

A tower had once stood on the corner above the choir, where another plaque indicated it had been struck by lightning in 1704, only forty years before. Barbara shivered to think of the noise and destruction she had heard, but barely remembered. Splintering wood, falling timbers, and the acrid smell of smoke promised to destroy her beloved church. But they did not.

The church had been founded by the ancestors of the von Niepperg family. Baron von Niepperg and his wife Helena Maria were names every Massenbach school child knew by heart. Barbara liked to sit as near as she could to the flat, inscribed tombstone embedded in the floor covering the Baroness' grave, and imagine what kind of woman she had been.

The von Massenbach family eventually took over ownership of the fiefdom and, of course, sponsorship of the church. Their grave slabs and monuments were still scattered throughout the sanctuary with figures wearing odd costumes and suits of armor. She thought again how hard life must have been for people during those difficult times in the distant past.

She had asked to speak with her present cleric, Pastor Kimmel at noon today and hoped he would not be late. The bell above her had just rung twelve times.

Barbara entered the church and walked over the cracked flagstones until she reached the line of three large benches sitting in front of the altar. These, of course, were there for the few wealthy families in Massenbach. She usually sat or stood in the nave along with the other peasants, but today she sat down on the very first bench.

Baron von Massenbach and his family occupied a small room, separated from the nave by a screen of thin, loosely woven, wooden slats, stained a beautiful reddish-brown color. There they would have their privacy, away from the prying eyes of the congregation. Everyone knew they were there, but no one could easily see them.

Barbara loved her church, loved to smell the sweat of hardworking men, the sourness of nursing mothers, the odor of dung tracked in by those who worshiped here. For her, this was the smell of salvation.

The lower portion of the walls was faced with stones dug from the fields surrounding the village. The steep, pitched roof composed of wooden beams had turned black from the smoke of a thousand tallow candles. Giant hand-hewn beams passed overhead from the top of one wall to the other.

Threadbare cloths, which changed color according to the church season, covered the simple altar. Barbara's favorite was purple, designating Lent, which lead to the resurrection of her Savior. A small, metal cross stood in the middle of the altar; it had once been gold, she was told, but that had worn off to reveal a brass ornament, splotched with green shadows.

The space between the stones and rafters had been plastered but was now showing its age. The grey plaster was slowly disintegrating and falling in pieces onto the floor or simply dissolving into the air.

Long ago, someone with remarkable skill had painted scenes on the plaster to remind congregants of their heaven to come. Faded paintings covered the walls, left over from the time before Herr Luther when everyone, except the Jews, were of the same religion. Angels with short, curly, golden hair flapped their silver wings above heaven's residents who were plump, well-dressed, and eager to begin

eternity. Some Bible stories were also depicted, reminding those below of the dangers of gluttony or greed. Part of the plaster on the
wall halfway down the nave had almost disappeared, but one could
still make out the den of Daniel as he walked through the door, un-
harmed by kittenish lions.

To the right of the altar stood the limestone baptismal font,
representing the love of God and the redemption promised to those
who were baptized. Both she and Jacob, along with their seven children, had been christened there, the Pastor dipping his hand in the
sacred water and sprinkling it over the head of Massenbach's newest
resident.

The large pulpit stood on the left, also made of stone, with
steps leading up to the platform where the priest delivered his mes-
sage. Barbara enjoyed these sermons, full of stories from the Bible
and instructions for how to live a saintly life so heaven would be just
beyond death's doorstep.

The stone of both was a natural, reddish-brown color, attracting her by its warmth. She hoped heaven would be filled with soft
colors like these along with the gold she knew would surely be there.

And what a wonderful day her confirmation had been! Standing right there on those steps in front of the altar, she became a mem-
ber of the Lutheran Church. Her parents glowed with pride along
with the other families of her catechism classmates. She was fourteen, then, passing from girlhood into the realm of a woman, wife
and mother. Not right away, of course, but starting down the path
she would walk to attain the maturity needed for these holy roles.

Most of the girls had a new skirt, or at least a freshly made-over
one, and the boys, new shirts. Her skirt was made of the softest linen,
dyed a dark blue, pleated over a new petticoat, with a soft green vest
embroidered with colorful mountain flowers. Barbara had improved
her embroidery skills on this vest, watching her mother slowly work
the complicated stitches and insisting from time to time that Barbara
try her hand at it.

The girls wore their braids fastened on top of their heads. Even though their new hairstyles were covered by white caps tied under their chins, everyone could see that childish braids no longer fell down either side of their faces and necks.

Barbara wished she had been given a woolen jacket like her mother's for the occasion, but that was not to be. Her mother's was made of the softest, red wool Barbara had ever felt, fitted down her arms to below her elbows and tailored to rest on the fullness of her hips. Thin pieces of cloth formed three sets of ties, which could be joined together to make the jacket even warmer.

Barbara's family was not as poor as others in the village, and, so, she had had newly shod shoes as well. Even though her father was only a schoolmaster, the family could provide more as she was the only child. The time had passed for her mother to have any more children, but her parents bore their barrenness with stoic resignation.

Now, how did that go, she wondered silently, trying to remember the first line of the verse she had recited at her confirmation. She was surprised she could not remember it right away, considering what an important part it had played in her life. Before her confirmation, she had practiced constantly, hoping she would not be one of the poor, unfortunate students who forgot her piece. Pastor Klein would have to break in and coach the poor child through her recitation, causing embarrassment and shame to herself and her entire family. Thankfully, Barbara had not been one of them.

"Now, they that look upon the Lord," she recited to herself. *No, that is not right.* "Now they that obey…" *No, not that word either.* "But they that wait upon the Lord…" *Yes, that was it.* "But they that wait upon the Lord shall renew their strength; they shall rise up with wings as eagles; they shall run and not be worried; they shall walk and not faint."

And then, knowing she had recited her piece flawlessly in front of the entire congregation, she proclaimed, "Isaiah 40:31." She thought she may have said that part a little too loud, but her mother assured her it had been perfect. Just perfect. Her father had smiled at her with rare acceptance, filling her with more joy than she could have ever expressed. Just perfect.

And then, in that very place, she became the wife of Johann Jacob Fridberg after the worship service on 24 November 1722. And that was truly the most wonderful day of her life.

————————

Barbara could hear Pastor Kimmel's slippers shuffling as he entered the church from the sacristy. He knew why Widow Fridberg had asked to see him. Noticing her belongings slowly appearing in the homes of his other parishioners, he had recognized the signs. He could not mistake the lovely pinewood box he had seen in Dewalt Konig's house yesterday, the one Dewalt helped Jacob make shortly before his marriage to Barbara.

The Fridberg cow was now tethered behind Frau Althoff's barn, right next to her own cow with the big, white spot on its rump. He suspected her cow was old and no longer gave milk, so she must have bought Barbara's. He wondered when Frau Althoff would be making the older beast into a nice stew or rouladen, thick with the perfectly seasoned gravy the women of his village made with exceptional skill. There was little in this life more important than a nice gravy.

That morning, he had seen Barbara's old cradle in another household. It had held all seven of her babies, at least for a short while. He thought her heart must have broken to give it up. Pastor Kimmel held his protruding belly under his loose-fitting robe as he sat down quietly and waited for her to speak.

She cleared her throat and began. "We are going away Sunday, Sunday night."

He had learned this through the village gossip, but only nodded to show he had heard her. Their nighttime departure confirmed his suspicions she was not moving to another village close by.

"I have come to ask for another set of baptismal certificates for my daughters and a reference for Ludwig. When we went to Schwaigern to get our passports last fall, the authorities insisted on keeping the certificates, although I do not know why."

And then she lowered her eyes, looked at the floor, and told him her second oldest daughter, Juliana, was not going with them. Pastor Kimmel had not known this.

"Baron and Baroness von Massenbach have been so good to her. The Baroness insists those who work in her home must be educated, peasant or not, and so reading and writing are encouraged. And, of course, now that Juliana does not have her family to support, she will be saving her money so she and Karl Schultz can get married as soon as he turns twenty." And to herself, "Hopefully, before Karl gets her with child."

At that moment, Barbara had a picture in her mind of Pastor Klein showing her the church's register book during one of her confirmation classes so many years before. It had recorded the baptisms, marriages, and burials of all the Protestants of the village for centuries. He told her he also recorded these sacraments for Catholics if he were asked.

She had seen for the first time the entries she had only heard of. Some births were recorded in the book either upside down or sideways on the line inscribed by the pastor. He recorded their little names and their mothers' names, and the fathers' too, if they were known. Spuria. The pastor wrote Spuria next to their names. Bastard.

Barbara did not know how those women could live with the shame. And to think their family members stood as witnesses. She did not know if she could ever go through that. Juliana was level headed, but Barbara worried about the temptation a young girl could be exposed to. She hoped God would watch over her, would watch over all of them.

"I will have the birth certificates ready in time for your departure," the pastor assured her, patting her in a friendly way on her shoulder.

———

Barbara was exceedingly grateful God had sent an unmarried man to take her husband's place as the village schoolmaster; he was willing to stay in a small room at the back of the church because he did not have a family. She and the children did not have to leave their home, which belonged to the church and served as the village schoolroom. He had only taken a small portion of the garden plot beside the church for himself, knowing the family needed to grow enough food to feed the six of them.

After the customary six-month mourning period, Barbara thought one of the village men might have taken an interest in her; after all, she had been only thirty-one with at least eight good years of childbearing left. But a timely marriage did not happen for her, nor the advantage of having someone to share the responsibilities of parenting.

CHAPTER 2

Making Ready

Four more days until they set out on their journey. So much to do. Barbara left the house that afternoon, taking the last of their unneeded belongings, hoping she could sell them for cash or barter for something else they needed.

Ludwig said he would stay at home to keep the fire going so the pot pie would cook evenly. Barbara imagined him sitting at the table, carving something incidental, like another spoon or a little doll for Christina. Odd jobs were scarce in Massenbach in the early spring, or at least the ones that would pay him anything, and he had spent a great deal of time lately at home.

As she entered the back door into her kitchen, she saw her son at the table, shaving pine chips of various forms onto the floor. He looked up and smiled at her, moving toward the broom to sweep up his small pile of shavings and toss them into the fire.

Ludwig knew supper would be a feast, unlike the meals they had had for the past several months. They were having chicken, a rare occurrence in their home. This time of year, greens had not yet begun to break through the earth, so the family would usually be left with only the leavings on the root cellar floor. Carrots had lost so much of their moisture they could almost be bent in half. Potatoes would be shriveled and soggy, sprouting gnarled fingers from their many eyes, but they were remarkably good at filling a belly.

All of the meat that was left, pickled, dried, or smoked, had been put away in the trunk to save for the trip. They usually had bread left from the last baking, even though it might be stale; it could be a while until they would have more. Their cow had been bred, but would calve and begin to give milk long after they left. And at any rate, Frau Althoff had taken theirs away Monday morning. Even so, he could imagine the creamy butter in all its yellowy goodness melding with the warm, fresh bread in his mouth.

But tonight they were having chicken, made into a pot pie with savory herbs. Knowing it was their old hen, Gretti, did not bother him in the least. His mother had filled the pie with carrots and potatoes, placing a latticework crust on top so the gravy would bubble through the spaces and not over the side. And their bread had been baked yesterday.

What a good boy, Barbara thought to herself. *So much like his father. So kind and strong.* She often wondered where she and her daughters would be if not for him. Probably living outside next to the city wall in Schwaigern, mired in the stench of the moat, begging for scraps from wealthy passersby.

Ludwig's blonde hair was growing darker such as a passing cloud darkens flaxen wheat drying in the field. His curls were gone, his long, straight hair pulled back with a ribbon now like the other boys in the village. Unlike his father, he was tall and thin, rippling sinew on a body that held no fat. Too thin, much like everyone else.

"Where are the girls?" she asked him.

"I think Christina must have fallen asleep upstairs. It it too quiet for her to be up there awake. Thea and Carlie are out some place, perhaps gone down to the river to look for those polished stones they like. I told them they could not take any with them on the ship, however; if they fell over the side they would sink much too quickly for anyone to save them."

With that, Ludwig grinned, but his mother shot him a glare hot enough to burn holes through his cheeks.

"I am only teasing, Momma."

"Well stop," Barbara demanded. "It is not funny. Could you go find the girls and wake up Christina? The pie will be ready soon."

After Ludwig sprinted out the back door, Barbara lifted the lid on her three-legged iron pot to check on the pie, as it spewed delicious smells into their darkening kitchen. It had been so long since they had had a decent meal.

Pastor Kimmel had finished the certificates and knew the best time to deliver them. He knew Barbara had not sold her last chicken and would not be taking it with her; he hoped he might be invited to dinner. Praying it would be covered with her smooth gravy and pastry top, he knocked on the side of the house, the door still open for the day.

"Ah, good afternoon, Pastor Kimmel," Barbara welcomed him. "Oh, come in. Please, come in," she said, putting the lid back on the pot and wiping her hands on her apron. "We are having chicken for dinner. Will you stay and eat with us?"

"Well, if you insist," he said." I have brought the certificates."

Barbara was relieved. She had been worried he might not have them done in time for the family's departure. "May I look at them?"

Barbara wiped her hands again on her apron and took the documents from the pastor's stubby, ink-stained fingers. She slowly opened one of the birth certificates; it was Dorothea's. She read to herself, "Baptized this ninth day of January in the year of our Lord, 1727, Bernhardina Dorothea, infant daughter of Johan Jacob Fridberg and his lawful wife, Maria Barbara Nellinger. Witnesses Herr Karl Ludwig, Baron von Massenbach, and his wife, Baroness Bernhardina Sophie. Pastor Augustus Kimmel, St. Georg's Lutheran Church, Massenbach, written this twenty-ninth day of March, AD one-thousand, seven-hundred, and forty-two."

Barbara smiled and nodded to Pastor Kimmel. Then, she opened a letter that stated: This letter will introduce Maria Barbara Nellinger Fridberg, widow of Johan Jacob Fridberg, late of Massenbach. She is a God-fearing woman who has raised her children in the love of Jesus Christ and the heart of God. I recommend her to those who may wish to admit her to their house of worship. She is a hard worker and willing to follow authority with just respect. Pastor Augustus Kimmel, St. Georg's Lutheran Church, Massenbach written this twenty-ninth day of March, AD one-thousand, seven-hundred and forty-two.

Barbara did not know this, but Pastor Kimmel had written on the last page of the church book, "The Widow Fridbergen has left for the New Land with her children." He prayed for their successful trip and relief from all the possible trials along the way.

Barbara smiled again and said, "Thank you, Pastor Kimmel." She felt an inward sensation of satisfaction, but had to hold her breath to keep from weeping.

"Well, I think this pie is almost done," she said as she stood up and called out the back door, "children, we are about to eat. And Pastor Kimmel is joining us."

Ludwig and his three sisters looked at each other and rolled their eyes. They knew they had to be on their best behavior when the Pastor came to dinner. He always ate a lot, and they worried they would not get their share. And this mattered even more because they were having chicken. But the bird had been a plump one.

Pastor Kimmel was filled with gratitude as he wedged his belly in close to the table and inhaled another lungful of the delicious smell. He smiled and handed his plate, the guest plate, the only one they owned, to his hostess. The cook at the palace had given it to Juliana; no one there would eat on a plate with a crack that big in it. As he put the first bite of food into his mouth, he could feel the spirit of warmth and happiness enter his hungry body. He rarely had anything to eat at home that was this delicious. And here was Widow Fridbergen with enough chicken to feed the multitudes. He did not hold back.

As Barbara was falling asleep that night, she suddenly came awake with a start. The word "weary" kept calling to her, like a nagging child pulling on her apron strings. Yes, she knew she was weary—weary of want, weary of fear, weary of waiting. But that would soon be remedied. She had worked all day until weariness overtook her, body and soul.

Yes," she cried sitting bolt upright. "...you shall run and not be weary, not be worried...you shall run and not be weary; you shall walk and not faint." And with that small, but important detail taken care of, she drifted off to a land where no one was weary, or faint, or, for that matter, even tired. Perhaps heaven on earth could be a bit closer to her doorstep than she realized.

CHAPTER 3

Saturday Morning

Long before the sun came up, Barbara sat in front of the fireplace, balanced on the small three-legged stool her father had made her for a wedding gift. A glowing coal near the back of the ash-strewn fire was stubbornly refusing to ignite any of the tinder she had just placed crisscross over it. She hoped it would light; she did not want to wake Thea to fetch another ember from a neighbor. The girl needed her rest; tomorrow would be a long day.

Barbara tried to hold her head up and find some solace as the tinder finally caught. Two more days, and then they would leave. Right at that moment, she did not want to go anywhere. She wanted to stay in her cold, damp house, eating the leavings on the root cellar floor and little else. Not even an egg. She just wanted to watch her children grow and prepare for the grandchildren who would soon come. If Ludwig ever went off to war, she was certain he would be safe. His intelligence and strong body would see to that.

But what if someone became sick, or all their teeth fell out, or they had nothing to eat? What if someone died of hunger? What if she died? What would they all do then? The Baron was supposed to provide for them during times of hardship, but he rarely did.

Why had she ever let Ludwig talk her into this? Was it too late to change her mind now?

Hearing a strange sound, Barbara turned and saw Christina, her youngest, perched on another stool, rubbing her eyes with one hand and sucking her thumb on the other. She sniffled repeatedly as she did every morning, curling her little toes again and again around the thin, worn, bottom rung of the stool.

"Come closer to the fire. The house was cold last night, and I expect you are chilled through." Barbara had found the small stack of firewood Ludwig had brought in before he left last night. The fire was now crackling, with thin tongues of red and orange licking toward the top of the thin chimney.

Christina toddled over and sat on her mother's lap, her thumb still in her mouth. And then Barbara stated, as she had many times, "You are almost in your seventh year. It is time to hold your hand in your lap like the Baroness von Massenbach. Do you not want to be a great lady some day?"

Christina only bowed her head and hoped she could meet her mother's expectations. She was not sure if she did want to be a lady; she had never actually met one and did not even know what they were like. True, she knew the great ladies of the von Massenbach family had been witnesses to her baptism and those of her brothers and sisters, but she had never seen them. They all sat far away from her in church behind a screen on the other side of the choir. The nobility came into the church before her family and the other peasants, so Christina was never able to see any part of them except for the tops of their headdresses.

This morning, Christina looked like one of the little cherubs painted on the walls of the church with short, blonde ringlets framing her smiling face. She had her mother's light blue eyes and creamy complexion, which turned red at the first touch of the sun.

Christina was always thinking, trying to put everything in its rightful place. All she encountered had to make sense to her; if it did not, she would tear it apart and put it back together again until it did. Sometimes, what made sense to her, however, did not make sense to others.

As Christina tucked her cold, bare feet into the tops of her mother's woolen stockings, Barbara thought how thin Christina felt against her bosom. All her children were thin with the possible exception of Carlie, who she thought had big bones. The other children in the village were thin as well, which she knew came from a sore lack of food. Juliana once remarked that the Baron's children looked fuller than anyone she knew, but, they, of course, had everything they needed.

Christina put her arms backwards around her mother's neck and said, "Momma, tell me again where we are going. I tried to dream of the New Land last night like you told me, but all I could see was our village and Frau Althoff's old cow. You know, the one with the big, white spot on her rump."

Barbara pulled her youngest daughter closer, wrapped her shawl around them both, and, choking back tears, began to tell Christina the story of their future.

"Tomorrow night after supper, once the sun has started to go down, we will take the wagon, packed with all our belongings, and begin our journey. When we are well out of the village, we will lie down in the forest and sleep until the sun comes up."

"And will we each take a turn at pushing the wagon?" Christina asked for what must have been the hundredth time. She wanted to be sure she would not be left out of the important task of moving their cart.

"Oh, of course," Barbara replied, pretending to be surprised by such a question. "Ludwig will push most of the time, but we all have to help him by doing our share. Even you." Christina felt sufficiently important, although she did not know she would spend most of the short trip riding atop the items heaped in the wagon.

"After we wake up," Barbara continued, "we will walk for about two hours to Heilbronn and the River Neckar. A big boat will be waiting for us there. We will all get onto it and ride north to the city of Mannheim and then Mainz."

"How many will there be on the boat?"

"Well, you and me and Luddy. And your two sisters, Thea and

Carlie. And Stephen and Hans. And, as you know, Adam Muller and Gabriel Kohler will be coming with their wives and children. There will be thirteen of us in all. Hopefully, we will all fit on one boat so we can travel together to Mainz.

"After we leave Mainz, we will get on another barge on the Rhine River to Rotterdam, changing boats along the way when we get to Koln. Rotterdam, I have heard, is a big beautiful city with a thousand people and streets that are paved with smooth, shining, river stones."

"Are the streets really lined with gold like Ludwig told us?" Christina wondered aloud.

"I do not think they are lined with gold, but they are very clean and pretty," Barbara replied, wishing Ludwig would not confuse his sisters with his tall tales.

"Once we get there, we will find a place to stay while Ludwig looks for a big ship to take us all the way across the ocean to the New Land. After a few days in Rotterdam, we will board the ship and sail to England, and then Philadelphia.

"When the weather is sunny, we will sit on the top deck of the ship singing songs and watching the men sail the ship. And, of course, working on your lessons. When the rains come, we will go down to the bottom of the ship where we sleep and take long naps and tell stories quietly to each other. Then after a month or so, a sailor man on the ship will call out, 'There is Philadelphia!' and we will sail up another river to our new home. As soon as we get there, Luddy will find us another place to live, hopefully a house we can have all to ourselves."

"And will the house be big?" Christina wondered out loud. "I want a big house, with lots of room to play."

"We will have to see. But now we have to start packing. And I am counting on you to help."

"Oh, I will," Christina grinned. "I will go put on my clothes right now, and then we can start."

"And tell Thea and Carlie to get up and get dressed. We have a lot to do today."

Thea was the first to come down from the bedroom upstairs the children all shared. She seemed to float down the steep stairway with the beauty and grace of a princess. Barbara considered her the most attractive of her four daughters with long brown hair and brown, almost black, piercing eyes. She allowed as Thea's looks came more from the darkness of her father's side of the family, than the lightness of her mother's. If Barbara had not known better, she would have said Thea was the daughter of a noble.

Unfortunately, Thea's gums often bled, and she was trying to hold onto one of her back teeth, which had loosened. Frau Waldheim said these symptoms, which mostly happened in the late winter and early spring, came from a lack of fresh food. Barbara did not know if she believed this or not, but in some way it made sense.

Following close behind Thea, Carlie put her foot on the top step and fell the rest of the way down.

Poor Carlie, Barbara thought, *none of the grace of her older sister. Nor her attractiveness, either.*

Carlie proceeded to good-naturedly pick herself up, dust herself off, and plant a weak smile on her face. She imagined her mother was calling her doppy under her breath; Carlie could not help it if she was clumsy.

Barbara sighed, always hoping Carlie could develop her talents so her lack of beauty would not keep her from a successful marriage. But a lot of work needed to be done. Unfortunately, her legs were bowed slightly, while her ankles and wrists appeared overly thick. She also had a protruding breast bone—most unattractive.

After they had cleaned up from breakfast, the packing began. Barbara had been working most of the past year knitting and sewing so her family would have what they needed for life on the ship and in Philadelphia. She had knit new woolen hats and mittens, made two of Thea's dresses over for the two youngest, sewn extra shifts, and even new caps for the girls. She had hoped to have Jacob's lederhosen remade into a smaller pair for Ludwig, but she did not have the money to pay the leather worker. So, she put them in the bottom of one of the cloth bags and hoped they would fit a Fridberg sometime in the future.

As Barbara sat at the table folding the children's shifts, she looked down at the clothing she was wearing. She had inherited her mother's clothes when Maria Sybilla died in 1728 and, over the years, had made them into costumes for herself. She had taken them in and saved the leftover strips to use for her daughters' garments. But during the last several years, this resource had shrunk away to nothing, leaving them all with their wardrobes seriously lacking.

Barbara's black, linen skirt, worn over another linen petticoat in the winter, was badly faded. The once-stiff, once-red, embroidered vest now draped shapelessly over her long-sleeved shift. A stained, grey apron, tied around her waist, helped to protect everything beneath it.

Her most prized possession was her mother's red, wool jacket. Frau Schmucker had helped her alter it to fit. It came down over her hips, the sleeves ending below her elbows. In the winter, she wore long, knit, fingerless gloves, which kept her forearms warm, but could easily be removed if the need arose.

What a piteous hole time had wrought in the fabric of who she had once been. She knew she was not that fourteen-year-old girl anymore, waiting for her life to unfold; but could seventeen years have made such a difference? Marriage, seven children, constant work with little to show for it, hunger around every corner, widowhood. When did this all happen?

Barbara no longer bothered with braids, but pulled her long blonde hair, much thinner now, into a knot on the top of her head. Over this, she wore a once-white cap that tied loosely under her chin. She had another outfit to wear to church and for special occasions, along with two more caps and aprons, but her Sunday costume was not much better than the one she wore every day.

After many years of toil in the house, helping in the fields, and hunched over in the dimness of a grease light trying to make a bit of money by sewing, her body had paid the price. Her face had fallen into small, fatty jowls under her chin, while her breasts sagged from the nearly constant swelling and shrinking of seven pregnancies and the five babies she had each nursed for well over a year.

Barbara had not nursed her first Carlina because she was working at the Baron's palace at the time. She left her with a neighbor who fed her from a rag dipped in a wheat gruel thinned with cow's milk. Given the baby lived only a little less than five months, Barbara wished she had been able to nurse the baby herself. Wilhelm, of course, lived only a few hours so nursing him had never been an issue.

Shortly after her marriage in 1722, Barbara conceived Ludwig. Both she and Jacob were delighted they had so quickly shown the village Barbara was going to be a mother. No one would be calling her an "old mule."

Even as a small girl, Barbara had known the most important job for any woman was to produce as many children as possible. Both she and her husband would have a chance at immortality through the birth of their offspring, a chance for someone to carry on their family names. Of course, they prayed for an easy delivery for her and the child, knowing some births did not end well. But Barbara had not been afraid to die, knowing she was fulfilling God's plan for her.

Barbara and Jacob knew God had heard their fervent prayers for a boy, and Ludwig Jacob was born in September of the following year. He was strong right from the start, nursing vigorously every time he was put to her breast. He had grown into a tall young man with broad shoulders like Jacob's.

CHAPTER 4

Saturday Noon

As the girls were finishing their morning chores, Ludwig slowly sauntered into the kitchen. Barbara knew he had not come home last night and imagined he had fallen asleep in someone else's barn. She wished he had come home; the soft, steady in and out of his breathing would have relieved her mounting anxiety.

The ribbon holding his hair had fallen off and odd bits of straw stuck out of his strubbly hair. His eyes were red, and he seemed to be holding his head with his right hand to keep it in place. Placing his other hand over his chest, he tried his best not to belch.

"How were the festivities last night?" Barbara asked, knowing full well what had gone on. The night had been both wonderful and sad at the same time—a going-away party for five of the best-loved young men of the village—all leaving the rest of them behind.

Yesterday, as the sun had begun to fade, Ludwig collected Stephen and Hans from their homes, and linking arms, they set off to wrest Gabriel and Adam away from their wives. They planned to meet their other friends at the deserted farm out beyond the marsh, the usual place for such goings-on.

Old Gottfried came with his pipe to liven up the festivities with some music. He attended such gatherings as long as he was supplied with plenty of beer, and he was.

The young men sang and danced, reminiscing over boyhood times, swapping stories about their sweethearts, and boasting about thinly disguised plans that did not exist. They drank too much beer and ate too much food.

"Remember when Adam was trying to sneak back into his

house after he had been out with Kitty, and he fell into Widow Miss-bach's bucket of stale urine she kept for her laundry. He smelled like a privy for a week."

Those staying behind boasted, "I plan to leave as soon as I get my inheritance, and I do not think Father can last much longer," or "As soon as I have saved enough and married Margareta, we will be on the next ship." But they all knew Phillip's father was as healthy as a horse and George had one of the finest farms in the village. And anyway, Margareta would never marry George and give up such a rich farm to seek their fortune in a place unknown to them both.

But despite the frivolity, those left behind felt a heavy sense of envy toward the five of them and their coming adventures, tempered with the fear their best of friends would fail fatally in their undertakings.

The young men hooted and hollered, letting out months of pent-up winter frustration. They hoped their fathers would not be too angry with them for taking the extra beer, and smooth things over with their mothers. The fathers, of course, had already told their wives they would be putting a quantity of beer aside for the celebration they knew would take place that night. The mothers, in turn, had packaged up as much food as they could spare.

When the fires from the party had gone out, and they were all sufficiently inebriated, the boys staggered back toward the village, shouting goodbyes over their shoulders to whoever was still standing. Quite a bit of time had passed since Gottfried had been able to play more than the same long note, and they knew they needed to be going. The five soon-to-be-adventurers followed each other back to Adam's where they fell asleep in the barn. Adam knew Kitty would be furious with him the next day for his intemperance, but he did not care.

———————

"I am going down to the river to wash," Ludwig told his mother. He knew the water would be cold; after all it was only the first of April. But he craved the coolness it would bring to his burning skin.

"But, wait," Barbara said. "I will walk partway with you." As they started down the path to the water, Barbara again choked back tears and said to Ludwig without crying, "Is it too late to change our minds?"

Ludwig was furious. After all he had done to keep this plan afloat, and here she was, sticking pins in it.

"About what?" he said, knowing full well what she meant. "Yes, it is too late," he answered her, glaring as much as he dared. "Much too late." He began to pace from the house to the path, wondering how his mother could be doing this. After all they had done to make ready for their journey, all the plans they had forged to make it work, all the fear they had overcome, how could she even think of turning back before they had even begun. He had put up with her simpering and whining for over a year, and now that the time had come to leave, she was withdrawing her support from him. But then, after all, she was only a woman.

"I am afraid, Ludwig," she said, beginning to weep. "How do we know we will have enough money? And food? And what of illness, the storming seas, and all the other barriers to our success? I fear we will fail."

"Now, now, Mother," Ludwig softened. "We will be just fine. People go back and forth over the Atlantic for many reasons all the time. We know people have made new lives for themselves in America, prosperous lives. How could we ever make that happen here?" He tried to keep his voice even, but knew in his heart he was not telling his mother the truth. People did die—by shipwreck, starvation, sickness—for any number of reasons. He knew the food would be inadequate in quantity and quality, and seasickness could prevail during most of their voyage. They might well run out of money and become paupers in the richest territory in the world. But he was not going to tell her about any of this.

"But Ludwig, I have not been any farther away than Schwaigern, and, then, only three or so times. And now I am to take all of us thousands of miles away, across an ocean to a new home?"

"But Momma," Ludwig said, trying to hide his irritation and calm her, "we are all going together. We will not be alone. We will be eight adults and only five children. Surely, we will be able to find our way together."

As Ludwig was about to put his arms around his mother in an attempt to quiet her anxiety, Juliana appeared out of nowhere, almost knocking them down, panting as if her lungs would explode.

"Juliana!" Ludwig cried. "Watch where you are going!" He was certain all of the drama that was about to unfold would be nothing but female hysteria. Did she not know how much his head hurt?

"Momma, Momma, I have to tell you…" Juliana cried as she grabbed her mother by the arm and dragged her into the kitchen, collapsing on the bench, her body craving more breath and less anxiety. "Momma, you have to leave tonight, not tomorrow."

"But why?" Barbara answered. "Why today? What are you talking about?"

Ludwig returned to the kitchen, hearing Juliana had news that could change their plans.

"Well, we cannot leave today. We are not ready," Barbara countered, looking very surprised.

"No, no, you have to leave today, not tomorrow. You cannot wait another day."

Juliana turned around and, grabbing her brother by the arms, yelled one more time, "You have to leave for Philadelphia today!" Turning back to her mother, she spoke at a furious pace. "The stable boy at the palace told me. I had not even lit the fires in the kitchen yet. The Baron's men are going out tomorrow. They will pick up the draftees for his army. Ludwig is nineteen, and they will surely take him away. What will you do then? You have to leave tonight, not tomorrow!"

"But we have registered to emigrate," Ludwig said. "They will not take me knowing I am soon to leave."

"Oh, yes they will. The stable boy said they will pick up every man who has registered to emigrate, but has not paid his fees. Have you paid yours?" she ended, knowing full well he had not.

Barbara's face turned bright red with embarrassment and then white with fright. She wanted to stop what they were doing, getting on one of those enormous boats and sailing for weeks and weeks across the ocean. But then, she felt sick to her stomach as she had a vision of Ludwig being dragged off by the Baron's men, left to bleed to death in a ditch far from home. Now she knew what they had to do.

"Quickly," she whispered, "we have to pack and get ready to leave by sundown. Today, not tomorrow."

Ludwig felt a sigh of relief course through his body. Maybe now his mother would finally understand they had no choice but to leave.

Barbara began giving directions to Christina and Carlie.

"Hurry upstairs and bring down all our clothes. Be sure to pick up the little piles over in the corners. Bring them down and start packing them in the bags in the front room."

She turned to Thea. "Go find Hans and Stephen and tell them what has happened. One of them can find Gabriel and Adam and tell them the news. Try to act calm so people will not think there is something amiss. Do not run, simply walk quickly. I will tell you what to do when you get back."

At this, Barbara began criticizing herself for her lack of planning. "I knew we should have taken that food down from the rafters last week. Why did I wait until the last minute?"

Even before his mother could direct him, Ludwig said, "I am going out to finish fixing that broken wheel. And as everything is packed, bring it outside. I cannot just throw things in the cart; they have to go in a certain order so we can get to what we need tonight. Just put everything beside the barn door."

Christina was beside herself with joy. "We are leaving tonight! We do not have to wait all the way until tomorrow."

Barbara turned and grabbed Christina sharply by the arm, causing her to whimper in pain.

"Christina, you must stay in the house all day. We cannot risk having you talk with anyone; no one must know we are leaving. Did you hear that, Carlie? That you must do as well. If anyone comes to the house, I want you both to walk slowly upstairs and stay there until I say you can come down."

And so the Fridberg family began their frenetic last day in Massenbach. Barbara's head was spinning with all she needed to remember—pack the clothes, cut down all the drying fruit and put it in the small bags, put the food for tonight aside.

Blankets, cookware, her box with medicinal herbs and other spices she used for healing. Honey for infections. Do not leave any rags behind, they may be needed; Thea would soon be starting her courses.

Barbara had been successful in trading away most of their possessions. What was left she would leave in the house, and the new schoolmaster would certainly make use of them.

What was she forgetting? Was she taking enough food? That worried her more than anything. They needed their own food for the trip up the Neckar and then the Rhine and once they arrived in Philadelphia. But, in truth, she was taking all the food they had; there was no more.

The golden nugget in their plan was Ludwig, Stephen and Hans; they would work any place along the route they could. It was the only way they would make it. Thankfully, the boys were strong and reliable and would work themselves to the bone if enough opportunity presented itself. And that was the other nugget that needed to shine for them. If God could provide the opportunities, she knew they would all do their best.

"Momma, I am back," Thea called, rushing through the back

door. "I told Hans and Stephen we had to leave tonight, and Hans said he would find Gabriel and Adam. He and Stephen are going to help the families with whatever they need."

Another good boy, Barbara told herself. But goodness would not get them where they were going. The men had to stay strong and healthy, or surely their venture would fail.

They stopped for a quick meal at noon and then went back to their assigned tasks. Barbara fried the last sausage she had saved out, and roasted some carrots and potatoes in the fire, making extra for their night in the woods.

As they sat at the table hurriedly eating, Barbara looked across the table at her children, feeling a surge of pride and love for all of them. What would she have done without them? But more to the point, what would they have done without her?

Barbara had washed the girls down using her lye soap the night before, scrubbing their heads vigorously, not trusting them to do an adequate job. She had seen more flea bites on Christina, but hoped their new home would have fewer of these little creatures. Ludwig declined a bath, but the girls had no choice.

Barbara carefully combed oil through Thea and Carlie's long hair before washing it and then combed it again, hoping to dislodge all the lice and nits. Then, she braided it tightly into long plaits, tying the ends with small pieces of ribbon she had put aside especially for the trip. Envious older sisters watched Christina's short hair turn into a mass of yellow curls, but they knew she would have braids before much longer.

CHAPTER 5

Saturday Afternoon

Once the meal was over, Carlie helped Thea quickly wipe the dishes and utensils clean and put them in the cloth bag. They used what was left of the vinegar in the crock to scrub the table. Barbara ran her palm over it to be sure it was clean. She did not want anyone saying Maria Barbara Fridberg did not leave a clean table. She scrubbed and rubbed as she grabbed and packed, hoping to get the cleaning done by the time everything was in the wagon.

As the afternoon wore on, the cart filled with their belongings. Bags of clothing, straw mattresses, food, and the other necessities, had all found a place. Every once in a while, Ludwig would take out some of what he had put in, having rethought his packing strategy. Eventually, the cart was almost full.

"It is time to go, Juliana," Ludwig said at last.

When Juliana visited, Ludwig would walk her back up the hill to the palace. He would do it tonight, knowing it might be the last time he would ever see her. He so wished she had not decided to stay behind.

"I will not get on that ship, or boat, or whatever you call it," she had repeated over and over. This was the first time Juliana had ever defied her mother's wishes and the first time Barbara had ever allowed her to.

Juliana Catharina would soon be fourteen and celebrate her confirmation in the Lutheran Church. It bothered her greatly her family would not be in the church when she professed her faith for the first time, but she knew Johannes and Margaretha would be there, and certainly Karl.

She had been born in May of 1728, a little more than a year after Thea, inheriting her father's straight, dark brown hair, which trailed down her back in a pair of long braids. She had his deep brown eyes, but, thankfully, not his ruffled eyebrows.

Juliana had been independent even as a baby, crawling and walking earlier than any of her siblings. Her father said he had never seen a child learn to read at such a young age. Unfortunately, however, she was taken with flights of fancy, emotional and unrealistic in many of her dealings. She did, however, manage to obtain a job in the kitchen at the Baron's palace, contributing significantly to the small income on which her family lived.

Juliana's life in Massenbach was full of promise. Her job was one of the few in the village that paid cash. It consumed all her energy on most days, but she was equal to the task. Her employers treated her well. The Baroness kept her clothed, gave her a warm, dry bed, not a straw pallet like at home, and the cook was good to her, as well. She and the other servants ate what was leftover from the Baron's table, something that did not happen in other wealthy households. Juliana received a fair wage, and, although she had given it all to her mother to support the family, she could now begin to save most of it once her family left.

She would be staying with Johannes during the time she was not working. It was a long walk, but she hoped he would pick her up with his cart some of the time. He and Margareta had always been kind to her, and she had no reason to believe that would end.

She and Karl had already pledged themselves to each other, but no one else knew. While she was only fourteen, Karl was sixteen, and they hoped the Council would approve their marriage in four years. After all, he was already working the farm left to him by his parents when they died. In fact, he was turning it into a showplace in the small community. His guardian, his father's brother, kept a careful eye on the property. Karl was expected to take his advice until he turned twenty-one, but Karl respected him and did what he was told without complaint.

Juliana finally turned around to her mother and sisters. They were all she had ever had, and Ludwig, of course. Tears began to form in her eyes as she looked at the four of them standing before her.

Would Karl be enough? She loved him with all her heart and soul, but would he be enough to take the place of her family? She had had a great many misgivings about staying behind while her family went forward with their lives in America, but every time it came back to one thing. She could not leave Karl, and he had made it clear he would not come with her if she left.

His farm had more potential than any in the village. She would be able to live a comfortable life, with perhaps a few luxuries. But even at the age of only fourteen, she knew her dream was much more stable than the flimsy vision her family had of "going to a better life." She was even making money and would offer it to Karl as her dowry to increase the profits from the farm.

Christina was the most forlorn of them all; Juliana was her favorite sister. The thought of living without this little sparkle in her life was more than she could bear. Running over to Juliana, Christina threw her arms around Juliana's waist and sobbed into her belly, repeatedly begging, "Please come with us. Please. Do not stay behind." She had been holding this emotion in for weeks, and now the dam had broken into pieces.

"Karl can come with us," she said, wiping her nose on the sleeve of her shift. "I will be nice to him, I promise. And Carlie and Thea said they would be, too. Please come with us. Please!"

The other three slowly formed a circle around Juliana and Christina, becoming one large hug they all knew would probably have to last in their hearts for eternity. They cried together while Ludwig stood in the doorway and faced the barn, trying unsuccessfully to hold back his tears. As their sobs started to abate, they pulled away from each other, wiping their faces on their aprons in unison.

But then, Juliana became more animated. "Do not look so sad. You will all be settled into a big, beautiful house in Philadelphia before you know it. Promise me you will write to me if you need money; I will have enough for all of us. And then in four years, you can come back for my wedding and spend the whole summer. Ludwig will be married and have four babies by then, although I cannot imagine who would have him," she teased. "Actually, all of you could be married by then, except for Christina, of course." Christina frowned, feeling left out of everything once again.

But they finally said goodbye with more hugs and kisses and tears. Thea ran up the stairs with Carlie following close behind. They flopped on the floor, holding hands as they had when they were younger, crying even more into the bare boards that had been stripped of all their comforts.

After wiping his face on his sleeve, Ludwig grabbed Juliana by her arm and pulled her out the door. Barbara sat down on the bench as Christina crawled into her lap, and they held each other and wept one more time.

Ludwig was anxious to get back to the house and finish packing, but Juliana wanted to poke along and chatter while they walked.

"Luddy," she said, becoming more serious now. "Please take care of everyone. I have Karl to take care of me here, and Cousin Johannes and Margareta, too. I will not always know what you are doing, even though I know Momma will write to me often." And then she threw her arms around Ludwig and began to cry again. "I am going to miss everyone so much. Even you!"

Ludwig could not remember the last time he had been hugged and that had probably been by his mother. He was surprised to find himself hugging Juliana back and placing a kiss on the top of her head. Then, he grabbed her hand and ran the rest of the way. She tried her best to keep up, anxious now to get back to the palace and have some time to read her Bible before she fell asleep. But she knew in her heart she would grieve for the loss of her family for the rest of her life.

CHAPTER 6

Saturday Evening

Ludwig returned home to a mass of screaming girls, more tears, and his mother's harsh words. He could easily understand what might have happened, but these ongoing displays of female hysteria had come to infuriate him. "I love them all dearly, but how will I stand to be cooped up on a sailing ship with the four of them. I will go mad," he silently screamed to himself.

Barbara was switching Carlie and yelling, "I am so disappointed in you. How could you be so selfish! I told you not to put any food in your bag. We all need to share this, and it needs to last. Take those dried apples and put them back in the box."

With that, Barbara marched back into the house, shouting another "Shame on you!" as she slammed the door.

Carlie was sobbing now, sorry for her lapse of self-control. Her mother had accused her of gluttony, sinning against her own family and, worst of all, selfishness. The other two girls looked down at the ground, wanting somehow to help their sister, but not wanting to be caught by their mother giving support to the sinner. They would pay for it if she did. Carlie quickly headed for the privy and tried her best to stop sobbing as she wiped her face with her apron. Her eyes had begun to hurt and her nose was red and chaffed from wiping it.

But finally, Ludwig called out to his sisters, "Come now. Time to finish this packing. It is starting to get dark."

Barbara looked around her little house. Even though it belonged to the church and was used as the village schoolroom, she had always thought of it as hers—hers and Jacob's. The downstairs was one large room with a chimney dividing it in two. The larger half contained the kitchen with the fireplace facing into it, vacant now except for the large table, the four student benches and her three-legged stool. How she wished she could justify taking this symbol of her father's love with them. The other half of the house was smaller. Jacob had used it for school in the warmer months, but during the winter, everyone huddled around the fireplace in the kitchen. The fireplace had a large hearth covered with flagstones, which had probably been pilfered from another building of an earlier time. The floor was made of rough planks, given to pushing splinters into the feet of little, shoeless children.

The walls were comprised of wattle and daub, covered with a thin plaster, without hangings or anything else to keep out the drafts. Because the house sat on posts at each corner, the floorboards were only a few inches off the ground. The dampness and chill seeping through from the earth meant the house was continually cold in the winter and damp in the summer. During the hot summer days, the upstairs rooms turned into an oven. The low ceilings on both floors condensed the heat, but that could be an advantage or not, depending on the time of year.

The back door let in a little light on sunnier days. The front room had another door, as well as a small window covered not by glass or a curtain, but by shutters hung on the outside. An old blanket covered it in the winter.

At the top of the narrow stairway were two sleeping rooms, neither with a door, one for Barbara and Jacob along with whoever was in the cradle at the time. The children slept in the other room on pallets on the floor, as close to the chimney as they dared. Jacob loved to see his children in their shifts with their little backsides pressed against the warm chimney stones, standing in odd positions while they tried to make their hands and perhaps a foot touch the heat as well.

During better times, the outside of the house had been painted, but now little decoration remained. Like most of the other houses in the village, theirs was made with half-timber beams, filled in between with wattle and daub and covered with plaster and paint. Parts of the finish had worn away so that some of the wattle poked through or was open to the elements entirely.

Thatch made from marsh reeds covered the roof, making all the homes in Massenbach highly flammable. A spark from a neighbor's fireplace was always a concern, one reason fires were always banked for the night. Bugs, mice, insects and other vermin burrowed in the thatch itself, often finding their way onto a sleeping body.

Barbara took one last look around the house, blew out the grease light, and walked out the back door for the final time. Maybe it had been nothing but a lowly peasants' cottage, but it had been her home for twenty years, and she was sorry to leave it.

Carlie was trying to compose herself as she moved to the front of the wagon. With no explanation, Ludwig suddenly dashed back into the house. He could barely see in the darkening kitchen and so felt around in front of the fireplace for his mother's stool. They had to take something with them to remind them of home and their life here. He felt for the bench and sat down, thinking how glad he was to be leaving behind this sorry excuse for a house.

But not everything that had happened here was regrettable. He remembered his father sitting in this very spot, holding his toddler son on his outstretched lap. Jacob would smooth Ludwig's blouse, and then begin their game.

Eye Winker, and Jacob would place his finger first on one of Ludwig's eyelids.

Tom Tinker, and next on Ludwig's second lid. Ludwig would begin to giggle.

Nose Smeller, and the finger would land on the tip of Ludwig's nose. Jacob would begin to laugh.

Mouth Eater, the finger touched Ludwig's quivering lips.

Chin Chomper, and three of Jacob's fingers would gently pinch the end of Ludwig's tiny chin. By this time, they would both be laughing uproariously.

And then, the pause…and the pause…and the pause. Jacob would walk two of his fingers down towards Ludwig's little belly, Ludwig squealing with painful delight.

And then, Gully, Gully, Gully! as Jacob tickled his son's little gullet until the two of them were out of breath from laughing.

Once Ludwig had caught his breath, he would yell, "Again, Poppa. Again!" And the game would continue until Barbara stepped in to quiet the commotion.

Oh, Poppa, Ludwig thought. *I hope we have your blessing. I hope we are doing what is right for all of us.*

With that, he ran back outside and tossed the stool on top of the mound of belongings inside the cart. Barbara smiled, knowing that all the little bottoms of her family loved that stool as much as she did.

"Are we ready to leave?" Ludwig asked his mother. She only answered with a silent nod as she stood at the front of the wagon.

Thea and Ludwig started off pushing. Little Christina could barely reach the bottom of the wagon, but stood between her brother and sister and went through the motions of pushing with gusto.

The Fridberg children, especially Christina, had been warned to be extremely quiet as they started out through the back alley that led to the road through the village. All the village residents would be in their homes by now, warming themselves in front of their fires, feeding their children and getting ready to lie down for the night. That night's emigrants had agreed to stagger their departures so as not to attract too much attention, but the other villagers knew what the odd noises out in the dark were all about.

Husband and wife looked at each other over their plank table, wondering, again, if they would be better or worse off if they left, too. The village children did not know that Carlie and Christina would not be in church the following morning and quietly took their places at the table hoping the cow had given a little extra milk for their suppers.

The night gradually became dark, very dark, pitch black in fact, as the family traveled the muddy road toward Heilbronn. It was full of ruts threatening to pull the wheel rims down into the quagmire. No moon lit their way. Barbara and Carlie walked side by side in front of the wagon, walking fast to stay ahead of the cart, keeping an eye out for any obstacles, and trying not to look at each other. Carlie could not see where she was going and eventually tripped and fell, scraping the side of her leg. She wiped the blood off with her hand and continued forward in the darkness.

The family walked for what seemed like hours, but once they passed over the brook roaring with the spring snowmelt, Ludwig told Thea to stop.

"There is a pine forest over there," he said pointing to the north, "and the needles will give us something soft to lie on."

Thankfully, the night was warm. Barbara and Ludwig spread blankets over the pine needles and covered themselves and the girls with those that remained. They all fell into an exhausted sleep, inhaling the sweet, familiar scent of pine and hoping fervently they would find pine trees growing in Philadelphia.

CHAPTER 7

Sunday

B y noon the next day, Christina was sitting on top of the wagon laden with everything the Fridberg family still owned. Suddenly, she began to stand up and started shouting, "Look, look! I think I see some water. I think it might be the river, with boats!"

Ludwig yelled at her to sit down. He stopped pushing and nimbly climbed on top of the cart, trying not to squash the food. He warily stood up so as not to upset the whole of the wagon.

"You are right, Christina," he smiled. "Mother, I think this is the Neckar. I can see the barges, too."

Christina smiled inwardly, congratulating herself on being the first to see their destination.

Ludwig hopped back down and put his stronger shoulder into pushing the cart for another quarter of a mile. Suddenly, he saw two men waving and running towards them. There were Stephen and Hans, yelling and whooping as they approached the small band of emigrants.

Stephen, or Johan Phillip Stephen Poppenmeier as he was called when his mother was vexed with him, was the most outgoing of the five friends. He could talk his way into or out of any situation and would be a valuable asset on their journey.

Stephen was shorter than Ludwig with a medium build, but then everyone was shorter than Ludwig He had inherited a feature from his grandfather, which was not often seen in the village. One of his eyes was brown and the other blue. The girls in the village teased him that God could not make up his mind when he made Stephen Poppenmeier.

"What took you so long?" Stephen laughed, finally reaching the cart. "We have been waiting since mid-morning and now it is after noon. Have you seen anything of the others?"

They had all agreed to meet at the depot on the river across from Heilbronn as soon as they could after leaving the village.

Ludwig replied, "No, but it is early yet. Have you found a boat for us?"

"Yes, there is one that will take all of us. They plan to leave by tomorrow at sunrise, so I hope Gabriel and Adam get here in time. Otherwise, we will have to decide whether to wait or leave without them."

"But where will we sleep?" Barbara asked, a question of great concern to her. Their neighbor, Herr Meyer, had heard stories of people sleeping with strangers on boats or in camps along the rivers. She wondered how they would protect themselves from thieves or, worse yet, someone wanting to have their way with one of her daughters. She had talked this over with Ludwig and Stephen before they left; they assured her they would take shifts staying awake to be certain nothing untoward happened.

Stephen answered, "The boat cannot navigate in the dark. It will stop shortly after sundown, and we will have to get off. We can find a place to camp with all the other passengers and cook whatever we need for that night and the next day. But we will be together, and if Adam and Gabriel find us soon, there will be five of us to fend off any n'er-do-wells. We will have to be up early with all our belongings in hand, ready for the river trip. The boat leaves at dawn, and we had better be on it."

The three men continued to worry about Adam and Gabriel. Where could they be? The three present had decided they would take this boat, not knowing when another one would come along. They could not afford to wait for the stragglers. But they lamented what might happen if they never connected with their friends before reaching Rotterdam. All of them had counted on traveling as a group, for safety, as well as the pleasurable companionship. They had promised the women everyone would be together for the trip, but that was looking less likely to happen.

As far as the night lookout was concerned, Ludwig, Hans and Stephen would each have to stay awake for a third of the night. They would simply have to do it for all of them to be safe. The Neckar was nothing like the small stream that passed through Massenbach; it was full of treachery and ill intentions. And they imagined the Rhine would be even worse.

Barbara was frowning at Ludwig, showing her anxiety at the new things her family was being asked to do. But she held her tongue. After all, she was only a woman. She had made a pledge to herself and God the night they left Massenbach that she would trust Ludwig and the other fellows and know that the Lord would give them wisdom and deliver everyone safely to America. She would not complain about every little thing but would show courage even though there dwelt within her a hellish turmoil.

"Do not worry, Frau Fridberg," Hans said, easily seeing she was upset. "God will take care of us."

Johannes Ludwig Schmaltzhafft, known as Hans, was Barbara's favorite of Ludwig's friends. He was usually agreeable and showed kindness to everyone. His positive attitude was his greatest asset. Barbara noticed during the past year he was slowly turning into a leader, having been a follower for most of his life. She was glad he had come with them.

Unfortunately, Hans was very short, but his tow blonde hair and deep, blue eyes helped him to stand out in a crowd, as long as the looker was not looking up. He had carefully followed how the girls his age in the village were growing in stature, always looking for the one that might be lagging a bit behind the others. He knew if he were to marry someone his own height, he would have to be vigilant. But perhaps women in Philadelphia would be shorter. He could always hope.

"What about our wagon," Barbara went on, "do you think we will be able to sell it for a fair price?"

Hans chuckled and pointed to the three carts sitting together by the riverbank. "No one wants to buy them. Anyone who had need of a cart bought one years ago. Apparently, you will have to leave it here. Someone will come along and take it for firewood."

Barbara was disappointed to hear this. She and Ludwig had carefully planned the trip based on what they knew, but she was beginning to identify factors they could not have foreseen. She only hoped Ludwig could find some work on the docks while they were in Rotterdam, if only briefly. She could do nothing to earn money in a strange town, especially where she did not know the language.

"Come, girls!" Ludwig shouted. "Help me unpack the cart and make a camp for the night."

The other boys helped, and shortly the wagon was standing empty alongside the others.

Stephen suggested, "We could break some of the wagon up and use it for firewood tonight."

Ludwig nodded and pulled his hatchet out of the pile. He began to chop while Hans and Stephen pushed and pulled until they had plenty of wood to last the night. Ludwig felt a twinge of guilt as he swung the hatchet into the first post. His father had made the cart when Ludwig was a small boy. He was certain, however, his father would understand.

Stephen and Hans had arranged to travel with the Fridbergs as part of their family. They would contribute money toward the food, and Frau Fridberg would cook for them. They could not have survived on cold sausages and dried apples for very long. She was happy with this arrangement, knowing the two would help her whenever they could. She had promised both of their mothers she would look after them, something she had been doing since they were all little boys.

Hans started a fire with the years-old, dry wood. Soon, a roaring blaze appeared. The fire was too hot to cook on at first, but as it died down, Barbara wiped off four large potatoes with her apron and buried them in the glowing coals. She started some of her bacon sizzling in the heavy, iron skillet, and when it was cooked, she poured the fat into a small crock. After mixing up some oat cakes, she fried several batches of them in the pan. By the time they were done, the bacon fat had cooled enough to spread on them.

The girls picked at their food, but Barbara and the boys were ravenously hungry. Barbara encouraged the girls to eat, knowing she might not be able to cook for another day or two or even longer, but they did not seem to be hungry. They appeared uneasy as they started to tell Juliana something and realized she was not there. The boys ate what was left on the girls' plates and sighed with contentment. Stephen, as Barbara was sure his mother had insisted, thanked her profusely for their wonderful meal. She only had to look at his face to know he was grateful.

The young men set about pulling leaves and other loose vegetation into a pile and added the straw pallets they had brought to make a bed for the three girls and their mother. The boys would each find a comfortable spot someplace else and roll up in a blanket for the night.

CHAPTER 8

On the River

Everyone was up before the sun, the girls trundling small bundles of belongings toward the boat while the boys hauled the boxes and larger bags. A huge crowd was ahead of them, but Ludwig had already paid their passage and been assured seven seats on one of the benches would be theirs.

Most of their fellow passengers were just like them, traveling north to board one of the ships sailing to America. Barbara noticed everyone looked as poor as her family, like serfs and free peasants with gaunt faces and thin bodies. The family ahead of them in line had been coughing, even before the Fridbergs came up behind them. Barbara noticed an elderly woman wiping blood-tinged spittle on her sleeve, which made Barbara nervous about the diseases she had heard were carried on these boats. At least everyone in their party was healthy, if not somewhat undernourished. Another little prayer fell from her lips.

The group had thought seriously of walking at least part, if not all of the way to Rotterdam. This would have saved them the boat fare and kept needed money in their pocketbooks. But, walking could have taken at least twice as long as the boat. Camping at night would have been even more uncomfortable, given they would have had to leave Massenbach in early or mid-February before the ground began to warm. And traveling by themselves would not have been as safe with who knows what kind of people using the same route. Certainly, Ludwig and Thea would have pushed the cart most of the way, with Carlie and, perhaps, Barbara helping from time to time.

But, in any event, it would have sapped the strength from them all, and they would have arrived in Rotterdam exhausted.

Just a few miles down the river, Ludwig realized they had made the right choice. They could see other families struggling along the narrow path beside the river, trying to manage their carts, which stuck stubbornly in the thick mud. He repeatedly heard children and babies crying, causing him to feel even sorrier for those who did not have the resources to ride the river.

And what of the Kohlers and Mullers? Even if they arrived right now, it would be too late. The barge was full.

Ludwig and the others fell into line and marched quickly up the plank onto the barge. One of the men was directing people as they boarded. "Put everything you will not need on the river trip into the hold. Keep out what you will need between here and Mainz."

The barge was long and narrow with a flat bottom and a fairly shallow draft. A mast grew out of the deck about two thirds of the way toward the bow, while oars on either side would be used to steer. Rows of benches were placed towards the outside edge of the deck, while passengers' baggage and all sorts of animals were found nearer to the center.

Cages of squawking chickens, spring piglets tied to the masts, goats bleating without any need to hold back; all filled the air with the deafening sounds of the barnyard. Christina was quite interested in making friends with all of them, but Ludwig and his mother made it clear she had to stay away from them.

All Ludwig had to say was, "One might break loose and chew off your leg," to keep her in her place. Even though Barbara did not approve of lying, she did have to admit the strategy worked quite well.

A crewman told the travelers to quickly find their seats as the barge was beginning to move, but Ludwig could not find seven places together; they had to quickly split into two groups. Barbara, Stephen and Christina found three places together while Ludwig, Hans, and the two older girls found another bench with four empty seats. Christina began to cry, thinking their being together meant in a side by side sort of way. But Stephen lifted her up, placed her on his lap, and all was well.

As Ludwig was finding his seat, he was seized by a strange feeling. Looking over the side of the boat instantly made him dizzy and queasy. As this experience continued to happen throughout the day, he wondered if he was becoming ill; by the time it had occurred several times, he began to worry. *Why is this happening to me?* he thought. Although he did not believe in spirits, his mind fought the fear that he had been possessed by some sort of evil entity. For the rest of the trip, he tried to stay toward the middle of the boat and avoided looking at the water while the boat was moving. He hoped no one noticed his odd behavior; that would have been humiliating.

They had boarded the boat on the left bank of the Neckar. As a few of the boatmen used long poles to push the boat away from the bank and toward the middle, the oarsmen guided the barge into the main channel of the river until it caught the current. They began to see Heilbronn itself as they moved closer to the other bank.

"What is that?" Carlie demanded to know, pointing at the enormous wooden crane that stood near the docks on the north side of the town. It had just picked up a large block of stone in a robust rope sling and was gingerly trying to maneuver it into the hold of a waiting boat, not much larger than theirs. The stone was swinging back and forth, and as all of them watched, they were certain it would never fall into the tiny square hole in the deck. But before they were out of sight, the stone had been put to rest, and the crane was swinging around to pick up another.

The docks of the town were bustling with activity, with more people than any of them had ever seen in one place, going about their business in an orderly, but frantic manner. Large carts loaded with wares from the country advanced toward the town from all directions. Huge houses dotted the waterfront, so unlike those at home. Christina decided they were probably palaces. Ludwig and Stephen thought the large, windowless buildings right on the water must be warehouses, gradually filling up with the bounty from the country farms and workshops.

Barbara was beginning to see this boat trip might not be as inconvenient as she had imagined. She had been afraid the girls would grow tired of sitting still, but there was so much to see, even as they left the town—more warehouses, large farms, and herds of sheep and cattle. The girls were enthralled with all of the sites, and the boys were kept busy explaining all of it to them.

As they traveled north, the city gradually turned into country, full of meadows starting to turn green. Clearly, the fields would soon be full of growing things such as grains, vegetables, fodder for the live stock, and even flowers. While the sides of the valley were not deep, they were steep. The passengers were beginning to see the signs of vertical, straight-rowed vineyards, so steep in fact that workers had to be tied to ropes to keep from falling down the slope and into the water.

The river was wide and slow moving, meandering along like it had all the time in the world. It was so shallow at points, the girls could lie down on the deck and watch the bottom of the river passing by. Every once in a while, a small fish would wiggle past them so close the girls thought they could reach out and touch it.

And so, the first day passed by quickly, with little complaint and much enjoyment. The array of boats on the river was astounding, all different shapes and sizes. Some carried passengers, while others were filled with goods and animals going to market.

Every once in a while, the boat would pull to the side and put down the gangplank so some passengers could leave and others could board. Often, peasants with carts filled with goods, unloaded them into the hold or added more noisy animals to the menagerie.

That first day, the barge stopped at a toll station, such as they had heard about. A man waved a flag as the boat rounded a bend and soon, the boat pulled to the side and stopped. The toll collector and a few of his helpers inspected the ship, the items held as cargo of more interest to them than the passengers' belongings. They got off the ship and put their heads together, deciding what the captain, and then each passenger group should pay. The captain was the first to pay up, while several of the men went from family to family collecting what was due. Ludwig was surprised how small the cost was considering all he had heard about boats being taken hostage and the huge tolls paid to redeem them.

"That was not terribly expensive," Ludwig said to one of the boatmen, feeling much relieved.

The boatman laughed and replied, "Oh, just wait. We have about twenty-five of these stations until we get to Mainz, and some of the tolls could ransom a king."

Ludwig laughed back, but was embarrassed he had shown his naïveté so easily.

Their first night on the riverbank was difficult for everyone. They had to gather all their gear and descend the gangplank, which in this area of the river went uphill.

Traveling families had made camp on the right side of the river for years, degrading the sometimes steep sides of the bank and trampling what was left of the vegetation into dust.

Ludwig was surprised to find they had to walk several hundred yards inland in order to find a comfortable place to sleep. Little wood was found by the bank, so they were required to walk even farther into the forest for that. They sincerely hoped the owner would not happen by and arrest them for theft.

Perhaps the worst part of the ordeal was the dampness; their clothes and bedding, and of course the food, suffered from the damp earth, the rain, and the constant spray from the river itself.

A small shower had come early that afternoon and pelted them for what must have been no longer than fifteen minutes. They were happy to see tarpaulins were provided, although sitting under one of them for even so short a time was tiresome. There was nothing to look at, but simply each other, with hardly any room to move around or air to breathe.

Ludwig had packed to minimize the chance of their belongings being peppered by spray or sliding into a puddle, never mind enduring a rainstorm. The two most important items to keep dry were the tinder box and the flour.

The wooden tinder box contained flint, a piece of metal with which to strike it, and thin sticks of wood. The tinder consisted of pieces of rag partially burned to increase their flammability. The flour had been packed in several small linen sacks that were distributed throughout their possessions to minimize the chance of it all getting wet at once.

Barbara knew wet flour had to be cooked that day, otherwise it would spoil. She would soon become an expert at making a messy lump of the white powder into something edible. Happily, a little bacon fat made everything tastier.

That night, the boys each took a shift to keep the fire going and guard their camp against animals, thieves or whatever else might harm them. They had no way of knowing how long they had been awake while the others slept, with no church bells or animals to provide them with cues. After the first of them thought a third of the night had passed, he woke up the second one, and then the second woke the third.

They found themselves close to other families traveling on the barge. After a while, the riverbank became quiet except for the sound of snoring men. Once asleep, nothing woke anyone up as they dreamed of a house in Philadelphia with a rain-proof roof and a blazing fire that burned all through the day and night.

Christina was the first to wake up. She slipped out of the communal bed, put on her shoes, and scuffled over to the boy sitting by the fire. It had almost gone out and the guard was asleep, but she would never say anything to anyone. She enjoyed sitting next to someone and having him all to herself.

Before long, everyone else began to stir. The fire was easily brought back to life, and Barbara had gotten up early enough to make a pot of porridge. Everyone was grateful for this small luxury, but thought how much better it would taste with a little cream or even milk. They simply had to make do with butter. Everyone ate quickly and then started pulling belongings together to take to the boat.

On this particular day, the clouds were becoming darker and threatening to turn the day into a wet one. Barbara silently said her morning prayer, thanking Him for bringing them all safely through the night and asking for Mainz to appear as quickly as possible.

After talking repeatedly to the boatmen, Ludwig was beginning to garner a sense of the goings-on around the river. He learned the large cities they would pass by were Neckarghemund, followed by Heidelberg, and then Mannheim where the Neckar met the Rhine. They would then travel on to Mainz, boarding another boat there.

While the girls were becoming experienced at spotting the oddities of the trip, Ludwig, Hans and Stephen were growing tired of their questions. Thea was the next observer to wonder after what she was seeing. She pointed it out to everyone saying, "Now what is that? Horses and mules pulling boats? Everyone knows horses pull carts, and boats float in the water pulled by the current, sometimes with the help of a sail. But what is this?" The boys were not close by to explain, so the girls had to figure it out for themselves.

"Well, we can float in this boat on the river because the flow takes us along at its will," Carlie reasoned. "But what about going the other way? How does that happen?"

Christina knew enough to be able to say a boat could not float the other way. "Back home, leaves only float one way in the stream, not in the other."

Thea was beginning to figure this out. Why could a horse not pull a boat? Someone steered the boat, which was attached by long ropes to teams of several horses or mules, walking one by one on a narrow path on the side of the riverbank. The boats did not have wheels, but they hardly needed them. At this point, she explained to her sisters that water had properties where objects could slide easily over the surface, unlike the muddy road where pulling them with a team was very difficult.

But odder than anything was the noise the drovers made to move the animals along. They screamed and yelled, sometimes banging old metal pots together to keep the animals moving. Occasionally, a whip came out, but only when it was absolutely necessary; the drovers knew beating the animals too much would send them to their knees. The sisters enjoyed watching the...well they did not know what to call them. But those men certainly had little pity for a weak animal pulling a heavy weight it did not want to pull.

After a week or so, everyone began to complain about the space, or lack thereof. Clearly, the captain had allowed many more on board than the boat could easily handle. Not enough benches were available to hold the passengers, and sitting on them was sometimes impossible as the boat pitched from side to side.

"This is terrible," the three boys confirmed in one of their many conferences. "You cannot hear anyone talking. The boatmen keep yelling, mostly at each other, but sometimes at the boat itself. Everything is sliding around, including those sitting on the benches. There is not enough space for everyone." So men walked around to give the women places to sit, and the women sat on the deck to give the men places to rest in comfort. The trip was becoming tiresome.

The boatman had been right; they were pulled over, sometimes more than once a day, for an inspection and collection of the tolls. Sometimes this process proceeded quickly, but at other times it seemed the collectors were more interested in cantering back and forth to their base station than getting on with it.

Soon, the passengers began to see the outskirts of what they were told was Mannheim, another river port busy with the commerce of the day. But here the Neckar flowed into the Rhine, the larger river, which would take them to their destination. Passing this mark helped them feel like they were making some progress. This city was even bigger than the ones they had already seen.

CHAPTER 9

Mainz: Day 1

On the sixteenth day of their river trip, the travelers began to notice more boats, some they had not seen before, looming large as they passed. More birds filled the air and people started appearing along the banks, busily on their way to whatever business beckoned their attention.

Mainz eventually appeared around the bend, and the boatmen seemed glad to have come to the end of their trip, this one taking longer than usual. After discharging the passengers, they would relax in the river port for a few days and then hoist their sails and head south to Basel to start the trip over again.

The boat finally came to a stop beside a large dock and the Fridbergs, along with Stephen and Hans, began to disembark. They hauled their belongings into another pile and drew together in a group to decide their next step. They only knew they had to leave the boat they had traveled on thus far and transfer to a larger one for the next leg of their journey.

"There is no place to camp here in the town," Ludwig began. "We will have to find a place to stay and another boat to take us the rest of the way to Rotterdam."

They decided Stephen would stay with the women and the belongings, Hans would look for a boarding house, and Ludwig would begin scouring the docks for an agent's office or another barge ready to leave tomorrow for Rotterdam.

Hans easily found a place to stay. He asked a fish monger where he could find a boarding house and the fish monger, whose name was Peter, knew of exactly the right place. His father's cousin and wife lived in a large house on Hill Street, and they sometimes took in travelers, mostly families.

Hans followed Peter's directions and soon came to a nicely kept house a short way from the dock. He knocked on the door and was greeted by a kindly looking man who appeared to be in his fifties.

"Peter said you take in travelers," Hans began. The older man smiled and asked how many there were of them.

"Myself, my friend, Stephen, and Ludwig with his mother and three sisters," he replied. "We have come from Massenbach on our way to Rotterdam and then America."

"America!" the man exclaimed. "Had the thought of going there myself a few years back, but never quite got around to it. Well now, I think we have two rooms for you. You boys can have one room and the females can stay in the other."

With that he yelled over his left shoulder, "Momma, we have guests. Looks like a nice young man with a few friends and four women."

A stout woman appeared, wiping her hands on her apron. "Well come in, then," she said to Hans. "Let me show you the rooms, and you can decide."

She led him to the back of the house where a long wing had been added. Opening the doors to two small rooms overlooking a small meadow beginning to turn green, she pointed out two beds in each. The price she quoted him sounded fair.

"I can include supper in the price, if you like," she offered, "and breakfast for a bit more. But you can decide about that once the rest of the group has arrived."

"This looks fine," Hans said, hoping the rooms would meet with Frau Fridberg's approval. He took several coins out of his waistcoat and paid the woman for one night. "If we need to stay longer, would that be possible?"

"Of course," she smiled. "I only rent to people I like, and I like

you." Hans smiled back, excusing himself and telling her he would
return soon.

Hans ran all the way back to the dock, grateful he had so easily
found a place to stay. "Frau Fridberg!" he called as soon as he saw her.
Out of breath he explained, "I have found us a good place to stay.
Two rooms, nice ones, for a reasonable price. We can have our meals
there as well, and stay longer than one day if we need to."

"Wonderful, Hans!" Barbara exclaimed. She trusted his judgement, but a small bit of doubt niggled at her thoughts.

"I have paid for it, so let me show you," he said. Stephen, Barbara and the girls helped Hans gather up their belongings as they
headed up Hill Street. Ludwig arrived just in time and ran after them
up the hill.

Barbara was delighted with their rooms. They were clean and
bright, much nicer than any of them were used to. She was especially
happy to meet Marta and her husband, Jan, who, she learned, were
Dutch immigrants. They had come to Mainz with their young children ten years ago and built an addition on the small house to ac-
commodate their growing family. As the children grew, they bought
homes and farms of their own outside the town. Marta and Jan rent-
ed out the extra space to those on their way to Rotterdam. But, only
to people they liked.

Marta apologized to Barbara that they had no servant. Maida
had up and left that morning for no reason. Just packed up and left.
Marta had decided they would have no guests until they found another maid, but Jan had sounded so enthusiastic about this family,
she decided to follow his lead. They would manage somehow.

"Our youngest, Jacob, left a year ago to move back to Rotterdam," Marta said with a sad face. "He was not able to find enough
work in Mainz and felt he could earn more on the docks in Rotterdam, even with having to pay for food and lodging. He is a restless
lad, eager for more adventure than Mainz or Rotterdam can provide.
He wants to seek his fortune in America."

She continued, "He returned for a visit last month and told us he had almost enough to pay his way on one of the ships going to the New Land. He only needed another two months' wages. Without Jacob asking, Jan gave him enough to pay his way and then some. Jan did not want his son arriving in America with nothing in his pocket."

The tired travelers were told to leave their belongings in the small barn behind the house and only bring what they needed inside. Christina's delight appeared in the form of a small cow whose sack looked like it was about to burst. She imagined fresh milk she could drink after such a long time without and felt it sliding down her throat, caressing her lips with its sweetness as it passed.

Jan and Marta welcomed them with open arms, helping the girls settle into their room. Marta appeared shortly with a fresh basin of warm water, imagining they must be dirty from their long trip. She thought the little one looked like she needed a thorough scrubbing. Jan came right behind her with several clean towels and told them to come down to the kitchen if they needed more. He told them the kettle was hot, and he had filled the extra one as well. They both left and returned in a few minutes with a steaming mug of tea in each hand. "We thought you might like a little refreshment after your long trip."

"I put some milk and a little sugar in them. If you want more, come down to the kitchen," Jan offered.

Barbara felt close to tears as she thanked her hosts for their kind hospitality. The mugs were made of pottery, not wood. And they were clean. She had not drunk out of a clean cup since leaving the village. The tea was, she was sure, a product of heaven.

Barbara and her daughters drank their tea, filled with gratitude Hans had found them such a lovely place to stay. She vowed she would never doubt Hans again. When they were done with their tea, Barbara unceremoniously stripped Christina bare in the middle of the room and started to vigorously scrub her dirty body. She did not see any flea bites and thanked God for that. Carlie washed next and afterward Barbara went off to find the kitchen to ask for another basin of warm water for herself and Thea.

She could hear Ludwig and Hans before she reached the large kitchen, one bigger than she had ever seen. A fire was blazing in the enormous fireplace with a delicious smelling stew simmering at the edge of the hearth.

Barbara greeted the three boys who had already introduced themselves to their hosts. Jan and Marta were happy with their choice of travelers to house; the two other young men seemed just as likable as Hans. Frau Fridberg and her daughters looked like a fine family, not unlike their daughters and grandchildren. They could tell their guests were peasants, perhaps even freed serfs, but not surly or ill mannered as others they had met from that area.

After the boys had cleaned up, they came down to the kitchen for supper. They were seated around a large rectangular table of oak, certainly large enough to hold a growing family. Each person had their own plate, real silverware, and a pottery mug. Juliana had told her family of such things, but none of them imagined they would ever have personal knowledge of them. She had even brought home a broken fork the cook at the palace had given her, and they had all practiced using it. The adults were given delicious mugs of ale with dried raspberries in them while the three girls had mugs filled to the top with milk, still slightly warm from the cow.

Marta placed a large helping of stew on each plate, smiled at Jan, and sat down. Jan bowed his head and waited for their guests to do the same. They did not look like Papists to him, so he assumed they were Reformed or Lutheran as he and Marta were. After a short prayer followed by a thankful "Amen," they all began to eat.

Little Christina picked up her mug of milk and drank the whole of it without stopping. Barbara was embarrassed by her show of gluttony, but Marta got up, took the mug, and refilled it right to the brim. Everyone else had started eating the stew, full of carrots and potatoes with plenty of parsley and more meat than they had ever had at one sitting, nevermind in one year. Marta had only to look at their clean faces to know they were each enjoying their meal immensely. She passed around a basket filled with fresh biscuits followed by a crock of butter, still cool from the dairy. The diners sopped up every last bit of gravy with small pieces of biscuit and sat back with stomachs fuller than they had ever been.

Marta offered a second helping to each of the boys, who accepted with enthusiasm. She always liked a young man with a good appetite and imagined they were all hard workers. Barbara and the girls declined more, especially after Marta told them to save room for warm apple pie. None of them had ever saved room in their stomachs for anything. What would be the sense of that? Hans, who, though small, had a voracious appetite, thought he would swoon with delight. His favorite was apple pie; it had always been his favorite.

Marta offered what was left of the stew, but everyone was satisfied. She rose from the table and started to clear the dishes, but Thea jumped up and said, "Please, Frau Hauck, please sit down. Carlie and I will clear the table." With that, Carlie rose as well, and helped her sister pick up each plate and set it carefully on the sideboard with the dirty forks and knives. Barbara was beside herself with pride, seeing her daughters take the initiative to help. She continued to sit in her seat and finish her ale as if their dinners at home played out in much the same manner.

Jan belched loudly, and when it seemed apparent this behavior was not frowned upon in their hosts' home, the three young men stopped trying to suppress theirs. They all smiled with satisfaction, especially Hans who was inwardly congratulating himself again on this fortunate find.

Marta said, "Who would like pie?" as she picked the largest pie any of them had ever seen up off the warm hearth. It must have been at least five inches high; Barbara stopped guessing how many peeled and sliced apples it contained once she got to nine. Martha cut and served it from her seat, passing a slice of exactly the right amount for each recipient around the table on more clean, china plates. She picked up a small pitcher of cream, passed it around, and told every one to help themselves. Christina's eyes were getting bigger and bigger as the pitcher made its way to where she sat. Barbara poured a bit on Christina's pie, anxious she would flood her plate if left to her own devices. Warm apple pie with cream. Cream on pie. They had never heard of such a thing. In their world, cream only belonged in the butter churn, and the butter was used in spite of any rancidness.

As soon as Barbara was finished with her pie, she stood up and began removing the small plates from the table.

"Marta," Barbara said, "I will do the washing up, and Thea will dry them." She did not dare let the two younger ones help, especially since Carlie had almost dropped a plate as she was putting it onto the sideboard.

Marta filled the basin in the wooden sink with hot water from the kettle and chipped some soap into it. While Marta's back was turned, Barbara quickly told Thea to be very careful with the dishes, but Thea had already judged how precious they must be.

Carlie took Christina who, at this point, could barely move she was so full of food, and they returned slowly to their room after thanking Frau Hauck for their dinner. The boys insisted on bringing wood into the house from outside and filled the boxes in both the kitchen and what they were told was the sitting room. Barbara could have burst, she was so proud of her family and the other two boys, as well.

Thank goodness Juliana had so often talked about the amenities at the Baron's palace, the beautiful dishes and silver pieces and how fragile and valuable they all were. Juliana had tried to impart an appreciation for the customs and manners of the nobility, and, apparently, her sisters had been listening.

For the next half hour, Barbara washed, Thea dried, and Marta put the dishes away in the cherry corner cupboard. It was painted a pleasing blue inside, and the three shelves on top were filled with beautiful dishes and glasses, cups and bowls with even a drawer in the middle for the cutlery. The bottom of it held serving bowls and platters on the two shelves there.

Before the boys left for their room, Ludwig informed Jan they would need the room for a second night. They had booked passage on a barge leaving not the next day, but the one after. Jan said that was fine and then hurried out to the kitchen to tell Marta the good news.

Once back in their room, Christina took off her clothes and crawled into the far side of the nearest bed. As she did, Carlie noticed the bed was made not only with a beautiful quilt, but also with clean, gleaming-white sheets. She had not seen a sheet since leaving Massenbach, and none they owned had ever been as white as these.

Barbara and Thea sat at the table and chatted with Frau Hauck for a few minutes and then excused themselves. They had both grown tired and were ready for a good night's sleep.

A tallow candle stood on the dresser in their room in a tall, pewter holder. Just as Barbara was wondering how she would light it, Marta appeared with another candle, and lit both the one on the dresser and on the table between the beds.

Before Marta left, she asked Barbara if they needed anything else. Barbara let out a sigh of contentment and thanked Marta for all she and Jan had done for her family. "No," she said. "I cannot think of anything else we could possibly want."

That night, as they all lay between the cool, white sheets, none of them dreamed at all. Their brains were too full of food to think of anything else.

CHAPTER 10

Mainz: Day 2

The next morning, Barbara awoke to find Christina was not in the bed beside her. She panicked for a moment, and then saw Christina's clothes and shoes were gone as well. Barbara quickly dressed and hurried to the kitchen.

There she found Christina sitting at the table, on a pillow this time, talking with Frau Hauck about their journey so far. Christina was starting to tell Marta about her mother falling in the river water, when Barbara rushed in to stop the conversation. She was glad they had never told Christina they left Massenbach without paying their fees.

"Good morning, Momma," Christina said.

"Good morning, Christina," Barbara replied. "And good morning to you, Frau Hauck."

"And to you, Frau Fridberg. How did everyone sleep?"

"Very well," Barbara answered.

"Yes, little Christina has been telling me the details of your trip so far."

Barbara hoped Christina had not shared all of them.

There her daughter sat, looking like a little princess, perched on a cushion that might well have been made of gold, sipping a mug of hot milk and sugar with chocolate chipped into it. She clearly was having a wonderful time.

Marta offered Barbara a seat at the table and, going to the fire, held up a pot of what Barbara guessed was coffee, although she had never had any. Marta poured it into a mug, added several spoonfuls of white sugar and at least two fingers worth of cream. Barbara sipped the steaming liquid, trying to make it last as long as she could. Thea, happy her growing maturity was being recognized, was offered some as well.

Before long, the rest of the boys and girls arrived. Marta told everyone to take a seat as she put a large pot of steaming, hot porridge on the table and began to spoon it into the bowls she used for breakfast. The boys watched as each bowl was passed along, eager for something to fill their bellies again. They realized all at once, however, it was not porridge with all its fillers but oatmeal, real oatmeal, not mixed with anything else to stretch it. At that exact moment, Jan arrived with a pitcher of cream from the dairy, along with a pail of fresh milk. Marta sent the crock of butter around the table as everyone realized they not only had cream for breakfast, but fresh butter as well.

After they had had their fill, Barbara again washed, Thea dried, and Marta put away. Christina sat at the table, her eyes dreamy with contentment, primly continuing to sip her hot chocolate, which Carlie now had as well.

After a vigorous belch, Ludwig asked what chores needed to be done. Jan, seeming almost offended, stated they were the Haucks' guests and not there to work. Ludwig replied, however, they had had nothing to do for over several weeks and would welcome the chance to help with anything he needed. Hans and Stephen nodded in agreement and rose from their chairs, ready to get to work.

"Well," Jan said, "if you insist. I do have wood left from last winter that needs splitting and stacking. And the barn needs a good cleaning out."

The boys almost tripped over each other, trying to be the first to get to the wood pile behind the house. Once there, however, they waited for Jan to come out and show them what he needed done.

The travelers spent the day and night with the Haucks, enjoying themselves immensely. The boys continued to beg for things to do, and Jan seemed able to continue with a good supply of chores.

He showed the boys his workshop, tucked away in a corner of the addition that faced south. It was a small, sunny room, full of woods, paints, and lacquers with an abundance of shavings on the floor. The smell of wood was pervasive.

Jan was a clockmaker, taught by his father to make not only the intricate inner works, but also the carved wooden cases so valued by the upper classes. Jan explained that every couple of months he would take what he had made up to Rotterdam to those who had previously ordered them. He would receive orders for more, mostly by referral from satisfied customers, and then begin the cycle over again. He sold some of his clocks in Mainz, but most of his living came from the seaport city.

Jan loved to work with his hands, loved to feel the finish on the fine woods, and see the colors he created on others. He showed the trio how he planned out the construction, chose the materials, sawed the parts, shaved, sanded, and finished the cases.

The boys could readily see how Jan had accumulated what he referred to as "modest wealth," through a lifetime of hard, continuous work. Jan wanted to teach his three older sons the craft, but none were interested as they seemed to have been born to spend their days outside. He had tried to convince his youngest son, Jacob, during his last visit, to stay and learn the craft while Jan was still able to teach it to him, but Jacob was determined to sail to the New Land as soon as he could arrange it.

"I suppose none of you are interested in staying in Mainz and learning to be a clockmaker," Jan said, half-jokingly. He could see the three of them were itching to cross the Atlantic and become English citizens.

The women folk spent their day with Marta looking at her lovely things. She gave them a tour of her china cupboard full of dishes with flowered patterns, bowls of pounded copper and silver, and flatware made of burnished pewter. The beauty of everything she put her hand on amazed the women, even Christina. She showed them her lovely linens, starched table clothes, and extra embroidered coverlets.

Barbara, especially, wondered why the Haucks had so much while they had so little. She felt no envy toward the couple, particularly since they had so generously shared their good fortune with the Fridbergs. They realized Jan had worked hard for the money to buy all the couple had, but how had he come to learn a skill which afforded him such a good living?

None of them knew of anyone who lived in such style as the Haucks. They were used to seeing only the benefits of nobility and all the attending amenities against the backdrop of peasant poverty. Juliana told them about the richness of life in the palace—the abundant food, beautiful clothes, rich furniture, and lavish hangings throughout the large, elaborate buildings. The Fridbergs had passed by the palace many times and knew it to be grand in scale and material, but only knew about what went on inside from Juliana. Although Barbara had worked there herself in the laundry, she had not paid much attention to the goings-on. Her mind was always back home with her children.

Juliana told them how a wet nurse was hired even before a child's birth. After that, other attendants, servants, and nurses would come to care for the child, leaving Baroness von Massenbach to recover from the birth. She returned slowly to her life of pleasure and luxury, never once having to muck out a barn or hoe a row of potatoes.

Dignified and important guests visited throughout the warmer months. They would eat lavishly, ride horses, hunt the wild boar in the forest, and revel in stories, with enough brandy and other spirits to keep them intoxicated until the sun came up.

These peasants had never experienced a way of life somewhere in between theirs of poverty and want and the nobility's of power and wealth. They had no idea it existed. Ludwig and the other men had visited Schwaigern, but even there an estate of abundance did not exist outside of the nobility.

But was this not why they had been doing without for years, so they could throw off the black, gnarled coat of near slavery and move into lives filled with bounty? Was this gem they had found in Mainz showing them what their lives might be like in Philadelphia? Could Barbara have a large kitchen with pretty dishes and a huge fireplace and be able to cook all the food her family could ever want? Might her daughters meet and marry men there who could support them and their children as Jan had supported his?

Ludwig, of course, thought of his successful butcher shop. Thea could see herself in a house like Marta's, full of fine things and all the time in the world to care for them. Carlie thought of the many children she would have, all of them dressed in warm clothes with full bellies every night. Christina wanted one of those feather beds like the one she had slept in those two nights and a cow that gave cream all day long.

This trip had given Barbara something she had never had before—time to think. Why had God made the world full of people without the basics of life and those with more than they needed? She had been told by Pastor Kimmel and the few other wise people she had met that God had made three estates in life—those who worked, those who fought, and those who prayed.

Her kind were the workers, protected by the kings and nobles, along with the Church who prayed for all of their souls. That was the way the world worked, and everyone had to accept his lot in life. But did they? Would they? Could their lives change simply because they took a boat to a place they had never been before, where, they had been told, abundance was available to all who were willing to work for it?

Barbara vowed if she ever had abundant wealth, she would share it, just as the Haucks were doing. She was well aware the Haucks had probably spent more money on her family than the family had paid them. Imagining how good a day would feel when she was able to help those she loved and those in need; she thought of all she could provide that they required to prosper.

After a breakfast of sausages and warm corn muffins, more cups of hot coffee with cream, and hot cocoa, the travelers gathered up their travel-worn gear and bid the Haucks goodbye. They had so enjoyed their time there; it had rested them and given them the spiritual and physical energy they needed to continue moving forward. In just three days, the Haucks had become increasingly fond of Christina, and Barbara had no doubt she would have been welcome to stay with them forever.

CHAPTER 11

The Middle Rhine

L udwig led the tribe to the dock where they found the barge he had engaged waiting for them. It was larger than the one on the Neckar, much longer with huge oars used for steering.

The center of the barge held several compartments, little houses, so to say. The crew would sleep in these as well as the few people of refinement making the trip. Tethered around this area were farm animals, and the ruckus the passengers listened to all day long. There was even a mule, Boris, which brayed unmercifully. Ludwig easily convinced Christina that Boris would bite off both of her legs if she ventured too close.

Once on the boat, everyone could see the accommodations were much better than those on their previous craft. Benches were set up in blocks with a piece of canvas nailed to a frame, which protected them from both the sun and the rain. The trip to Koln would be about the same length as the one to Mainz had been. It was rumored another month would pass until they reached Rotterdam, but Ludwig did not believe this as so many things they had been told were not true.

Fellow emigrant passengers populated other parts of the deck with their belongings in the hold or lashed to the deck. Barbara hoped those on this boat would be as agreeable as they had been on the previous one. But, unfortunately, this boat was just as crowded as the other had been. Two adults and a child had died of fever on the Neckar; Barbara prayed all would arrive at their next stop in Koln safe and sound.

The days were even hotter now, as April turned into May, with the sun beating down on their sunburned bodies and hat-covered heads. As before, the benches could not seat everyone on the boat, and so they took turns sitting under the awning away from the sun.

As the trip wore on, many gave up sitting on the benches and reclined on the deck, leaning against the softer parts of their baggage. They chatted in the morning and dozed in the afternoon.

Ludwig, Hans, and Stephen spent a good part of their day talking to the other men on the boat, swapping the tales that men swap, and, of course, what life would be like in America. Barbara entertained with her time-worn stories and even made up a few new ones. But they were all bored and cramped at the end of a long day spent sitting on something wooden.

This time, passengers were allowed to sleep on the deck of the boat, but had to get off in order to cook their food. After only one night spent on the river, however, the Fridberg party decided sleeping on something that did not move would be more to their liking. They knew their three days with the Haucks had spoiled them but swallowed their pottage each night with acceptance.

The fifth day on the Rhine, three men in uniform on beautiful, grey horses cantered to the edge of the river and held up their riding whips, signaling the boatmen to stop. Ludwig knew at once these were more of the toll collectors; they were a bit more official looking than the peasants who had collected the tolls on the Neckar.

As before, an inspection took place followed by the gathering of the tolls. Their captain told them that lining the route they would take to Rotterdam were about thirty-five different states, territories, duchies and other political units, each taking its cut of the lucrative toll business.

Ludwig and Barbara had planned for these tolls, but visibly winced when the senior officer told them the amount of their fees, much larger than those on the Neckar. Jan had told them not to argue with the officials, but pay whatever the collectors asked. The inspection could last most of the day, so they were often able to move only a few miles down the river before they had to stop again for the night.

Stephen talked to the captain the first evening out of Mainz about the lengthy waits; they were certainly slowing down the trip. The captain just laughed and told Stephen the waiting time so far had not been "lengthy"; sometimes the inspection took two days or even longer depending on the motivation of the officials. Some of the stations had chains across the river, hanging from the right bank to a toll house on a small island in the middle, and then on to the other side. After the inspections had taken place and tolls were paid, someone had to undo the chain, row over to the riverbank and secure the chain there. Only then could the barge pass.

Eventually, the Rhine became a narrow, twisting gorge with a faster current. Some of the bends were so severe, the boatmen feared they would not see the boats coming from the other direction until it was almost too late. Steep hills grew from the river's edge with ancient castles and fortresses at their tops.

Even more surprises awaited the Fridbergs as they floated along. As they were all dozing one lazy afternoon, Christina thought to sit up and look around. To her amazement, she saw an entire village floating down the river ahead of them.

"Look, Momma," she said, shaking her mother awake. "It is an island made out of wood. And it moves."

Barbara squinted through the sun to see what Christina was talking about, and Ludwig snapped at her to go back to sleep. Floating villages simply did not exist. But Christina continued and so all of them, including a few neighbors, were awakened.

When Ludwig saw for himself what he had just told Christina was not possible, he jumped up and rushed to the side of the ship, but not too close to the edge.

"Christina, you are right," he reluctantly told his sister. "But what is it really?"

A passing boatman explained. "Timber is floated down from the Black Forest in Bavaria, lashed together to make the journey easier. Smaller rafts join together at the Rhine and continue on to the coast."

Ludwig could easily see all the other boats in its vicinity gave it a wide berth, including the one he was aboard. If one of the boats, such as his, collided with the floating behemoth, the larger raft would certainly not be the loser.

Amazed, Ludwig expounded on the scene before him. "There must be hundreds of people on it, with huts where they sleep. Mother, get up and come see this. Goats, chickens, all kind of small animals, tied to the sides of the huts. It is a floating village."

Once they had gone through the gorge, the river valley spread out on each side, filled, as before, with fields and meadows. The travelers could see people who seemed to be wrapped in long ropes working on the grape vines. Another passenger explained that the vineyards were on such steep slopes, the workers had to be secured by ropes connected to the harnesses they wore. The long ropes were attached to posts on the top of the hill, and the workers let out the line as they worked their way down to the bottom. Without this configuration, they would have tumbled straight down the side of the hill, bypassing whatever pruning or picking needed to be done.

This leg of their journey passed no more quickly than the previous one had. More stories, more naps, more talk. Their sunburned bodies finally turned a tawny brown, while more freckles appeared on their noses.

Every day or so, more men appeared on the banks, ready to collect the tolls. Some wore colorful uniforms and rode liveried steeds, certainly an indication of heftier tolls.

The beautiful, expansive palaces and castles dotted the upper parts of the steep cliffs surrounding the river. Made of massive stone walls with slate roofs, some had glass windows through which the inhabitants could enjoy looking at their flower gardens and manicured bushes. Christina, with Carlie's help, was counting the castles on their trip and had already found twenty-seven.

Thea imagined what the handsome lord must be like who lived there, and his wife, resplendent in robes of velvet and gold. All the grandness Juliana had told them about seemed to abide in those massive conglomerations of stone. Ludwig attempted to make out the stables and other outbuildings. He could easily see himself as the lord of one of these mansions, riding out with his retinue to hunt a wild boar or deer. Carlie's game was guessing how many people lived there—how many children and servants, how many vassals, how many fields surrounded it. Barbara could not imagine herself living in such a place; she allowed as it must be dirty and drafty, even worse than their small village house back home.

One afternoon, three men rode close to the side of the river and signaled the barge to stop. Another toll station. The men, all elegantly dressed in official garb, got off their horses and crossed the gangplank put down by one of the boatmen. They wandered around the deck, down into the hold and up again, picking up items belonging to the passengers and dropping them as they went.

A tall man, obviously the most senior of the lot, with a fashionable powdered wig and tall, polished black boots, strode up to the Fridbergs and began talking. Gradually, he moved closer to Thea and managed to steer her away from her family in the direction of the bow. One of the boatmen nudged Ludwig to be sure he was paying attention.

Never had a grown man Thea did not know stood so close to her. Her body stiffened, and she had difficulty keeping her balance as the barge moved about in the choppy water. His sneer was unnerving as he made attempts to touch her. Thea began to understand why he had herded her away from the pack.

The captain explained to Ludwig, "These toll agents, rascals and scallawags that they are, think they can easily have their way with attractive girls on the barges. They are rarely successful, but threaten to delay the boat's passing if their demands are not met. And this one in the green jacket is the worst of them." The captain knew immediately Ludwig would protect his sister with the last breath in his body and went to tell his crew members they might be there for a while.

Ludwig strode quickly down to the bow, followed closely by Hans and Stephen. Ludwig was as tall as the official, something the man was not used to. He invariably used his height, not to mention his considerable bulk, to bully anyone who stood up to him.

Ludwig aggressively insinuated himself between the official and his sister, pushing her behind his back, handing her off to one of his friends behind him. The official looked at him and laughed, but he knew he was not dealing with one of the usual dummcups who traveled on the river. He saw Ludwig knew exactly what was going on and was not going to have any of it.

Smiling more broadly, the official pulled Ludwig aside as he placed his arm around his shoulder. Ludwig shook his arm loose and stared back with resolute defiance.

Still, the official went on in a low voice, "You know, young man, I could make this worth your while. Your sister looks delicious. She probably has not even been plucked yet, and I would pay handsomely for the opportunity to do that."

Ludwig was furious. His face became redder, almost purple, while he clenched his fists behind his back. He knew violence on his part would only bring trouble the three of them could not handle, and so he did his best to slow his breathing and calm his racing heart.

"She is not for hire," Ludwig replied, turning redder with anger and embarrassment. He had never talked about any woman like that before, nevermind one of his sisters. Trying to think the scenario through before anything untoward happened, he wondered if the official knew how old Thea was, but then maybe he did. Ludwig thought of her only as his little sister, certainly not a woman in any position to give the man any pleasure.

"I said she is not for hire. So take our money, get back on your horses, and be on your way."

The official was obviously irritated with Ludwig. "You know, young man. We could take an awfully long time to inspect this barge. It could hold you up, keep you from getting to your ship on time." He was guessing now, but was fairly certain Ludwig was simply another useless peasant, on his way to a good thrashing in America. "And I am willing to pay; I would not want to use up your precious asset without making it worth your while."

With this Ludwig shouted, "No!" and turning around, grabbed Thea by the arm. He could feel her shaking and wanted to put his arm around her, but did not want this brute to think any of them were afraid of him.

"Have it your way, then," the official scoffed. He gathered up his men and headed for the horses left on shore, telling the captain the boat needed to stay where it was until he returned. As he rode off on a narrow path up the hill toward the castle, he became even more determined to have his way.

Thea, of course, was shaken to her core. She knew men desired women in certain ways, although she did not know the details. But the way he was breathing, the way he looked at her, and how he kept licking his thick lips with his even thicker tongue, terrified her. His long, black mustache was frothy with what she did not know was desire, but she knew it did not bode well for her safety.

"Are you all right?" Ludwig whispered, finally putting his arm around her shoulders.

"That man is terrible," she answered, beginning to cry. "I felt so ashamed and uncomfortable by his attention I wanted to die."

"Well, the three of us will see to it that pig does not bother you again."

"Do I have to tell Momma what happened?"

"If you say anything, it will upset her. No need of that. Just keep your own counsel and act as if nothing has happened. I have already told the other two to keep what happened to themselves."

The captain knew they would be stuck there for days and vowed, as he had the last time this happened, he would no longer allow any attractive frauleins on his boat. It simply caused too much trouble and delay. Time was money,

Ludwig resisted the urge to hurl insults at the official as the four of them returned to the stern. Barbara, Carlie, and Christina were lying back on their pile of belongings, trying to find recognizable shapes in the clouds.

The boat sat there for days, the passengers baking in the sun. Barbara kept wondering why this stop was taking so long, but none of the young people ever let on they knew. Every afternoon, the official came by and asked Ludwig if he had changed his mind. Ludwig not once answered him; he only scowled and looked like he was about to spit in the official's face.

On the fifth morning, the official and his retinue reappeared, did a cursory inspection and demanded what everyone knew was an outrageous toll. Still, all onboard paid without arguing, even the captain. The captain had made up his mind once and for all only ugly girls would be allowed on this barge from now on—that was certain.

Barbara had found a sheep in the clouds while both of her daughters had spotted cows, one that looked suspiciously like the hind end of Frau Althoff's. They laughed at their silliness, unaware of the unpleasantness that had gone on for days right beneath their noses.

CHAPTER 12

The Lower Rhine

A t Koln, transfer to another boat was necessary. This craft, referred to by the boatmen as a *samoreau*, was larger still, with two masts and a more sophisticated steering system. Everyone onboard was tired of moving their gear every night and now they would have to, yet again, move all they had brought.

As they left the deep valleys of the middle Rhine, the river widened as it neared the sea. Finally, they left the German states behind as they poised to enter the territory of Holland in the Netherlands.

Their next toll station was an enormous stone fortress, Fort Schenkenschanz. It was larger than any structure they had ever seen, as if all the castles and palaces on the cliffs of the Rhine had been combined into one structure. The children had no words to describe what they saw, simply small gasps and questioning noises in an effort to make sense of this enormous edifice.

"Is that a big castle?" Christina asked, pulling on Ludwig's pant leg. "How many people live there? Are there little girls there, too?"

"No, no. It is a fort, a fortress. During times of war, hundreds of men fire guns and canons at their enemies on the outside. As for now, it is being used as a toll house."

It is so big, they must collect an awful lot of money, Christina thought. She wondered if they had cream and apple pie there, but decided not to ask. Momma had scolded her because all she talked about was cream and apple pie, something which would not be in their future for a while, if ever. *I know, gluttony is a sin.* Christina wanted to enjoy thoughts of her mouth filled with the delicious mixture, but then thought it would surely be there in heaven when she arrived, so she did not want to sin now and ruin her chances of getting in.

As they continued to travel north, the river divided, and then divided again into smaller river courses. The tides were beginning to have an effect on the water level, which confused Ludwig; he had no knowledge of why the water level would rise and fall as it did.

After a while, the captain told them they had reached the River Maas. This was the best sight of all, leading soon to the city of Rotterdam, near more small waterways that led to the sea. Ludwig was waiting on pins and needles to see this enormous ocean he had only heard of. How large was it? Did it have banks? Or beaches? How deep was it? He had no way of knowing any of this. Surely, he would soon put his pride aside and ask one of the boatmen about the mysteries of the sea.

They heard Rotterdam before they could see it, a cacophony of shouts and yells, commands to this one and that, softly echoed across the water and around the bend to the line of boats filing into the harbor. Horses objected loudly to cracking whips while ropes and lines clanked rhythmically against the ships' wooden masts and beams.

Slowly the sound increased until the travelers could see the harbors, wharves and all the delightfulness of a city in the midst of action. The harbors were enormous expanses of ship-filled berths, boats large and small, everywhere the eye looked.

People were rushing back and forth, over the quays, pushing and shoving in a swarm of humanity. Some workers carried trunks up and down the gangplanks, while others rolled huge barrels onto the deck. Sellers hawked food, everything from bread and butter to a peppery soup. One of the boatmen grinned widely, as he thought of the two or three pasties and mugs of ale that would be part of his immediate future.

Captains in expensive blue coats with shiny brass buttons supervised what needed to be done. Others were simply poor laboring ship hands who swabbed, cooked, wrangled long ropes, and climbed the lines and beams to the top of the slippery masts for hardly a pittance.

Gentlemen and refined ladies in beautiful, expensive dress, with dainty handkerchiefs covering their mouths and noses, wound their way through the crowd with a servant acting as the bow of a ship, cutting through the oncoming surf. They were obviously on their way to something extremely important at which the travelers could only guess.

Grimy street urchins dressed in rags ran here and there over the wharves like herds of rats. They yanked on coattails and petticoats, begging for a few pennies or something to eat. Older beggars were also in abundance, some seasoned pickpockets, while others were too tired and sick to move away from the sides of the ancient wharf buildings against which they leaned.

The boat, which had been their home for almost a month, finally pulled alongside the wharf in an out-of-the-way spot. Ludwig looked up and knew they would have to climb the short ladder, which flapped from side to side. The three boys helped the women to the top and then managed to transfer their possessions from the rocking boat up onto the deck.

None of them were prepared for the smell that met them at the top of the ladder. Rotted fish, greasy sweat, oily galleys, and messes from an abundance of mongrel dogs filled the hot, steamy air. People smelled as though they never bathed or changed their clothes. Whenever any man not designated as upper class needed to relieve himself, he simply turned around and faced the nearest wall. The smell of urine was everywhere.

Even the senses of the three young men were assaulted, and they had seen more of the world than Barbara and the girls. Little Christina began to cough and choke, crying intermittently, her eyes stinging as she buried her face in her mother's skirts while she tried to catch her breath. She was acting out the overwhelming feelings of the others.

For the third time, they had to deal with being subsumed by a large crowd of people. They saw some with coal black skin or slanted eyes. Some had hardly any clothes on at all, while others had layer upon layer of coats and jackets they were trying to sell without any of the authorities discovering they had been stolen. So many different costumes and colors, all swarming together in a kaleidoscope of humanity. Barbara had told the girls Rotterdam contained at least a thousand people, but now she thought that thousand were all on the wharves of the city alone. All she saw were the dirty, wet, slippery wooden planks on the quays, none of the beautifully paved streets she had heard about.

As they traveled north, they had usually been able to understand the dialects spoken on the river. But now that they were in Rotterdam, the differing languages were swarming together such that they understood nothing.

One of the boatmen directed them to a good boarding house once they landed. "Up that street ahead of you and then turn right at the sign of the Fox," was all he could manage to say as they hurriedly tried to move their boat out of the way before another rammed it. They neglected to tell Ludwig the name of the boarding house, but he was confident he could find it.

Barbara hoped they could find a place as nice as the one in Mainz. She knew the Haucks' "boarding house" was not the usual in a large city. It was more like a travelers home for the merchant class. She knew her family had been fortunate to find it.

The dirty, exhausted tribe managed to pick up all of their belongings and start down the street. Christina had nothing to carry; her job was simply to hold on to her mother's apron and not let go. Ludwig told Thea and Carlie to stay close to him, and if anyone tried to touch or pull them away, they were to scream as loud as they could. Barbara quickly shot Ludwig a disapproving look, but just as quickly decided he was right to speak as he had. She knew they were in a completely different world from what they were used to and needed to be wary. Her throat started to tighten as she asked herself for the first of many times if leaving Massenbach had been the right thing to do.

As they rounded the turn, Ludwig could see a rather dilapidated house a short way down the street with broken grey shutters and dirty windows. A pile of immigrant possessions like theirs sat on either side of a doorway, and he reckoned this must be the boarding house. He left his family with the two other men to guard them and gingerly stepped into the dark, steamy hallway. A line of people rushed past him and out the door, speaking quickly in the German he knew. He continued down the hall until he was met by an old woman in a gaudy, powdered wig sitting crookedly on her head. She began talking in a language he did not understand, but then changed to halting German.

"One room, second floor, two beds." Ludwig tried to establish if there were any way to cook, and she yelled back, "No kitchen! No cooking in room! Forbidden!" Ludwig was disappointed; they had hoped to find a room with some way to cook so they would not spend their money on expensive meals.

But when she told him the price, he thought he would lose his temper. The one room was more than twice what they had paid at the Haucks. And there, they had had twice the space.

Ludwig almost choked when he said, "What a ridiculous price!" and turned as if to leave.

The landlady had obviously been practicing. In perfect German she stated with confidence, "Take it or leave it. You will not find anything better, I promise you."

Ludwig rethought his strategy. It was almost the middle of the afternoon, and they could wander until sundown without finding anything better. He finally nodded his head several times and said, "Yes."

"Right now!" she yelled again, holding out her swollen, shaking hand with dirty, broken fingernails. Ludwig fished the coins out of his waistcoat, hoping he was doing the right thing. *Well,* he thought, *we can always move to a different place tomorrow if need be.*

After Ludwig collected his roommates from out front, they pushed through the hall, dragging their belongings up the narrow, crooked stairway. The woman opened the second door on the left to the room on the front of the house, and then proceeded to march back down the stairs, determined to rent the one room she had left.

The room was small and dirty. Barbara looked at Ludwig with surprise, but he simply shrugged his shoulders. They both realized their understanding of a boarding house had been skewed by the Haucks. Two small beds with mattresses, two chairs, and a wash stand with a stained, cracked basin were all the room allowed for comfort.

Barbara said she and Christina would sleep in one bed, Carlie and Thea in the other, and the three boys on the floor on the now thinner, but drier, pallets. She was glad they had their bedding as they would have had to pay extra for that.

The room contained a small fireplace, which looked as if it had not been used in years. They wondered where they could find wood to burn, but soon realized heat would be the least of their concerns.

One good-sized window with a frayed, dirt-stained curtain looked down on the street. Barbara tried to open it further to let in some fresh air, but it would not budge for either her or the boys. The noise and the smell, however, wafted in through the small opening, and they all hoped these would diminish as night fell. With that, Barbara began to beat as much of the dust out of the mattresses as she could. She dared not beat too hard for fear they would burst. Then she began to clean the room, sweeping up the dirt, mattress dust, and other objectionable litter from the floor with the small broom she was glad she had brought from Massenbach.

Barbara was hoping they could get some warm water for the basin, but did not feel quite ready to climb down the stairs and ask the landlady for some. Someone would have to go down to use the privy, and they could ask her then.

The sun was starting to go down when Barbara realized none of them had eaten since breakfast. After conferring with Ludwig and the others, they decided to go out while it was still light and find something to eat. They could still hear the hucksters peddling their wares on the wharf and, so, headed in that direction.

Within a few moments, they found someone selling bread with butter right outside the boarding house door. Ludwig bought a thick slice for each of them, two for the boys, and found someone to fill a few of their mugs with ale, one half full with water. Christina dropped her piece and a trio of hungry dogs devoured it at once. Ludwig got another piece for her and told her not to be upset about the one she lost, but complained to himself about the money that had been wasted.

The family devoured their food standing in the middle of the wharf, glad the butter had been spread on thickly and was not even rancid. The price, they discovered, was reasonable.

As they trundled back into the house, they passed the landlady's open door. Barbara asked as nicely as she could if they might have some warm water to wash with. The landlady simply slid the arm holding the kettle over the barely warm fire and said, "Only one a day. More, you pay extra." Barbara nodded and hoped the water would not be cold.

In a few minutes, the landlady appeared with the kettle held in her bare hand and quickly filled the basin. One per day. Seven people. Carlie and Thea started first because they were the cleanest followed by Christina and then Barbara who was finally able to locate that piece of her lye soap. It was useless, however, because the water was not warm by anyone's standards. By the time the boys were finished, little water was left in the basin, but they had managed to get off the first layer of grime. They wiped their hands and faces on their shirt sleeves and tried to smile at each other.

Looking out the dirty window, they could see the sun had gone down; the room was beginning to darken. Barbara had forgotten to ask if candles were included in the price of the room, but decided not to go back downstairs and just burned one of the grease lamps she had brought. They began to undress down to their shifts and find their places on the mattresses.

Barbara reminded them to say their prayers and thank God for their great good fortune. They had all arrived in Rotterdam, together, with everyone well, if a little tired, and were making ready for the next leg of their journey. Barbara especially thanked the God of her ancestors for taking away most of her fear as she blew out the light and settled in for the night. She dreamed of a large, sturdy table, set with a gleaming white cloth and more food than she had ever seen. The sauerkraut looked delicious.

None of the women slept well. The room was hot and stuffy, and they and their belongings were still damp. A baby cried throughout the night in the room below them while his mother tried to soothe him. Some of the noise outside the house began to quiet, but then grew louder as drunken men wandered around the wharves, yelling and swearing, trying not to fall in the water. Women could be heard calling out to men in lilting, suggestive tones, for what, none could understand, except for the three young men who were able to miraculously span the language barrier. And for that reason, the three young men, usually able to snore their way through any amount of noise, slept poorly as well.

CHAPTER 13

Rotterdam

A s Barbara opened her eyes, the sun was just beginning to burn in the sky; the noise was beginning as well, although it did not seem as loud as the day before. Christina snuggled up against her mother, wishing she could sneak down the little stairway in Massenbach and find her sitting there by the fire instead of here.

The others began to stir. All except Christina wished they could have a cool splash out of the dirty basin, but knew the expense of that every morning would diminish their funds. They would have to do with a wash at the end of the day.

"I am hungry," Christina moaned, sitting up on the side of the bed and dangling her toes in the dust, which had accumulated since the night before. Barbara rubbed her eyes and tried to sit up, but fell back against the mattress, too weary to get up and begin the day.

"I am, too," both Ludwig and Hans said together. With that, Christina scrambled over on top of her sisters who groaned with peevish displeasure.

"Leave me alone," Carlie complained, as she tried to bury her head under the coverlet. She had already begun to wonder how long they would all have to stay cooped up in this airless room.

Once they were all up and had pulled their clothes on, Stephen suddenly stood up from where he was sitting on the floor lacing up his boots. "Shush," he said. "Shush," louder this time. Everyone wondered what was wrong, but they could see Stephen's mouth had suddenly broken into a grin. He hurriedly put on his other boot and bolted from the room. He could be heard out in the hallway calling,

"Adam, Jurg Adam Muller!" as he pounded on the door of the room next door.

Barbara realized the Mullers must have arrived during the night and become their new neighbors. She had been afraid something had happened to them, and now here they were within pounding distance. She pulled her costume into some semblance of order as Catharina Christina, known as Kitty, burst into the room.

"We did not know where you were!" Kitty cried. "Or what to think when we finally got to Heilbronn and you had already left. The mud was awful. One of the wheels on our cart came loose, and we had to keep stopping so Adam could fix it. I am so glad to see you all." Christina hopped up and threw her arms around Kitty's swollen belly. Kitty was one of her most favorite people.

Kitty was one of Barbara's favorite people as well. She was petite, but almost overwhelmed by her thick, brown, curly hair, equally curly lashes, and large brown eyes. Barbara had always felt bad for the little thing; her mother had one of the sharpest tongues in the village. Somehow, though, Kitty had always been the kindest, most even tempered, sweetest girl in Massenbach.

Barbara thought this must be due to Kitty's father, a kind, sensible man and a good friend of her Jacob. Kitty's brothers made it a point to be out of their mother's grasp whenever possible. And their father helped this to happen. Poor man.

Kitty and Jurg Adam Muller had been married last January, and God soon blessed them. Since the change in the rules for military recruitment, Adam had been afraid he would be drafted. The idea of taking a new wife with child across the ocean did not seem right to him, but he felt he had no choice.

Adam was as big as Kitty was small. He was stocky, with brown eyes, dirty blonde hair, and a full, bushy beard. When they were seen together, the difference in their sizes was not lost on anyone. Adam was simply besotted with Kitty and had been since they were in school together. Through hard work, he had been able to amass some property, and so had been able to marry where others his age could not.

The young men shook hands with Adam and all wondered where the Kohler family was, rehearsing individually the dangers of being on the road. They tried not to think of anything too sinister. Ludwig realized the missing family had best appear soon or the ship would leave without them.

What Ludwig and the other two, now three, needed to do that morning was to first find a ship and sign contracts for the trip to America. They were filled with excitement at the thought of finally engaging a ship that could take them away from all the ugliness in their lives. Their second task was to find jobs, ones that would be steady and pay them a good wage.

They had planned for the three families and Stephen and Hans to travel together on the ship to Philadelphia; they would have to go ahead and reserve their spot even if the Kohlers did not arrive on time. The group had decided before they left Massenbach they would stay together, but not at the expense of a missed opportunity.

Hans and Ludwig went out and found another bread seller, and the bread was truly warm this time. The yellow, fatty butter had melted into the spongy centers of each slice, flowing in rivulets, running down the holders' wrists. They proceeded to lick it off their skin with vigor. Once they reached the room, they passed the bread around along with more mugs of ale, one half filled with water.

The girls knew the first order of business was to find a ship to the New Land, and their disappointment landed all over their mother once they learned they would not be going along to look for it.

"But Momma," Thea pleaded, "we want to help pick out the ship we are going on. How can we stay locked up in this stuffy room all day?"

Carlie agreed with her older sister and added, "Please, we all want to go out together."

Barbara knew after they had gone out last evening into the swirl that was Rotterdam, they would have to stay put in the room most of the time. Once she saw what the wharves were like, she discovered a stronger sense of fear. Taking the girls out on the quays, nevermind herself, would not be safe. They were all used to being among the same five hundred or so people, most of whom they had known and trusted all their lives. Barbara was not prepared for the onslaught of humanity that roamed outside their door.

"No," Barbara said. "We can go out once a day for a short walk when the boys are with us, but that is all. " She knew being crammed in their room together would try her patience, but the situation could not be helped. "This is difficult for all of us," she said, putting emphasis on the word all, "but it will not be for long. I wish the three of you would remember that and stop being so selfish."

Barbara wished she could simply walk out the door and slam it in frustration, but that would not do. And this was only the first day. She wished she knew how long they would have to wait. A few days? A week? Longer than tomorrow would be tedious. The girls turned around and flopped down on the beds as the boys hurried to get out of the room to what they hoped would be a small taste of freedom.

None of them knew which way to go. The New Landers, who had come to the village last fall, said to go down by the docks, but that meant little to any of them. The four, however, sucked in their stomachs and puffed out their chests to give the impression they knew exactly what they were doing.

After wandering about for over an hour, they finally found the area where the large sailing ships were berthed. They saw several more anchored out in the harbor, larger than any boats the four villagers had ever seen. Three ships of varying sizes floated in the filthy harbor water. Two of them were actually ships, while the third smaller one was known as a snow. They laughed together to think a boat could be named a snow.

They could see other emigrants such as themselves milling

about the gangplanks, talking to a finely dressed man with sheaves of papers in his hands. They sidled up to the Englishman talking in loud, halting German, flanked by their countrymen. "No, no," the gentleman in the soft yellow jacket and stylish waistcoat said. "You do not pay your fare now, simply a deposit. You will pay 8 florins for every adult, and half of that for children three to fifteen. Babes are free. The rest of your fare is due when we leave port."

A disgruntled man with a shaggy beard asked, "Well, can we get on the boat and see what you provide? How can you expect us to take it sight unseen?"

The gentleman laughed a little and said, "This boat, as you call it, is the ship *Francis and Elizabeth*, and it has only been in port for five days. Not even completely unloaded yet. And then we have to build the accommodations so you will be comfortable, which will take at least another three or four weeks. That takes us until about the middle of June. Once the bunks and other passenger areas have been completed, we will load 'er up and head to England."

Stephen thought he would choke as the words, "Three or four weeks," burst out of his mouth. He could see their funds diminishing before his eyes as they paid their surly landlady for four more weeks and bought who knows how many terrible, inadequate meals. They could not live on only bread forever.

The other three had the same thoughts and wondered how they would all bear the wait. Four weeks was a long time, especially when they were all so anxious to get on with their lives. They did not have to wonder how the women-folk would take the news.

The man continued with his sale's pitch. "Now, that is four weeks assuming everything goes well. The last trip we had trouble finding enough seamen to make the voyage. And all the wood and nails and such needed to refit the ship are difficult to find. We have rounded up enough experienced men to make the alterations, but then you never know when someone will become ill or decide to be on his way back to wherever he came from.

"And do not think, my friends, you will find another ship leaving sooner than this one. Yes, the ship *Loyal Judith* is right over there and leaves tomorrow, but it is full and has been for weeks."

Another man shorter than Hans waved both his arms in the air and yelled, "How do we know there will be a place for us when the ship is ready to sail?"

"We will sign you up with a contract so you know how much space you will need and how much you will have to pay for it. We will need that deposit when you sign the contract, so you do not decide to go back home and leave us with empty bunks we are unable to fill at the last minute. I have a few blank contracts right here you can look at if you wish."

The four crowded around the sheet of paper the gentleman had given to Adam and tried to make sense of what they saw. The contract was written in Dutch, which, of course, none of them could read or understand.

"I have one in English, too," the man offered with a smile, knowing he was probably not being helpful.

"Do you have a copy of this in German?" Adam asked, trying not to let the exasperation show in his voice.

"Of course, of course," the man replied. "Meet me here tomorrow at about noon."

The four men were as excited as they had been when they were little boys and school let out for the summer. And yet the uncertainty, the language barrier, and their poor knowledge of prevailing customs quickly put a damper on their enthusiasm.

Stephen mocked in a whiny voice, "Here is a copy of the contract in either Dutch or English even though I know you cannot read either of them."

"Tomorrow," Hans said. "We will have our answers tomorrow."

CHAPTER 14

Waiting

The quartet traipsed back to their rooms, each of them trying to focus on the positive aspects of their situation. They knew they somehow had to go forward. So much money had been spent to get to Rotterdam, they doubted they had enough to make the return trip to Massenbach. And the money they did have had to last. None of them wanted to spend the next seven years of their lives working for a master who paid their passage when they got to America and then kept them as indentured servants. The thought of any of their female relatives having to do this, as well, made them all quite sober. Stephen had not told Ludwig he had heard children as young as six, just like Christina, were taken away from their parents and made to work under horrible conditions.

When they arrived at the boarding house, Kitty was visiting with the Fridbergs in their room. They all perked up and assailed the four young men with questions. How long before we leave? Tomorrow? What kind of food do we get? How much does it cost? What will we do if the Kohlers do not arrive on time?

Ludwig, who was now the spokesman for the group, told them all to sit down, and he would tell them what he knew.

"First of all," he began, "Mother, Thea, and I will be charged the full fare while Carlie and Christina will pay half of it."

Christina's heart jumped when she thought she and Carlie would have to pay their own fares. Neither of them had ever had any money. She suddenly had a fleeting glimpse of what life would be like with the two of them living in Rotterdam by themselves, begging on the wharf, and sleeping in the alley by their boarding house. Her horrified look turned her mother's head and forced Barbara to smile as she realized what her youngest daughter was probably thinking.

"No, Christina," she reassured. "You do not have to pay your fare yourself. Ludwig and I will pay it for you."

Christina quickly calmed her screaming mind and cast a grateful look at Ludwig. "I do not have any money of my own," she said to him under her breath, as if it were a failing. Carlie tried to look non-plussed by the situation, but knew God had recognized her heart beating at breakneck speed along with Christina's. Ludwig walked in one stride over to his two younger sisters and smiled while he put a comforting arm around each of them.

"And second of all," he began, steeling himself for what he knew would be a large dose of female hysteria, "we will not be leaving for at least three, possibly four weeks."

He watched their faces fall and turn into looks of surprise, fear, disappointment, and despair.

Barbara spoke first, feeling her temper rising in her chest. "But how can we wait that long? We have to pay for this filthy room and eat cheap, rancid food that will not fill us up. Our money will all be gone before we even get on the ship." Sweat was beading up on her forehead as she tried to calm herself. "So, there is no other ship we can take before then?"

"No," Ludwig replied. "The ship *Loyal Judith* is leaving for Philadelphia tomorrow, but she is filled to capacity. Everyone has paid a deposit, which, by the way, we will have to do as well. No one is going to forfeit their deposit unless they have good reason."

Kitty looked lovingly at her husband, summoning up a small smile to let him know she was still behind him.

Thea started to cry. "How can we sit here for four weeks? What will we do all day? Listen to Christina whine? Or maybe Carlie complain about how hungry she is?" She turned to her mother, hoping she would have a ready solution.

Her mother asked in a slightly shaking but even voice, "Why do we have to wait four weeks?"

Ludwig went on to explain the delay was caused by the need to convert the ship from a cargo to a passenger ship, find supplies for the journey, and employ sailors willing to cross the Atlantic. He purposely did not include the line, "Four weeks if everything goes as planned."

Both Carlie and little Christina were upset by their sister's unkind remarks. Carlie fired back, "Well maybe we can listen to Thea cry like a baby all day."

Christina went over to her mother, who was sitting on the bed, and buried her head in Barbara's lap. Christina did not like to see people fight.

Barbara gave the other girls a reproachful look over the top of Christina's head. "This is going to be difficult for all of us."

Ludwig said to Adam a bit louder than he had intended, "Could I stay with you in your room tonight?"

Another reproving look came in Ludwig's direction as his mother's eyes began to fill with tears.

At this point, both Christina and Thea were sobbing, Carlie's face was turning red, and Kitty was looking lovingly again at her husband.

"We can do this," Barbara spoke up after a long silence. "We must ask the Lord to help us brave this setback and deal with our disappointment." But she, too, was worried about the money running out. What were they going to do? That fear gripped her for a second time.

Hans, who hardly ever spoke said, "Look, all four of us are going out first thing tomorrow. I am certain we will find work and earn a fair wage. These docks are a busy place. None of us are afraid of hard work, and all these ships need to be loaded and unloaded. Stephen and I will share what we earn with you, Frau Fridberg. You know that. Maybe we will be able to buy better food, maybe even

some treats like apples. That would certainly cheer everyone up."
They all seemed to be getting used to the radical change in their plans
as they dried their eyes and tried, however haltingly, to put their faith
in God. They knew they had no other choice.

Ludwig waved the other men toward the door as they grabbed
the mugs and set out to forage for their suppers. His mouth began to
water as he thought about how good a bowl of hot broth with rivels
would taste right then.

The shoppers decided together everyone needed a boost. They
would spend a little more than yesterday to make that happen.

They soon returned, laden with food and smiling faces, having
found a man with sore, swollen feet who was selling cooked sausages
and wanted to go home. They bought all of the sausages he had left,
enough for a feast, and bought them at a low price, too. In the few
minutes they had spent with him, they learned he had immigrat-
ed in '39 from Ittlingen, a village close to their own. His feeling of
closeness with these strangers may have affected the price he charged
them.

Along with mugs of ale, one half water, they found hot biscuits,
fresh from the oven. Finally, they found the apples their mouths had
been watering for.

None of them wanted to rush back to the boarding house, but
knew the women were hungry. They picked up their pace, hoping
they would be regarded as heroes with the food they carried. A silent
prayer went up from the four of them, "Please, God, let us all find
work tomorrow."

CHAPTER 15

The Contract

The next day did not dawn as they had hoped. The red sun slid through the soggy air and disappeared before it had a chance to shine. The four young men knew, however, that regardless of the weather, they would all get up early, put on cheery faces, and head to the docks. They had to find jobs and return back to the *Francis and Elizabeth* at noon to look at their contracts.

They did not know where to begin. They found the area where ships were being loaded and unloaded and started asking passersby if they knew where any work might be had. They were met with some sneers and a few grunts, but their questions were mostly ignored. They finally found what looked like the captain of a ship who was talking in halting German to a few scruffy-looking workers about how much he would pay for how much work. Apparently, the wage was not to their liking, and they were on their way amid shouts and insults, shaking their fists at the captain as they left. Without even thinking, the four scurried up to the official and asked if he was looking for workers. He allowed that he was and told them what he would pay for men to unload his ship. The young men had no idea if this was a fare wage; they had never worked for money before. But they eagerly took his offer.

"I only need two more. You, the big one," he said pointing to Adam, the most rugged looking of the four. "And you, the tall one. That is all I need. And to be sure this is understood, I will need you for only two days." Stephen and Hans tried to smile at the others as they turned and trudged on down the wharf.

They found their way back to the *Francis and Elizabeth* at noon, where the representative for the ship was standing at the end of the gangplank just as he had said he would. He recognized them and had a copy of the contract ready.

Stephen was a fairly good reader and began pulling apart what was rather a long, complicated document. The heading of the page said " The Ship Francis and Elizabeth" and under that "Capt. George North, Master." The ship's name meant nothing to either of them, but they did not want to bother the agent over who Francis or Elizabeth might be.

The contract outlined what the fare would be for each of them according to their ages. It described the sleeping arrangements, which they both knew would be difficult for all of them. They had been told before they left Massenbach to expect bunks 6 feet long by 1½ feet wide, one for each adult or two children, but this contract stated they would be allowed a bunk 6 feet by 6 feet. That would mean all the Fridbergs would have to sleep together in an area of 36 square feet, hardly enough for all of them. The Mullers would have to share their bed with Hans and Stephen and the Kohlers, if they ever arrived, with a stranger. That seemed awfully crowded to them. They asked the official how so many people could sleep in such a small space, and he explained half of the family slept during the day and half at night so they would have more space. They both wondered how well that would work, especially with the children. But being slim would, for the first time ever, work to their advantage.

The contract went on to explain the victuals would be handed out by way of "messes." A group of four or five would receive a certain amount of food and drink each week. One person would do the cooking, but the passengers would have to share the braziers on deck when the weather permitted. When the weather was bad, they would use the fire pit in the hold. A list of the foods they would be given included salted pork and fish, dry beans, rice, flour, and the most popular, cheese. They would receive beer or ale and water, some for drinking and some for cooking. None of the food seemed fresh, but Frau Fridberg had brought extra, fresher food along with her, and they knew she would share it with everyone.

The official said he would allow them to take a contract away with them, but insisted on a small deposit to be certain they returned it, whether signed or unsigned. Stephen quickly handed the man the money, then folded the contract carefully and put it in his shirt.

The duo wandered around for a while longer. Finally, soaking wet and chilled to the bone, they made their way back to the boarding house. Stephen realized the contract had gotten damp inside his shirt, so he carefully unfolded it and lay it flat to dry under Barbara's bed.

Barbara insisted they take off their wet clothes and wrap up in some blankets. She tried to hang their clothes up, but had little hope they would dry in the steamy, dark atmosphere of the small room. She knew the other two would probably arrive in much the same state and wished, despite the heat in the room, she could start a blaze in the fireplace.

When Ludwig and Adam returned hours later, they appeared to be in a much dryer condition than the first two. Ludwig explained they had worked down in the hold, rolling barrels over to the base of the gangplank to the main deck. Their workspace had been dark and fetid, but they were glad they had endured when the supervisor put the coins in each of their hands.

Adam went back to his wife with a feeling of satisfaction in his ability to provide for her, while Ludwig was just as happy to show his mother the day's wage. He let her know, however, the job for him and Adam was only for that day and the next. With some of the sausages left from the night before, together with the coins they had earned, the anxiety of spending money on food began to dissipate.

Barbara felt encouraged. She thought if two of them had found work that day, even if it was only for a few days, they might be on the road to a better situation. She tried to overcome her irritability from listening to her three daughters quarrel most of the day, but had little success.

After they had eaten, Stephen surprised everyone by bringing out the contract for the voyage. Ludwig and Adam were eager to look it over and spent quite a long time studying it, asking questions of Stephen as they went along. Finally, they began to read out loud so Barbara, Kitty, and the girls, too, would understand. They stopped from time to time to discuss the details and answer questions.

They were in agreement the contract was fair, given what they would have to pay. It seemed to everyone there would be plenty of food and drink in addition to what Barbara and Kitty had brought. They saw the main problem would be the sleeping arrangements, but agreed they could manage somehow. Ludwig said he would doze at night on the floor or sitting up, and then have a few hours of good sleep during the day. Kitty was not happy to be sharing their bunk with anyone, but was glad it was Stephen and Hans and not two strangers. Barbara, who had remade their straw mattresses from home into five now thinner pallets, knew they would have to somehow be remade to fit the area allowed.

The three girls did not know what to think. While the adults knew they would be thrown together with a mass of strangers, living on a strange diet, and sleeping in an even stranger arrangement, the young girls made up pictures in their minds of how the ship would look. None of them had ever seen a boat other than the fishing boats on the rivers and lakes around Massenbach, and then the river barges.

Ludwig vowed he would sign the contract for his family and pay the deposit on his way to work the next day. The official had told Hans and Stephen they should all sign on as soon as possible given the ship was filling up quickly. The excitement of thinking of himself and his family on the ship, on their way to America, made Ludwig beam with joy and a feeling of success. He knew his father would be proud of him for leading the way to a better life for all of them. In a sense, he began to feel more and more each day that he was taking his father's place as head of the family.

The other three, however, did not feel the same. How many days would pass before all of them had consistent jobs with a good wage. But then, maybe a ship would come in the next day, or the next. Ludwig said they needed to be patient; jobs would come to them soon.

CHAPTER 16

Discouraged

Ludwig and Adam spent two days working on the dock, while Stephen and Hans walked the length of the wharf several times, hoping to see someone official who would hire them. They had been told by riders on the riverboats and several men in Mainz, including Jan, that work opportunities in Rotterdam were abundant. But that was not what the two men saw. There were plenty of strong men working at various jobs, but Stephen and Hans could not tell where the jobs without workers could be found. Could there be another portion of the dock they had not discovered, or perhaps another wharf altogether?

By the end of the third day, Ludwig and Adam's jobs had ended and the other two still had found nothing. How they wished they knew how to find Jacob Hauck; he would have known where to look. They tried to keep each other's spirits up, frequently commenting on the same old saws—having faith in God, and faith in their abilities.

The two workers had been happy to bring home their pay, but now all of them would have done anything to avoid showing their gloomy faces to Barbara, who knew as soon as they entered their room what the news of the day would be. Chatter continued about how they would certainly find good jobs any day, but inside everyone's head lurked the voice of the devil himself.

"Why do you not give up and go home? You had better go now before you spend all that money on food." They could hear his evil laughter as they wracked their brains to find a solution.

They counted every day as it passed by along with the money they had brought and the little they had made. The boys thanked God they did not have to spend time during the day in the room with quarreling girls, but felt sorry for their matriarch who did.

On the tenth day, they came home to find Christina under the bed crying, Carlie shouting at Thea, and Barbara in a terrible state of anxiety, sweating and gulping air in an effort to stop yelling. The four of them, as usual, rushed up to the two before they had even crossed the threshold.

And the questions. "Did you find anything?" The women had to know the answer to that from the looks on the boys' faces. "Did you see any other men working?" Of course we did. That is why all the jobs are taken. "Do you think there will be work tomorrow?" How would any of us know?

But one evening a thought came to Ludwig that would change everything. If they could find out when the next ship was arriving, they could be standing on the dock to welcome it. If they were lucky, they could locate the first mate, or even the captain to get a head start. Surely, if they arrived at the ship just at dawn, someone would have to notice them and see what excellent workers they would be. But how could he find out?

Hans said he would go to the *Francis and Elizabeth* and ask how one could find this information. And as luck would have it, God was waiting there to help him.

The foreman of the work crew was cursing at a man with a carpenter's bag who was sauntering away at an easy pace.

"God damn you!" the foreman shouted after him. "Why did I ever hire you in the first place? All you did all day was to look around for lovely ladies, and that is all you did."

Hans could not believe his brazenness, but he walked right up to the foreman and said in his most sympathetic tone, "Looks like you just lost one of your carpenters. Must be difficult to manage your workload when all you have to hire is fools like him."

The foreman looked sideways at Hans, seeming to be sizing him up. "You know anything about carpentry?"

Hans pulled himself up to his full height and, much to his own surprise, declared himself to be an experienced carpenter.

"I have only just finished my apprenticeship," Hans lied, "but I am hale and hardy and willing to work hard."

"You look pretty puny to be a carpenter," the foreman stated. "How do you manage?"

"Well, sir, I have very long arms and work very hard," flew out of Hans' mouth. He hoped the head man would buy what he was selling.

"Well, where are your tools then, Master Carpenter?" the foreman snidely questioned. "You have to have tools if you are going to work."

Hans answered him quickly on the chance his excuse might sound plausible. "They were stolen," was all he could come up with. "Yes, stolen. Some thief came in the night while we slept on the riverbank and took them all. The bastard," he added for effect, socking his right fist into his other hand.

"Well, I am taking a chance, for certain, but I am behind now and Captain North is getting on my nerves. He is always poking at me with something. 'You have to work faster. My ship needs to leave the first week in July.'

"How about I hire you for a week, and then we will see after that."

Hans shook his head in agreement and nodded again when the foreman said, "Tomorrow morning before dawn. We have a lot to do. Oh, and do not worry about your tools. We always have extra ones hanging around."

The day back at the house had unfolded as usual. The Fridberg girls ate their skimpy breakfast, and then Barbara began to entice them into working on their lessons. After Barbara had been ignored for a time, the girls usually quarreled for about an hour, begging to be let out of their prison. After an equally skimpy lunch, Carlie and Thea whispered to each other for a while and Barbara told Christina a Bible story. Today it had been the raising of Lazarus. Then the girls took a nap, and Barbara, thankfully, had a little time to herself. Today they were sleeping well past their usual time, but Barbara was not about to wake them.

When Ludwig and Adam returned, they quietly tiptoed into the room, waving at Barbara. Their plan was to go next door where, as it turned out, Ludwig now spent most of his free time.

"Ludwig," Barbara whispered. "I want to talk with you. We can go outside where it is a bit cooler." Ludwig was afraid to find out what she had on her mind. She had been awfully quiet lately.

They went out and stood under their window. It was hard to hear each other with the noise of the wharf going on about them, but they managed. Barbara knew the girls would tap on the window when they woke up as a whipping might be theirs if they ventured down the stairs and out onto the wharf.

"I have been thinking," she began. "What if none of you finds a job? What will we do then?" She took a deep breath and then said what she had been waiting all day to say. "Ludwig, I think we should go home."

"What?" he bellowed. "How can we possibly go back when we have come so far?" He had been telling himself this would not be coming, but expected most days it would.

"But right now, we do not have enough money for our fares. Can we ride without paying and then get a job there to pay what is owed?"

"And why would you think we would have enough money to travel back home? Remember how much we spent on tolls? We would have to do that all over again, buy our food and pay the barge captains as well."

"But Ludwig, what will we do if we cannot pay our fares? Could we travel on credit and then pay the shipping company back over time?"

"No, Momma, it does not work that way. If we cannot pay, the Captain will find someone to pay our fares, and then we will work for this master for five or six years. I hear it is not that bad."

"What about the girls?" she asked. "What will they do while we are working?"

"Oh, they will probably have small jobs to do, or help out in the master's house."

At that moment, he sincerely hoped God was not listening. He was lying more than he had ever lied in his entire life. Indentured servitude was terrible. Families were sometimes split up and were never able to come back together again. Children as young as Christina were made to do horrible jobs. Some were fed poorly and even beaten. He certainly did not want this for his family, but above all they had to get to America. Some way, they had to do it. He was not going back to that hole in the wall they had come from.

Just then, Hans came barreling down the street, happy to see his two friends looking as if they were expecting him. "I have good news!" he cried. "Very good news. I found a job, and a good one, right on the *Frances and Elizabeth*, of all places. I will be a carpenter!"

"What?" Ludwig laughed. "You do not know anything about being a carpenter. All you ever did was farming." He laughed again and told his mother, "Hans does not even know which end of the hammer to hit the nail with."

"You and the others are going to teach me everything I need to know."

"By tomorrow morning?"

"Of course not," Hans said. "Just enough to get started. You can teach me the rest of it as we go along."

Barbara and Ludwig looked at each other and shrugged their shoulders. This was a crazy plan, but if anyone could make it work, Hans could.

The girls were awake and tapping now, so the three of them started up the stairs. Ludwig had already begun. "All right. You hold onto the wooden part and hit the nail with the metal part. That is called the head. You have to hold the nail while you try to hit it and hope you do not hit your thumb. The pointed part of the nail goes in the wood and the flat part…" His voice trailed off as he moved into the finer points of how to straighten a nail.

Ludwig was inwardly jealous that Hans had gotten a job, and he had not. But carpenters made a good wage and were in high demand, so at least one of them was working. Hans could not get them all to America, but he could keep them fed. And he could use his skills for telling tall tales to find out when the next ship would arrive in port.

Despite their lack of any tools for demonstration purposes, Ludwig, Adam and Stephen tried to turn Hans into a journeyman carpenter. They found, however, that using the girls' slates for illustration purposes was very helpful.

Hans left the next morning, armed with information and the will to succeed. He was given the task of building false walls in the bunk area, which he did with a likable young man named Philip, who knew exactly what he was doing. A few times Hans had to ask a question; there was surely no way around that. Philip answered the question easily and did not seem to take notice it had been something a master carpenter would have easily known. Hans kept a close eye on what Philip did, and had a tutorial running through his head at all times. At the end of the day, the two shook hands and said goodbye, as Hans sprinted back to the boarding house.

Everyone, including Kitty, was waiting for the report on Hans' first day. He said he thought it had gone well, especially thankful for Adam's tutorial on dropping a plumb line. He had had to do that repeatedly throughout the day and was only corrected on two occasions by Philip.

That evening the four of them sat in a small circle on the floor, reviewing the fine art of nail pounding, followed by a summary on using a level. Hans was exceedingly proud of this day's accomplishments and was looking forward to the start of the next day. And tomorrow he would surely find the chance to ask someone about how it could be known when the next ship would arrive.

The following day, Hans returned home more confident in his skills and full of information on how to find a job. He said the smaller boats, passing by an incoming immigrant ship, would, for a price, seek out the office of the ship owners and let them know when to expect arrival of that ship. So all the other men had to do was call at the various shipping offices and inquire when their next ship was expected, if this was known. The men would then present themselves early on the day of arrival and wait for something to happen.

Within the next week, Stephen, Ludwig and Adam all had jobs unloading ships. They worked from dawn to sundown every day until the ship was empty and work could begin on refitting it for the passengers' use. The money was not very good, but the long hours made up for this in the end. Barbara finally stopped poking at Ludwig to return home. Her faith had been restored.

CHAPTER 17

An Offer

God seemed to be watching over them; Ludwig, Hans, Stephen and Adam all had good-paying jobs working on the waterfront—unloading or loading ships, pounding nails or sawing boards, or whatever was needed. But most importantly, each one of them worked most days without layoffs or being outright fired. Their goal, always their goal, was to earn enough money to take them and their families to America. Frustration, however, seemed to grab Ludwig at every turn. He wanted jobs for all of them with a better wage and longer hours that would provide them with more income. They had to do whatever it took to reach America.

As Ludwig was rolling a large cask onto a ship one day, a stranger came up to him and began talking. He spoke perfect German, but looked more like an official or businessman from Amsterdam. His person was immaculate, dressed in britches, waistcoat, and jacket of the finest quality wool, all topped off with a fine, powdered wig. Ludwig could not help but imagine himself in such fine attire, a Philadelphia businessman owning several butcher shops, all staffed by his workers, the smell of blood and offal following them all through their days and nights, not him.

"Must be awfully difficult rolling those casks around all day," the man began.

"It certainly is," Ludwig replied, surprised anyone else could appreciate how hard he worked day in and day out.

"I am Friederich von Battenburg," he said. "Happy to make your acquaintance, sir."

Sir, Ludwig thought. *Not even close to being a sir.* But he finally found his manners and introduced himself to this man, von Battenburg.

"You must work very hard for little reward," the man continued with a smile. "Have you ever thought about trying to better yourself, young man?"

Ludwig thought to himself, *Yes, that is about all I do,* but responded out loud, "Oh, yes, but opportunities are scarce."

"Now you look like an intelligent man," Friederich said. "Mind if I offer a suggestion?"

"Of course not," Ludwig replied, looking around to be sure his supervisors were not keeping an eye on him.

"Have you ever thought about training to become a sailmaker? I own a business that employs smart men like you. We make sails, which are sold to ship owners around the world."

"Well, yes," Ludwig said, his mind beginning to think in serious terms now. "But how would I do that?"

"Just leave it to me," von Battenburg said. "All we need is to get you set up with the tools you will need. You will have to pay for them, of course, but you will earn back your investment in only a few weeks."

Ludwig thought this man's offer was too good to be true, picturing himself in a sail loft, working with his hands, not his whole body, returning home at the end of the day with energy leftover to do more than eat and fall asleep.

Von Battenburg quoted him the price for the tools, which made him wince, but he quickly assured himself this was an outstanding offer, which he had better not let get away.

The price he was quoted was a week's wages. A lot of money for him, but well worth the investment.

"What say you then?" von Battenburg asked. "Are you in or out?"

"Oh, in," Ludwig said. "In indeed."

"Excellent!" von Battenburg said. "Meet me here tomorrow, first thing in the morning. Bring the money, and then I will arrange for your tools. We can meet again the following day, and then walk over to the sail loft, about a mile from here, and you can see where you will be working.

"Just one thing," von Battenburg said. "It would be best not to discuss this arrangement with anyone. Apparently, someone has been going around pretending to offer the same opportunities as I. But unfortunately, he takes a man's money, never provides the tools, nor does he return the money. It would be too bad if someone got the two of us mixed up and talked you out of this wonderful opportunity."

"Of course," Ludwig said with hesitation. He thought the man looked trustworthy, but how could he know for sure this man was telling the truth? Well, he was not going to do anything to spoil this wonderful opportunity.

As he arrived home, his mother was waiting for him, ready to receive his day's donation. Ludwig had thought about what he would say and launched into his story as soon as he had shut the door. He could feel his face growing red like coals in the fireplace and his voice a bit shaky, knowing he was about to lie to his mother. Disgracefully, in fact. He hated lying and knew it was probably one of his worse character failings. He had never been able to successfully lie to her when he was little. She always found him out, and he never could understand how. What would she do today?

"Mother, something has happened," Ludwig began.

"Oh," Barbara said raising her eyebrows. "Something?"

"Well," he said looking at the floor. "I knocked a carpenter's bag full of tools over the side of the ship today. The foreman said I had to pay for them or I would be fired." And just for good measure, Ludwig added, "I am afraid the authorities may come after me as well."

"Ludwig, that is terrible. Do you have today's wages? So I shall give you four day's worth?"

"Yes, please. I am sorry this has happened, but it was all an accident."

"And an expensive one, at that. Well, it cannot be helped. We cannot have you ending up in the jail."

With that, she pulled her purse out from under the mattress and gave him what he needed. When Ludwig took it from her hand, he was certain it was going to burn a hole right through the middle of his palm. How he hated to lie, but it certainly was for a good cause. And he believed God would forgive him. At least, he hoped so.

"Oh, and Momma, please do not mention this to anyone. I would feel so embarrassed if my friends were to find out. What a fool I was to kick those tools into the water."

"Of course," Barbara replied, and then to herself, "yes, a very great fool. How could he have mistakenly kicked a bag of heavy iron tools off the boat? He needs to be more careful."

The next morning, he was up bright and early, fairly running all the way to the ship where he had been working. He started his day as usual, not wanting to look like anything was amiss. He was thrilled beyond belief; he would soon have a new vocation that paid well in Rotterdam and could help him to get started in Philadelphia.

Von Battenburg arrived after a few minutes, and Ludwig handed him the money. He could feel the excitement surge through his body; he was soon to have a vocation that would get him to America even richer than he expected.

As Ludwig began work the following day, he kept stumbling into the man in front of him. But shortly, that would not matter because he would no longer be working on that ship. The day passed and even though Ludwig kept a sharp eye out for his new employer, the man did not appear. Ludwig told himself that something must have happened. The next day was the same, and Ludwig was becoming nervous; that man had his money.

As his workday was ending, he nudged the fellow he had been working with all day. "I wonder if you know anything about a gentleman who offers men jobs in the sailmaking industry? I was supposed to meet him here yesterday, but he has not returned."

His partner laughed and said, much to Ludwig's chagrin, "I hope you did not give him any of your money. That man is nothing but a fraud. Shows up here every week or two and cheats workers like you and me out of our hard-earned money."

Ludwig could feel his face falling, but tried not to let on that his partner's words had caused him any dismay. "No, of course not," he replied, feeling the bile rise in his throat. *What a fool I have been,* he berated himself silently. *Giving a man I do not know my money on the chance he might just keep his word.* He had never been this angry with himself.

Ludwig chatted with his friend a bit longer and, even though he did not want to go home, he knew he must. He just hoped no more lies would be necessary to keep his story afloat.

Ludwig slowly slogged on home, feeling embarrassed and angry. "What a fool I have been," he repeated over and over.

As he entered their stifling hot room, he handed his mother his pay for that day, hoping she had not yet figured out his deception. "Another day closer to America," she always said. Well, thanks to him, they had been becalmed for a week before they even set sail.

He was certain his mother did not suspect anything, but knew God was looking down on him with disgust. *What a fool I have been, a stupid, greedy fool. I hope God will find it in His heart to forgive me, but I could understand if He did not.*

As the days passed by, Barbara asked Ludwig repeatedly how his new job was progressing. Ludwig always had a ready, "Fine" to placate her with.

But after two weeks, he could not stand it any longer. "Mother," he began as soon as he walked in the door. "You will not want to hear this, but there is no sailmaking job."

"No job?" Barbara barked. "What do you mean 'No job.'"

"There never was a job. There were never any tools, either."

"But, what happened to the money I gave you?"

"I gave it to the sail master, but I never saw the tools or him again."

"What have you been doing these past two weeks?" she fairly shrieked.

"Working at my old job. And here, here is my last two weeks' pay. But, yes, the week's wage you gave me is gone." He had hoped the sight of the money would calm her, but he could tell by the fire in her eyes it had not.

She raised her right hand, as if she were going to hit him, as she might a naughty boy who had misbehaved, but something kept it from striking out.

Oh, Ludwig, what have you done? She thought. And then, through the Godliness of her heart she saw a twelve year old boy with a tear-stained face standing before her. His father was gone from the earth, and he was left with the burden of caring for his mother and very young sisters, one as yet unborn. He was thrust into responsibilities he had not asked for, but had never shirked.

And now, he had taken on the job of shepherding his family across the seas and onto the coast of America. Some may have thought she was taking the upper hand in this, but both she and Ludwig knew it was him, and not her, who had succeeded in quelling their fear and moving their project onward.

And so, due to his young age, he had made a mistake, albeit a bad one. The money they lost might someday mean the difference between success and failure. Or not.

And with her arm still in the air, she folded it around his middle in a soft motherly hug, followed by the other. She could see the anger and self-reproach in his eyes and vowed she would do nothing to make these worse. To her surprise, he hugged her back, as they stood in the small steamy room, wondering what would become of them.

She then stood back, looked at her son, and said how she wished she had a nice bowl of broth with rivels to give him. They both smiled at the thought of it.

CHAPTER 18

Success

The days passed slowly as June wore on, making the wharves and the small rooms above them hotter and hotter. Even on dry days, the young men returned to their rooms soaking wet, anxious for anything they could put their hands on to drink. Their good luck continued, and, while each one did not work every single day, their little piles of coins grew along with the heat. They felt their bodies growing stronger from the loads they carried up the gangplanks and down, and driving nails into wood over, and over, and over again. They bestowed their wages on Barbara as the time had come to pool their resources without any mind to who had contributed what. Barbara hid the piles of coins in her mattress, even as she complained with a twinkle in her eye about how uncomfortable her mattress had become.

Hans kept the tribe apprised of the growing changes on "their ship." He described how more bunks were being built day by day along with a few tables with benches. Areas were being fenced off to hold the supplies of food, water, beer, and some of the cargo the ship would carry.

As time went on, he tried to imagine how the ship would look with adults, children and sailors passing their days and nights together, sleeping, working, eating or talking the hours away. He could not imagine how they and all of their belongings would fit. But, he kept his own counsel on this, and was glad he had once the ship got underway. He tried to make Kitty's treasured trunk fit somehow amid the upright and horizontal beams on the passenger deck, but knew this was not to be. He kept this to himself as well.

As the travelers adjusted to their temporary life in Rotterdam, they continued with worry over Gabriel and his family. Gabriel would have continued down the Neckar if he had not found the others within a few days. All kinds of tragedies filled their minds—the Kohlers had been stripped of their money and belongings by thieves and gone back to Massenbach. Or, perhaps, their riverboat had overturned, and they had all been lost. Someone could have taken ill, or Gabriel could have broken his arm or something else horrible could have happened. As they went through the day, the men looked around the docks, trying to catch a glimpse of Gabriel or his family. Barbara, Thea and Kitty took turns looking down from their window for the sight of any family resembling the Kohlers. But the time had come to where no room might be left for them on the ship.

Toward the end of June, Hans said one evening after their meal that Capt. North had announced the ship would sail the morning of the second of July, given the winds were right and everything else went as planned. The tides had to be just right to carry the ship along the northern coast of Holland and across the English Channel to Deal. He told Hans this could take anywhere from two to four weeks as the winds on the channel could be somewhat unstable this time of year.

They were all elated, as much from knowing they were beginning to move as from knowing they would not have to bear each other's close presence for much longer. Barbara thought they would finally have some room to breathe, maybe even to be alone for a few moments. Christina had become even more clingy than usual, which had tried Barbara's patience to no end. Thea and Carlie failed miserably at adapting to their surroundings, either fighting with each other, crying, or giggling. Barbara did not know which was worse.

The girls and their mother had started out in Rotterdam with daily lessons and Bible reading, but that quickly ended. No matter how much Barbara berated and shamed them, nothing seemed to work. They still had nothing to occupy their time, nothing to get ready for the trip or even clean up after themselves.

As the second of July approached, the girls begged to be taken down to "the ship" so they could see for themselves what one looked like. Adam, along with Ludwig, had taken Kitty, now more visibly pregnant, to see the scene for herself. She tried to answer the other women's questions, for which the men thanked her profusely.

Finally, Ludwig, Barbara and the girls made a pact; the girls would be shown their ship if they promised to work faithfully on their lessons until the day came to leave. They could go together along with Hans and Stephen. Adam and Kitty would stay home to guard their money.

Christina was jumping up and down by the time they left, but Barbara could not bring herself to scold. Ludwig gave strict instructions as to their configuration for the walk. The girls nodded, and assured Ludwig they would comply with the plan. He gave them his usual talk about strangers, and how they should scream if anyone touched them. Christina halfheartedly hoped someone might bump into her so she would have the excuse to scream, something she had been wanting to do since they first arrived.

They walked quickly, weaving in and out through the crowds as they had on their first day there. However, now that the boys knew where they were going, the little entourage quickly found the ship.

"There she is," Ludwig called over the din of the wharf, "the ship *Francis and Elizabeth*." The women looked with mouths agape over the expanse of the ship, bow to stern, up and over the many masts, beams and sails. Smiles came to their faces.

"Yes, sir, that is she. Three hundred and fifty tons with eight guns."

None of the women, even Barbara, could imagine what a ton was, but knew the guns were there to protect them. Barbara had heard pirates sometimes set upon immigrant ships, but did not relay this information to her daughters.

"We will be back in a week," Ludwig continued. "We will walk right over that gangplank onto the deck with all our possessions and down onto the passenger deck. After we find our bunk and places to store our belongings, we will be on our way to Deal in England."

Christina felt two little jumps escape her body while her mother was looking up at the top of the masts. How good that felt!

"Those are the crow's nests," Ludwig explained, pointing to the round devices attached to the masts, almost to the top. "That is where the sailor will see America and yell, 'Philadelphia, everyone!' Then we will get ready to leave the ship and start our new lives as subjects of King George the Second."

Christina was beside herself with joy. Not simply a baron or baroness, but a king. They would be living with a king in their new town! She could not imagine anything better. No one could find it in their hearts to tell her the king would actually be over thirty-five hundred miles away in England. But perhaps he might come to visit Philadelphia some day.

Everyone continued to look for the Kohler family and pray for their arrival. They kept seeing what they thought was Gabriel in a new jacket or one of the children skipping along the wharf, but still, they did not appear.

CHAPTER 19

Ready to Leave

Hans arrived at the boarding house at just past noon, five days before they were due to depart. He looked devilishly happy and suggested the five women might want to look out the window because a surprise awaited them. Below them on the wharf were Gabriel and Lisabeth. He was holding Anna Margaretha's tiny hand while his wife held Catharina Barbara in her arms. Everyone shouted at once as Hans raced down the stairs and brought the newfound family up to their rooms. After a great deal of hugging and kissing, they finally settled down.

The Kohlers had been in Rotterdam for almost three weeks, boarding at a house a few streets away. Their late arrival was due to Lisabeth who had twisted her ankle outside of Massenbach. It took both of them to push their cart, and so she had needed to rest until she could bear weight on her foot. When they finally came to Heilbronn, a boat had been available the next day, and so they arrived in Mainz in time to get another ride to Rotterdam.

"We looked for a ship to take us to England as soon as we arrived in Rotterdam, but did not find one," Gabriel explained. "We looked all over for you, but finally signed a contract on the ship *Francis and Elizabeth* even though it meant a long wait. We asked if any of you were already on the ship's list, but they would not say. Probably too much trouble. But, here we are, ready to be your shipmates after all."

Gabriel was the oldest of the five men, almost as tall as Ludwig, but not quite. He was the best looking of all of them with white, even teeth and a broad smile. Perhaps due to his age, he had the most knowledge of the group and had done the best in school of all of them. He had done well for himself, apprenticing as a weaver in Bonfeld before he met Lisabeth.

Lisabeth was anxious to see her brother, Stephen. She had worried about him as he had worried about her. "We stopped by the ship today," she told Barbara, "to confirm the departure date. Hans was standing at the top of the gangplank, and when he looked up and saw us standing there, he stopped and spoke with us for as long as he dared, even though his overseer was angry. We would have found each other once we were all on the ship, but being reunited today was even better."

Lisabeth had been born a Poppenmeier and looked amazingly like Stephen, except that both of her eyes were blue. In fact, all the other children in the family had the blue eye, blonde hair combination so prevalent in the village. She had a medium build and Stephen's happy, outgoing personality, making friends wherever she went. Both brother and sister knew this would help them aboard the ship and in America.

The following day, Barbara began lessons for her daughters. They had held up their end of the bargain and responded to Barbara's efforts much better than they had before. Now that the departure date was close at hand, she thought they might be taking their responsibilities more seriously. And she was so happy they had something to do; she had frequently lost her patience and struck out a few times. She reminded them almost daily that everyone in America could read and write, and if they wanted to become real ladies in Philadelphia, they would have to work hard. More often than not, Kitty came by and helped Thea so she could move along more quickly. But the tension in the room was palpable by the time the men returned for the day.

The day before they left, after organizing and packing up most of their belongings, they began their final lesson in Rotterdam.

Christina was working on Isaiah, Chapter 41. She read a bit haltingly, "But they that wait up on the Lord shall renew their strength," and then stopped, wanting to know what "wait up on" meant. Did it mean God was late and you had to wait for Him?

Barbara explained the verse meant you stayed close to God. You listened to Him and did what He wanted you to do. Christina seemed to understand that and continued, "...they shall mount up with wings as eagles." And here, to the horror of her mother, she began to wave her arms up and down as if a huge bird had suddenly descended on them all. Thea and Carlie giggled, and Kitty had to put her hand over her mouth to keep from laughing.

Barbara gave Christina the look they all knew meant someone had stepped over the line. Even Christina had to admit, if only to herself, no eagle had ever acted as she had, especially in the Bible. She put on her more reverent face and continued, reading "...They shall run and not be weary; and they shall walk and not faint." Christina seemed satisfied with her rendition of the verse, and her mother smiled and rubbed the back of her hand.

Barbara began to think about the verse, verse 21. She had not thought about it since leaving home. The verse meant God would give her strength and keep her from failing if she followed His ways. And He certainly had.

She realized, now, how little she had known about life at the age of fourteen. She did know sometimes there was not enough food, even for her and her parents. She sensed her parents sometimes did not let on how hungry they were so she could have a larger share of the meal. Remembering the cold nights when firewood was low, she could see her father pushing her stool closer to the small blaze as he moved their bench farther back into the cold, dark room. She did not know the wolf lived just outside the front door of every house in the village or how much trouble could be had simply by picking up a stick of wood you had no right to.

As Barbara grew older, she came to know her parents had received their strength by turning to God and His Son. She, too, eventually turned in this way toward a power so much greater and grander than herself, and even her parents.

Barbara looked back at her difficulties—hunger, cold, Jacob's death, and the early deaths of two of her children. She had been given the strength to overcome these trials and live a life that sometimes, although sparingly, included safety and abundance. She came to understand God was served best when His children lived in hope and gratitude.

As she sat in that stuffy little room, she could honestly say she was grateful for much in her life. Her oldest child and only son had grown into a man, seeming more each day like his strong, faithful father. Her daughters, though trials to her at times, were growing in the spirit of God and their Savior, learning the skills they would need as future wives and mothers.

They had floated in boats up unknown rivers to a city that both terrified and exhilarated them. And now they were ready to start the next leg of their journey across an enormous ocean to a strange place they could not even imagine. There they would live, hopefully in harmony, for the rest of their lives.

She had almost lost her faith, but God had come through for them again. They had amassed enough money for their fares with a little leftover to begin again in Philadelphia.

Christina reminded Barbara she had promised to tell them the story of Noah again after they finished their lessons. Thea and Carlie lounged on their bed and whispered to each other while Kitty sat in the chair, resting her swollen, burning feet on the side of the bed and closing her eyes.

Barbara began the story of the greatest voyage of all time. Christina piped up, "We are like them, Momma, going on a big ship to a new place." After a few thoughtful moments, however, she looked sideways at Barbara and wanted her assurance their lack of animals would not pose a problem.

And there they all were, just climbing down off one of the mountains of Ararat when Ludwig, Stephen, Adam and Hans burst into the room and declared they were hungry enough for six people.

July 2, 1742. The Massenbachers had been waiting for this day for such a long time. All of the men, and they were all men now, were thinking about the ground they would plow and the businesses they would start. The three single men could see their beautiful, faithful wives sitting by the fire holding their children into the night. Thea and Carlie imagined the strong, successful men they would marry, the houses they would own, and the babies they would have. Adam and Kitty thought about the child growing in Kitty's womb, the one they hoped would wait to be born a citizen of Britain. Christina, of course, was planning different strategies to get to know the King and perhaps even play with his children under the fruitful apple trees in their back garden. Barbara hoped they would all arrive together, safe and sound with enough money leftover to begin again.

CHAPTER 20

The Ship Francis and Elizabeth

Here I am in the Rotterdam harbor, waiting to pick up my next delivery of human cargo. My stern begins to swivel from side to side, rocking the huge rudder in one direction and then the other, as if I am trying seductively to lure patrons aboard. The blue-green sea churns around my hull, splashing up my side and over my rail, as a lover might run his hands over the fullness of my body.

But no one, not even the Captain, wonders how I feel about my impending journey, nor do they care. Will I founder in a storm taking myself and my cargo to the bottom of the sea, never to be heard from again? Perhaps I should have left well enough alone and stayed tied up to an out-of-the way wharf or been dismantled in a distant dry dock. But if one were looking carefully, he could see my bow swelling with the determination to fill my sails with the breath of the sea and begin to move the three hundred and fifty tons and more of wood, metal, rope and humanity west to the North American coast.

I can see a group of thirteen emigrants walking over the gangplank. The little one, the girl with the blonde curls, is full of uncontainable excitement. I doubt she knows the reality of the voyage she is about to take, but she is alive to all its possibilities. No fear in her soft blue eyes, just exhilaration at beginning what she is told is her new life.

The woman holding her hand, a mousy, housewife type, probably her mother, does not look as happy. Her face is twisted into a compote of fear. She looks obsessively in all directions, careful not to miss anything important to the well-being of her family. Her expression shows, somehow, that she knows what lies ahead, what the possibilities of a horrible death on the seas could be. Her mouth is jumbled in pain, her eyes little slits against the harshness of the visions before her.

Two other girls, who look to be about fourteen and fifteen, huddle close to the mother, trying to keep up. They both feel lost, not knowing what their future really holds or what they have just given up. They are calling on their faith in God, as good girls their age are wont to do. Neither of them looks well. One has bloody gums and the other looks swollen in her limbs.

A young man about twenty seems to be in charge of the whole group. He is tall and thin, strong and wily, with a voice that demands respect. "Everyone stay together," he says. "Hold her hand. Look, you have dropped that bundle. Pick it up. Hurry, the line is moving." No fear on this face, only determination to move forward into the future. And his smile. The broadest of them all.

A young couple, the husband as large as the wife is small, creeps along with the others. She is obviously pregnant and, unless she is very lucky, will have her baby on one of my decks. I have a way of coaxing those little mariners into the world before they are ready. Nothing I do on purpose, mind you. It just seems to happen that way. Her husband and another man are carrying a small trunk, probably full of her most-prized possessions. She most likely does not know her world will fall apart in just a few moments. Her husband, though he tries, will not be able to help.

Another young family with two small girls are so intent on staying together and holding on to their baggage, they have no time to think. They are taking things one at a time; first up the gangplank, next down the stairway, next waiting to be shown to their bunk, next finding their new home. I imagine it will be "next this" and "next that" as they creep their way to America.

Two other young men bring up the rear. One is average in every way, but the other is exceedingly short. His scruffy beard is all that informs he is an adult. He seems to know his way around. "Yes, down to the bottom and then turn right," he guides the others. The average man is carefully and calmly taking in the sights, slowly turning to the mast and then to the stern. You can see from how his eyes move he is thinking, processing, putting the entire scene into perspective. He shows neither fear nor joy as if he is just along for the ride.

Finally, everyone is aboard and the Captain takes his place on the bridge, ready to work with the pilot boats as I am pulled away from Rotterdam, into the wide channels that lead to the sea. I, too, begin to feel the excitement. The Captain thinks he is in charge, but on the ocean I am; everyone reacts to me. My sails are pulled to the tops of the masts and begin to fill with the sea air that will push us along to the coast of North America.

Sailors are running all over the decks, pulling on one rope, fasting another to a large peg. They do as the Captain directs, calling to each other trying to synchronize their efforts. They yell to the passengers, "Out of the way! Do not stand here, stand there!"

The one part none of us can control, and we all know what this is, Captain and passenger alike, is what the weather will bring. Blisteringly hot, frigid for the summer months, winds that promise to blow me to pieces and take me to the bottom. Or we could be calmed for weeks at a time. A pleasing time for me, but it makes for a longer journey and people become bored and hungry.

Passengers settle in, the quartermaster distributes food, sailors haul up water in buckets to pour into the large tubs that sit by the on-deck braziers. A large mastiff sniffs around the deck, forcing his nose into places it should not be going. He finally settles down near the little girl with the blonde, curly hair. Putting his head in her lap, he readies himself for a nice nap and a long voyage ahead.

But I never sleep. I am always on guard, on duty so to stay. I always have to be ready for whatever comes our way. But once we reach our destination, I can go back to bobbing and rest languidly in the waters of the New Land.

CHAPTER 21

Embarking

E veryone awoke early, even before the sun. They ate some of the bread and butter purchased the day before to take on the ship, not knowing when they would have their next meal. Saying a thankful goodbye to their temporary prison, they hobbled down the crooked stairway and out into the now uncrowded street. Barbara summoned a smile in the direction of the landlady as she passed her door, almost feeling sorry for her; they were leaving, and she was not.

As they neared the water, their hearts began to pound and excitement mixed with the blood in their veins. Other groups such as theirs milled about, making last-minute adjustments to this and that. Sailors on the ship scurried here and there making final preparations. Suddenly, there was the ship, towering over them

Captain North stood at the base of the gangplank, asking for names and consulting with his assistant to be certain everyone's contracts were in order. He checked all the children's birth certificates, but thought that Fridberg girl looked bigger than a ten year old should and wondered if they were trying to sneak an older girl on at half price. But her baptismal certificate did say her stated age, and he decided not to make an issue of it. He let the Fridberg family pass over the gangplank and down into the darkness of the passenger deck.

The families, now joined by the Kohlers, were jostled and pinched by the crowd, holding onto their possessions with all their strength. As Adam and Kitty began to cross the gangplank, they were stopped by one of the sailors in charge of assigning bunks to each family.

"Sorry, Missus," he said in German, "but you cannot bring that chest into the passenger area." He casually spit a mouth full of tobacco juice onto the deck, just missing Kitty's foot.

Kitty looked at Adam with panic in her eyes. Her father had made that chest for her as a confirmation gift when she was fourteen. She could not let it out of her sight.

———————

Hans Jerg Stocker had scrimped and saved to buy the wood to make his only daughter a chest, piecing together the different kinds and planing them so they flowed together as one. He was a carpenter, and that showed in his workmanship; but the details he had so painstakingly added showed the love he felt for his daughter and the sorrow for she would soon cease to be a girl and become a woman right in front of his eyes. The thought had never occurred to him that she would leave him forever.

The box itself sat on ball feet, carved out of four different ends he removed when he was repairing the beams in Herr Steinhilber's house. The top was not flat, but fashioned into a shallow dome. Inside on the left, he had installed a till with a lid where she could keep money, small objects, and her most precious possessions. Although he would have liked the color to be brighter, he settled for the impurities in the grayish-blue surface, knowing he could afford nothing better. On the top, front and ends he painted open squares in brown. He knew his painting skills were not adequate, but he managed to fashion the likeness of a stem with small blue flowers on the stalk inside each square. When he was finished, he attached small, leather straps to each end for lifting it.

Jerg began to work on the chest in the cow shed, hoping Kitty's mother, Anna Maria, would not notice. He was afraid she would be angry that he had spent even a penny on the materials seeing as she had to pinch every one that came her way.

"What are you making her a chest for, you stupid man?" Maria had ranted. "Why are you spending money we do not have? So she can have an empty box to take to her home once she is married? Or are you going to fill it full of linens, pots and pans, tinware and knickknacks we also cannot afford? And I suppose we are assuming she will have a candle or two in this beautiful hovel of hers so we can all come by and admire the lovely decorations none of us can see."

"Be quiet, Maria!" Jerg ordered. "Everyone will hear you. I can see Frau Ritter hanging out her upstairs window now."

"I do not care, you idiot!" she screamed back. "You cannot fix the hinge on the back door, but you have all the time in the world for that spoiled daughter of yours."

Jerg stopped working on the chest for a while, but resumed painting again as the time neared for Kitty's confirmation. Because Anna Maria knew he would finish and likely present it as a gift from both of them, she tried to hold her tongue and accept the inevitable.

But then he appeared one day with a lock and key. He knew he should have installed it before he painted, but felt this would have sent his wife into a frenzy. She was waiting for him when he returned from Schwaigern, knowing he never went anywhere near there except to buy something.

"You spent money on a lock and key? When will she ever have anything worth locking up? What an ignorant man you are."

With that he hit the side of her already red cheek with the back of his hand, making it even redder. "Enough!" he yelled. "You will never talk to me like that again. If you dare, you will know more than the back of my hand."

Maria moved away from him slowly, knowing she may have gone too far this time. Pastor Kimmel had stopped by the week before admonishing her about disobedience to her husband and her habit of criticizing him so the whole village could hear. For a few days she was afraid she might be punished by the Council for her scolding tongue, but that fear dissipated almost as quickly as the paint on the chest had dried. Pastor Kimmel also reminded Maria their daughter most likely heard their disagreements, and expressed his concern Kitty might learn ungodly ways from her mother.

Kitty, of course, heard their fights and cried throughout every one of them. She had decided at the age of five she would never ever be like her mother. She would treat her husband with respect and honor her marriage vows, never calling him stupid, even if he was.

———————

Kitty stood looking at her chest, wondering what they would do. She knew she should hold back and allow Adam to speak for them, but found herself shrieking, "Why not? I need my chest to stay with us near our bed. My father made that for me! What am I supposed to do, leave it on the wharf for anyone who wants it?"

Adam put his hands gently on his wife's shoulders and asked the sailor in a more measured tone why they could not move the chest into the passenger area.

"No room," the sailor answered. "There is hardly enough room for all the passengers, nevermind any furniture. Or did you think perhaps you could stow it in the Captain's quarters?" He was growing irritated with all the demands of the passengers and had no patience for anything as insignificant as a chest.

"You can put it in the storage area, but I can tell you now you will not be able to get to it once everything else has been packed in around it. You will have to take what you will want during the voyage now," he explained, emphasizing the word *now*. "When you have taken what you want, I will throw the chest in with all the others we have no room for."

As she heard how the man was going to carelessly throw her chest into the hold, Kitty began to cry as she tried not to, holding onto her mid-section, fearing the sailor might say there was not room enough for this either. Someone behind them in the line was yelling, "Hey, what is the hold up there?" Others called forward with other complaints.

Adam began to take some of their belongings out of the chest and piled them on the floor. Stephen and Hans picked up as much as they could carry, given their arms were almost empty.

CHAPTER 22

Settling In

A nother sailor came along and led Adam, his wife, and their friends around the corner to a bunk not too far down the corridor. Hans had gotten to know some of the men on the ship, and with a little help from his pocket of coins, was able to reserve the most advantageous areas for his friends. They were close, but not too close to the stairway and the opening onto the deck. Hans knew the hatch would be covered during bad weather, but would allow them a little sunshine and fresh air when it was open.

Hans had sorted out how the room on the ship would be allocated. The broadside he read in Rotterdam advertising the ship *Francis and Elizabeth* stated the sleeping quarters were "private and comfortable," neither of which would be true. When everyone had to stay on the passenger deck during storms, a certain number would have to be lying down in their bunks, while the rest stood, sat, or lay on the floor in order for everyone to fit.

There was little room to put any belongings, especially large ones. Passengers would only have parts of the areas between and under the bunks, which had to be shared by sixteen people. Other areas had been sectioned off toward the stern for storage, but he feared anything put back there might well disappear. He had again kept this all to himself, not wanting to scare or upset any of them. He wished now, however, he had told Adam about Kitty's chest; she was behaving as if her heart would break.

Hans had also not told anyone about the lack of ventilation in their living quarters. But the new passengers found out about it the minute they descended below the top deck. That first wave of heat rushed past them on its way to freedom in the space beyond the ship. With it came a stale smell of mold and rot along with the odors human bodies are want to excrete. It had been almost a year since people had been carried on the ship, but the odor prevailed. The air, if you could call it that, was stiflingly hot and moved not at all. It reminded the women of the huge oven at the baker's where they took their loaves to be cooked. Barbara wondered what it would be like once all the passengers had found their bunks.

The two-story bunks were arranged with one side up against a false wall, then a space of a few feet, and then another bunk. There were upright beams and another thin wall that separated the next suite configured like the first. Adam and Kitty, along with Stephen and Hans would have the bottom of the first six by six foot beds, and the Fridbergs would share the top. The Kohlers would have three quarters of the opposite bottom bunk with a fourth person or even two children assigned to them later on. The top bunk would hold people who would be strangers to all of them. At least a few areas with tables and benches would be available where everyone could take turns sitting down to eat. What a luxury given the lack of amenities anyplace else.

Adam easily saw why the chest could not come with them. There simply was no room. If they could find ways to squirrel away the things they needed, especially their extra food, they would be doing well. He prayed silently the chest would still be there when they went to retrieve it.

Barbara got busy, sweat pouring down her face and neck into the bodice of her shift, and started organizing both people and belongings. The bunks seemed high enough off the floor so that much could be stored under them.

Barbara set Thea and Carlie to pulling their pallets and blankets up onto the family's bunk, spreading them out to provide a little softness between their bodies and the floor of the bed. Barbara knew, however, the arrangement would never amount to more than a jumbled mess. And clearly, they would all be lying with the blankets under, not over them.

A feeling of suffocation began to overtake Barbara's previously quiet and grateful mind. There was no room, no room for anything. The Fridbergs would be able to at least sit up, but the Mullers bunk left only a few feet of headroom. Yes, there was plenty of storage room under the bunk, but they would have to take out the things at the edge and front to get to the things in the middle.

Suddenly, one of the girls on the top bunk screamed and tumbled over the side followed immediately by the other. Thank goodness Christina had been lying down with Kitty on her bed.

"Something moved!" Thea yelled, trying to even her breathing so she could tell Ludwig what had happened. "It wiggled, and then moved, and then wiggled again. I think it was an animal!"

Ludwig tried to act nonplused by the event, but said he would see what was happening. He climbed partway up the ladder and then heaved himself up onto the platform. As he did, he saw a slick, brown, furry figure with a sharp, pointed nose spring out from the bedding, jump to the beam above his head and scurry along it out of sight. Ludwig knew these ships carried vermin—mice, rats, and other small mammals—which made their homes among the passengers. While the animal was too large for a mouse, it was about the right size for a rat. He did not have a good feeling about this.

He leaned his body over the side of the bunk and called down to the sea of faces staring back at him, "No, nothing up here that I could see. I think it was only a lump in the blankets." He tried to look as if he believed what he was saying, but he knew from the expression on his mother's face she did not.

"No!" Thea barked. "It moved. I saw it move. I know it was an animal. It looked like it was going to bite me!"

Carlie had never been bothered by small creatures, not snakes, not mice, not spiders. Anything moving that was smaller than a cow, however, had always sent Thea up on a stool or running hysterically into or out of the house. Carlie thought wryly to herself, *At least Christina would be pleased now that an animal had been sighted.*

Ludwig did his best to straighten out the bedding and then climbed slowly down to show everything was all right.

Just at that moment, a different sailor appeared and said, "You," pointing to Ludwig, "how many in your family?"

"Three adults and two children," Ludwig replied, wondering why he needed to know.

"Good, you will be a mess of four. Report to the quartermaster on deck. He will give you your food for today. You will get enough for the rest of the week tomorrow." With that, he turned around quickly and scurried off like that small, furry animal. Barbara had heard the sailor give his instructions to Ludwig, so she grabbed some plates and containers and followed him up to the deck.

Emigrants such as themselves, some with trunks, were still coming over the gangplank, although the line seemed almost to the end. She was glad she had left her trunk behind. Ludwig had told Barbara back in Massenbach he was not sure her trunk would fit on the ship, so he and Stephen moved it over to Johannes' for Juliana to have. It had belonged to Barbara's mother, and Barbara wanted to be sure it would remain safe. She thought briefly about the daughter she had left behind, but hurried on to keep up with Ludwig.

The quartermaster stood in the middle of the deck, surrounded by barrels, crocks, and a sea of stoneware pitchers. Many of their fellow passengers had lined up to receive their rations for the day. Barbara held out one of their trenchers, and a sailor put a large scoop of rice into it followed by a medium portion of salt pork. They also received a sizable piece of hard cheese and two small loaves of bread with a ration of butter. Finally, they were given a pitcher of ale along with two pitchers of water.

The quartermaster directed them to the braziers, which were burning on the deck. A large barrel had been cut in half and placed on a hearth of bricks. After the bottom was filled with several inches of sand, a fire was laid on top. Around the fire stood several large tubs of water, ready to quench any stray flames.

Barbara put the rice and most of the water into her three-legged pot and put it over the coals. She would have soaked the pork to get rid of some of the salt, but the quartermaster told her that was not necessary; the pork had just recently been packed. Going back down to the passenger deck, she collected her frying pan; she might have boiled the pork, but only a small amount of water was left in her pitchers.

Kitty joined Barbara at her fire, and Ludwig stayed with them while they cooked. He smiled and nodded at some of the men as they walked by, wondering where they had come from and why they had chosen to risk crossing the Atlantic. People were milling about all over the deck, learning about their new neighbors. Ludwig realized most of the passengers were men, single men. Many couples, of course, had their children, but few women were on their own. He hoped his mother and sisters would meet people like themselves. As for himself, he would be talking crop rotation and cess pit construction with the other men before England was even sighted.

Barbara, Kitty and Ludwig carried the food back to their bunk where Thea, Carlie and Christina were waiting patiently. No room was available at any of the tables, so they spread out on the two beds and leaned against the upright supports. The food was hot and surprisingly good, if a little salty. No water was left in either of the jugs, so the girls had to drink their ale full strength. While the ale had been watered down before it was put in the casks, it was still much stronger than they were used to.

Barbara instructed them, "This is all the food we are allowed for today. We need to eat half and save the other half for this evening." Everyone nodded their heads in understanding. "We will get the food for the rest of the week tomorrow, so we will have to ration it carefully."

Everyone had a belly a bit more full than they had had in weeks. The girls crawled into their bunk, and without even talking, promptly fell asleep. Kitty followed suit, while Ludwig and Adam went up on deck. Barbara was glad to sit down, if only on the three-legged stool she had installed at the side of the Mullers' bunk, and closed her eyes for a moment. She was grateful for her little stool, which at least kept her off the floor and away from the dirt that was already beginning to accumulate there.

CHAPTER 23

The English Channel

Ludwig and Adam stood by the ship's rail, watching the pilot boats starting to pull the huge ship out of the harbor and into one of the channels that led to the sea. Ludwig had been on several ships while working in Rotterdam and had felt none of the giddiness he did on the river. But now that he was again on a moving boat, that feeling had returned. It almost felt as if he were walking, but not touching the ground. Floating, in a sense. Suddenly, he felt dizzy and began to sweat profusely. Gripping the rail tighter, he tried to look more comfortable than he felt and hoped Adam could not see how uneasy he was.

Ludwig still did not know what was happening to him. He attempted to breathe deeply, but realized he was breathing faster and could not make the swimming feeling stop. When he began to feel sick, he moved away from the rail, looking as if he were interested in seeing some of the ship's rigging.

After a few moments, he began to feel better, but did not go back to standing by the rail. Adam had wandered off somewhere, and Ludwig was glad to have him gone. He felt a keen sense of embarrassment at this unmanly show of weakness.

As Ludwig continued to stand on the deck, he began to see snippets of a scene from his childhood. He tried to fight it away, but it would not go.

One beautiful day in July when he was twelve, he and Juliana had gone out on the river in a small boat with Wilhelm Gross, a boy about Juliana's age. This was an unusual activity for them given they needed to be working almost every moment of the day. They tied the boat to the stump of a tree in order to stay close to the riverbank as they lazily floated away the afternoon in the sun. They had no need to move away from the bank as they would not be fishing; all of the fish in the river belonged to the Baron. And, of course, they did not want to drift out over their heads because none of them could swim.

All of a sudden, Wilhelm stood up and started to scream. He had been stung by a wasp. He must have thought he was on the ground because he tried to run around the small boat, immediately tipping it over and pitching the three of them into the middle of the river. Juliana began to screech, terrified of going under. While Ludwig could barely swim himself, he was able to find his footing, grab Juliana and pull her back onto shore. When he turned around, Wilhelm was gone. He tried to look under the water but knew he could not swim out over his head, and so watched helplessly, waiting for Wilhelm to appear above the surface.

Both he and Juliana called for help, yelled and yelled for help, and finally someone heard them. Several men appeared, all of whom could swim, and they dove for another half hour trying to find the poor, unfortunate boy.

After a while, the search party knew their efforts were useless. They took Ludwig and Juliana back home, finally realizing the missing boy was Wilhelm Gross. His father, Johan, would be devastated; he and his wife had just lost another child to an early birth and now this had happened. The news quickly passed through the village, and another cadre of seasoned swimmers hurried back to the river. They found Wilhelm's little body, a short way downstream. He was cold and blue, something those men hoped they would never see in their own children.

Thankfully, Barbara was home, starting to cook the family's evening meal. The man who brought Ludwig and Juliana home, quickly explained what had happened, and then left to join the others at the river. Barbara screamed for Jacob out the back door. He was at the other end of the garden hoeing potatoes, but dropped his tool and sprinted in the direction of Barbara's voice. When he heard what had happened, he kissed both of his children on the head and ran back out the door. Barbara knew Jacob was on his way to find Pastor Kimmel for Jacob would have been useless at the river.

Once back home, Ludwig tried to be brave, but Juliana continued to scream and cry, gasping for breath as if she were still trying to keep her head above the water. Barbara could only hold and rock her back and forth on the bench. She thanked the Lord both of her children were alive and prayed for Johan and Philippina to endure this terrible day.

———————

Ludwig was finally able to shake that long ago afternoon out of his mind and push away the feeling of being over his head in water. He knew he had to overcome what he now recognized as fear; he was going to be in water over his head for a long time. Despite his feeling better, he did not again look over the railing at the water churning by for the rest of the voyage. When he thought about Juliana back in Massenbach, he hoped whatever she was doing, she was safe.

Those on the passenger deck could hear everyone walking, stomping and otherwise milling about above them. Barbara could feel a heightened movement in the ship and hear ropes squeaking and squealing as they slid against the masts and beams. She heard several commanding voices ordering this and that while a strange sound she had never heard before began. While she could not imagine what it could be, the sound reminded her of clean clothes flapping in the breeze on the line back home.

Just as she was dozing off, she felt the ship lurch, first to one side and then to the other. That sound grew louder, and she realized the flapping and banging must be the sails as they tried to catch the bits of wind that would carry the ship *Francis and Elizabeth* across the English Channel. The ship lurched again, harder this time, and seemed to move in another direction, and then another. The sound of boots sliding over her head and stomping on the wood convinced her the ship was definitely taking on wind. She thought of going up on deck to watch the goings-on, but did not want to leave her daughters alone.

Barbara reached for her shawl hanging off the end of the bunk above her, and wrapped it around her shoulders, already beginning to feel the dampness and chill of the water. It seemed that the coldness of the ocean would mitigate some of the heat. But within minutes, her shawl was back on its peg.

And then, that ongoing question began again. How could she be sure she had done the right thing by leaving her home? She went back and forth over her decision, following her thinking over the past few years. Although she knew for certain life in Massenbach was cold, hungry, and mostly just difficult, happy moments had been interspersed with the hardships. Her love for her family kept her from giving in to the despair, which seemed to follow her everywhere.

Every day in the village was just like the next, interrupted by a birth, a confirmation, a warm spell, or the first ripe apple. But the peace the church promised and her yearning for something in her life beyond mere subsistence was only a dream. Would she have to wait for death for the peace and happiness she craved? When Jacob had been there to encourage her, she seemed to manage, but since his passing, her ability to cope sometimes dwindled away to nothing.

CHAPTER 24

Underway

Barbara had heard stories about America, but was not naive enough to believe them all. Most immigrants she knew, or had heard of, left Philadelphia and went out to settle in the areas of fertile land in the country, almost free for the taking they said. She was a female with three daughters. Her only source of support was a young man who seemed devoted to his family. But could that last?

Could the five of them strike out into the wilderness? Could she deal with the Indians she had heard about? What would they do if they stayed in Philadelphia? She was good with a needle, but did not believe she could make a living with it. How many jobs could she do? At forty-one, she was not as strong or nimble as she used to be; she did not have the body to work all day and night with little rest.

Thea was old enough to work as a servant, and Carlie would be in another year or two. How would she feel if she only saw them from time to time? Would they have to sleep on a pallet on the floor in a strange house, work all day and night, and bring what they earned home to their family so others could eat and have a roof over their heads?

Ludwig could and would earn a living by way of his strong, young back. But how much could he earn to support his mother and sisters? Granted, he had learned a lot about how to butcher meat from Johannes, but could he make a living with these skills in Philadelphia? There was so much she did not know.

Would they end up right back in the same situation they had left? At least in Massenbach, they had fresh air and the beauty of the countryside to make their lives a little better. Philadelphia, she had heard, was a noisy, dirty and expensive place to live. Would they be paupers in Philadelphia, while they had been able to keep the wolf from the door back home?

Barbara knew she had to change her attitude, to look foward to everything positive about their new lives. She did not know what the apprenticeship customs were in Pennsylvania, or even the guild restrictions, if there were any, but perhaps Ludwig could find a job working for a butcher and learn what he needed to run a successful stall of his own. She imagined Ludwig standing in the market with a sharp knife, poised to cut up a quarter of pork while she disjointed chicken parts to sell to those with the money to buy them. Could this be possible?

Thea's beauty and even disposition would certainly take her far. Although Carlie was big for her age, Barbara felt she would soon grow into her body. She had a good head on her shoulders and would make a man without unrealistic expectations a good wife. Either of them could work in a shop as they both knew how to read and write and make simple computations.

Just as Barbara was beginning to doze again, she felt something wiggle over her toes. She cringed as she thought what it might be. Ludwig had, in no way, convinced her the "mysterious animal" on their bunk had only been a lump in the bedding. She knew vermin were frequent riders on these ships and that little could be done about them. Ludwig had done a passable job of comforting his sisters, but they would soon know the true story.

Coming down the corridor along with all the other noise of the ship, was another family such as hers looking for their bunk, dragging along the parcels and luggage they had been holding all day. The sailor with them pointed to the empty space above the Kohlers, and said this must be theirs.

"But remember," he went on, "seeing as there are only the two of you, two half freights and a baby, you will probably have to share with at least one more person. Sometimes it takes more than a day or two to get everyone shifted around and settled, so do not get too comfortable with all the room you have now." With that, he turned around and scampered off to his next assignment.

The father, who was tall with a full beard, nodded at Barbara as she got up off the stool. If Ludwig had been there, he would have spoken to their new neighbors, but as she was the only adult present, she began to make some introductions.

"Hello," she said, hoping she would become more comfortable speaking to people she did not know. "My name is Barbara. We come from Massenbach. My son Ludwig is on the deck right now, but he will be down soon, I imagine. My three daughters are having a nap on the top bunk."

Initially, the man seemed a bit anxious, but settled down as Barbara went on.

"You will have the top bunk," she explained. "I know the Kohlers left space under their bunk so you would have some storage." Thankfully, they did not seem to have much with them. "If you are hungry, the quartermaster might still be handing out food, and the fires are supposed to be lit until six. In any event, if you are going to have anything to eat tonight, you had best take a look."

"Hello," he finally offered. "I am Johannes Eckert and this is my wife, Angelica. We are from Langenselbold where I'm a cooper, or rather, used to be." Angelica looked at Barbara with enormous eyes and nodded her head. "And back behind Angelica, burrowing into her skirts, are Magdalena, Valentin, and baby Conrad. We have had a terribly long day."

Barbara responded with a knowing smile. "Have you ever heard of our village? I am not familiar with yours." Johannes shook his head and shrugged his shoulders.

"Several of us came from the Reformed Lutheran Church in Langenselbold, seven single men and six families. Some are going to Berks County, but others, like myself, do not know where we will be.

Perhaps Berks. It would nice to be around people we know and can depend on, though."

The man put down their belongings and shoved them under the bunk and into the corner. He nodded again and said, "Come Angelica, come children," and off they went.

CHAPTER 25

England Bound

B arbara took hold of the six feet at the edge of the upper bunk and shook them gently. She did not want the girls to sleep too long, fearful they would be awake late into the night. Christina, of course, was the first to appear, climbing down the short ladder.

"Come now," Barbara called to the other two. "We can go up on deck and see what is happening. I do believe we have left the harbor and, who knows, perhaps we can see England already."

After the Fridbergs were all standing on the floor and had straightened their caps, they went off in a line heading for the stairway. Christina raced ahead, but Barbara called her back with the reminder she must hold her mother's hand at all times until they knew what to expect aboard the ship. They climbed into the cool, fresh air and shielded their eyes as they looked out into the bright sunlight.

The foursome began to look for Ludwig, but he was not to be seen. Barbara led the girls around trying to keep her head down while looking for Ludwig at the same time. They heard his voice calling just as they were beginning to get used to the brightness.

"There you are," he said. "Did you have a nice rest?"

The girls and their mother, their mouths agape, looked in awe at the scene before them. They were far out into the channel now, although they could just barely see land in the hazy distance behind them. The grey sails were partially raised and were full of the strong wind blowing the ship along. The top deck was crowded with people, just like them, experiencing the movement of a large ship for the first time.

The passengers had been so overwhelmed by settling in, none of them had had a chance to look at the ship herself. She had three tall masts of differing heights with three square sails on each mast, the smallest at the top. Off the front of the bow was a short beam set off at an angle with a small sail shaped like a triangle.

While they had been waiting in line to board, the man behind them explained the configuration of the ship's body. Under the main deck was the passenger deck, and below that the hold where cargo and provisions for the trip were stored. Near the stern on the top deck was a compartment that belonged to the Captain, along with another cabin for a first mate or well-to-do passenger.

Sea gulls in the hundreds surrounded the ship, waiting for more of the tidbits of food they had stolen off the docks of the city. As the women looked up into the sails, they could see men in brightly colored shirts standing in what Ludwig had told them were the crow's nests. Thea marveled at a strong young man, probably her own age, skittering along an empty beam and then up the large ladder-like structure, which ascended into the sky. Although he was moving farther and farther away, she could still see his strong, sinewy arms and legs pulling him upward.

They could see in every direction; in front of them, to the side, and behind was nothing but water. Nothing. Just waves and the spray of the ship as it moved forward. This beautiful grey-green liquid of silent waves with small white caps riding atop was new to them. The ship's hull moved in an even rhythm, side to side, and up and down, as it plowed through the surf. Christina gasped with delight as they shared the exhilaration of the moment.

Ludwig thought his family might be frightened by the new experience on the ship, but was glad he was wrong. They were enjoying the scene immensely. No one seemed to be bothered by the motion, but then they were barely out of the harbor. Carlie tried to drag Ludwig over to the railing, but he simply held on to her as she looked over the ship's side. She wanted him to move beside her and kept tugging on him, but he forcefully held his ground.

The light was blinding. Barbara was glad she had brought along the straw sun hats they wore during harvest time and thought she would insist her daughters wear them. She could see some of the men and their families had already put theirs on. Carlie had lost the ties on hers, but Barbara was certain she could find something to hold the hat on her head. Clearly, hats would be floating in the ocean unless they were firmly attached to something.

The breeze they felt on the deck was strong and fresh, a gift from God after the time they had spent in Rotterdam, roasting in the juices of their small room or, now, in the hold of the ship. They walked around for a while still in formation—Ludwig on the inside—trying not to get too close to the ship's side or touch its rail.

Just then, they saw the Mullers talking to a young man who looked familiar. Adam waved them over and laughed. Here was Wolfgang Kobber from Berwangen, a village northwest of Massenbach. Ludwig knew him as well. Wolf's sister, Apollonia, was married to Karl Neumann, one of the young men at their last-night party. Wolf earned his living as a day laborer, owning no land or anything else of value.

Wolf had often come to Massenbach on Sunday afternoon to visit his sister and had gotten to know some of the young men in the village. He wanted to move to Massenbach, but while the officials in Berwangen would have been happy to see him go, those in Massenbach would not have allowed him permanent entry. Massenbach did not need another mouth to feed. Overpopulation was already causing great hardship, and the village did not need another man without a job. But worst of all, he could be another man just waiting to father an illegitimate child.

"Wolf!" Ludwig exclaimed clapping him on the back. "What are you doing here? Out for a boat ride, eh?"

Wolf chuckled and replied, "Ludwig Fridberg, the giant of Massenbach. How are you? Who else is here from your village? I had no idea anyone so close by was emigrating, too. Of course, I did not let it be known I was leaving because," and at this he lowered both his head and his voice, "I had no money for the fees." He looked sheepish, staring down at the deck, as did the other adults around him.

Adam began, "Well, the Fridbergs are here, and also Stephen Poppenmeier, Hans Schmaltzhafft and Gabriel Kohler and his family. We all tried to come to Rotterdam together, which did not work out well. But now we have found each other and are together for this wonderful voyage."

Wolf asked if they knew their destinations in America. He was going to Lancaster, west of Philadelphia. A few fellows from Berwangen had settled there and had written, encouraging him to follow them. They said he could work as a laborer for a few years and earn enough money to buy his own plantation. He might even be able to marry fairly soon.

Ludwig began, "Stephen and Hans are planning to go to Dillingersville in Northampton County. Stephen has some family there. I am going to try my luck in Philadelphia, maybe find work as a butcher's helper until I can set up my own stall in the market. My mother and sisters may be able to find work, as well, at least until I can get on my feet. Adam is still not sure what he wants to do, but with all the farming he has done, he could certainly make a success of that. Or maybe he will keep me company in Philadelphia."

Adam laughed and said what they had all been thinking. "At least there is plenty of land there, cheap land, and the right to make the best living a man could without having to give most of what he earns to a baron. If you need firewood, you simply go out in the woods and cut down a tree. Even if the tree belongs to someone else, he will not mind a bit. What is one tree when you own a thousand, or even more? No more freezing nights with no way to stay warm."

They all realized this applied only to those living in the country. City living was another matter. Both Adam and Ludwig knew Philadelphia had its own set of hardships—poverty, high food and housing costs, and worst of all, crime. They would just have to see when they got there.

A short way down the deck, Barbara could see the Eckert family holding out bowls to the quartermaster and then heading toward the fires. They had at least another hour until the fires were left to go out at six o'clock. She felt in her heart they were fine people and would be good neighbors. Ludwig said the single men were constrained to another section of the ship, so Barbara did not have to worry so much about her daughters.

The Eckerts had a child Christina's age. Thea and Carlie were growing closer to each other, which made little Christina feel left out. Carlie and Christina, three years apart in age, had been best friends, but now that Juliana was no longer about, Carlie had moved up to take her place. Even though she was five years younger than Thea, she was happy to be separated from "the baby." Now, perhaps, Christina would have children more her own age to spend time with. She would not, under any circumstances, be allowed to roam the ship, and friends would help to keep her close.

The group from the State of Wurttemberg continued to stand on the deck, chatting, reminiscing, and sharing dreams of their futures. The younger children played together, organized by Christina, and the older ones huddled together talking. This would prove to be the configuration they would follow throughout the voyage.

Barbara felt happy and satisfied. Everything was going so well. They would have old friends to make the trip with while she was certain they would make new ones. Surely, the most difficult part would be having nothing to do. No cow to milk, no vegetable garden to hoe, no house to clean. What would she do with herself? Most likely, stand at the side of the ship's rail and marvel at the beauty of God's universe.

As the sun began to sink into the water, Barbara gathered everyone up and herded them down below for supper. The meal had been much better hot, especially the greasy salt pork, but they had saved their day's ration of cheese for the evening meal and were all content making that disappear.

Each bunk, up and down, was given a lamp to share. Either someone was holding it, or it was hung on a nail close to the corridor. Christina was forbidden to touch it, but made little attempts to tap the side when she thought no one was looking. However, once she burned the tip of her little finger, she decided a new game was in order.

Barbara thought they would have an early night, given all the physical energy they had expended in getting their belongings onto the ship and stowed away. They would sleep as the girls had that afternoon, with their heads at the uprights and their feet at the edge, Ludwig's hanging over. She only hoped they could all bear the heat and stale, stifling air. Once they had gotten settled and both Ludwig and Barbara had silently prayed for any rodents to stay where they were, Barbara began the nightly ritual of Christina's story.

"What story would you like to hear tonight, dear?" she said pulling Christina a little closer. The others, as they always had, secretly listened to the whole of the story even though they had heard the same ones since they were young themselves.

But tonight was different. "Tell me a story about our new house in Philadefeluh," Christina said. "What will it be like?"

So Barbara began. "Once upon a time, not long ago, a little girl named Christina Catharina lived with her kind mother, her strong brother, and her two beautiful sisters in a little house in Massenbach. One day, they all got on a big ship and traveled across the ocean to the beautiful town of Philadelphia in America.

"Christina's brother found them a lovely house to live in, built of bricks and mortar with marble steps leading up to the freshly painted red door. On the first floor was a large hall, a fancy parlor, and a stately dining room with an enormous fireplace in each room. Costly furniture was everywhere, with beautiful pictures on the wall, and warm, cozy rugs on the floor.

"In the basement of the house, where it was cool and dark, was the kitchen. An even bigger fireplace filled almost an entire wall. Clean white cupboards were attached to the walls and various tables and utensils were scattered about the room. A cool place to keep the milk and butter was located through a small door in one of the outside walls.

"On the second floor were three bedrooms—one for the mother, one for the brother and one for the two older sisters, who did not mind sharing. Again, the rooms were filled with beautiful furniture and luxurious draperies; the mother's room even had a cage with a song bird in it."

Christina interrupted, wondering where little Christina's room was. Certainly not in the basement!

Barbara continued, "And little Christina slept in the best place in the whole house. On the top floor was another lovely room. It took up the entire floor with windows that looked out over all of the city.

"Her bed was made of beautiful, dark walnut with a mattress full of fluffy little feathers and two pillows stuffed with the same material. Even though no small creatures filtered down on her while she slept, the bed had a canopy with frilly ruffles around the edge. The sheets were cool in the summer, and the thick quilts, which were the same fabric as the canopy, kept her warm throughout the winter. In the summer she would open all the windows, and the cool breezes off the harbor would flow over her little body as she slept."

"What did she do in the winter? Did she have a fireplace?"

"Yes, a little one in the corner. She could not have a big fireplace because of all the windows."

Christina's golden lashes started to flutter, and her eyes finally closed. Her sisters had fallen asleep as soon as they heard what their rooms were like. Ludwig was still awake, wondering which side of his stall he would hang the fowl on and which would hold the cuts of beef. He wiped his hands on his apron and fell asleep to the sound of steers moving slowly through the rustling grass.

Barbara turned to the wall and continued the story to herself. *If we could please have one room all to ourselves with a fireplace and maybe a room or two upstairs we would be ever so grateful. The cow could come later.*

CHAPTER 26

The Unexpected

Suddenly, Christina sat up, moaned, and vomited all over the bunk and everything in it. The blankets, their shifts, the stockings on their feet, and even the walls were now covered with her stomach contents. The greasy salt pork was having its way with her little belly.

Barbara covered her own mouth and clambered down to the floor the best she could to retrieve the slop bucket hanging on a hook below the lantern.

"Christina!" Barbara yelled, holding up the bucket. "Here, Christina. In here!"

Christina struggled to her knees and crawled as fast as she could to the edge of the bunk. She continued to retch until her stomach was empty, and then some.

The other children had been raised by the noise and Christina's cries. The smell was terrible. They tried to cover their faces with the bed clothes, but whatever they touched was sodden with bile and putrid food. Thea began to gag, but managed not to vomit, as she desperately tried to hold onto her supper. Ludwig, over against the corridor wall, was the farthest away from Christina and the last to wake up. He pulled on his britches, jumped down to the floor, and attempted to help his mother hold up the bucket and comfort Christina. He ended up using it himself.

By this time, the Mullers had woken up. Kitty was feeling unwell. Adam felt around on the floor in the dim light for another slop bucket, wishing he had located it before he lay down. He eventually found it hanging under the lantern, hoping it was not the last allotted to them. Kitty was lying as still as she could, holding onto her bloated belly and trying not to cry. Hans and Stephen had already left the bunk, heading for the fresh air of the deck; Kitty could now spread her swollen body on the bed and try to find some coolness.

Of course, all of the ruckus had woken up the two families on the other side of their common area. Gabriel, on the outer side of the bed, was rubbing the back of one of his daughters and whispering softly into her ear, while Lisabeth did the same to the other. In the bunk above them, Johannes and Angelica were readying themselves for what they thought was coming their way. Fortunately, the children between them continued to sleep soundly.

Barbara did not know what to do to help her family. She had not expected this sickness. All of her children had strong stomachs and were rarely sick, but the increasing action of the boat's motion as they moved farther out to sea had made them ill. She found a few rags she had brought, dampened them with the last bit of the water, and tried to dab at the bed clothes and Christina's face.

Carlie crawled down from the bunk, putting her foot right in the middle of Adam's stomach and, struggling through her embarrassment, tried to reach the corridor away from the smell. She found, however, the stench was no better there. As was happening with the Fridbergs, other families tried to comfort each other with their children crying and retching into more slop buckets. Carlie had avoided most of Christina's spray and counted herself among the fortunate for this bit of good luck. She was the only one of her party who did not vomit, not even once, during their entire trip.

Ludwig lifted his sister down from the bunk while Barbara tried to make a place to sit with her on the stool, wishing she had some water so Christina could rinse out her mouth. Just then, Adam's strong arm moved out and bestowed what was left of his own water on the mother and child. She gave Christina a small sip and told her to spit it into the bucket, not to swallow it. Soon, Barbara could see the color returning to her daughter's cheeks, even in the dim light of the passenger deck.

Ludwig bent down and spoke softly to his mother. "What are we going to do, Momma?" he asked. "We have little water and nothing to clean anything with."

"We will have to use sea water," Barbara said. "Take the pitchers up on deck and bring down as much as you can from the tubs." Barbara leaned her head back against the wall and tried to think. This was only the first night. Would the situation become better or worse over time?

Barbara felt Kitty push past her. Kitty grabbed the downstairs bucket and fell to her knees as she held it close to her face. Adam was quickly beside her, rubbing her back as if she were a child herself. Thank goodness he had a strong stomach.

The rest of the evening was a nightmare. Child after child, and most adults, succumbed to what they would soon come to know intimately as a frequent state of affairs. Every once in a while, one of the sailors would come by with an extra bucket or two, and Ludwig was able to grab another one for their common use. He had a feeling Johannes Eckert and his family would get to know the Fridbergs and their friends much better than they had anticipated.

The night slowly turned into day as the ship plowed through the surf, up and down, up and down. The entire vessel was in disarray. As soon as the light came, women, and even men, began dragging their bedclothes up to the top deck to get them out of the passenger area. They soon realized the large fire tubs also served to rinse their fouled bed clothes.

The blankets were then spread on the deck, heavy enough with the water they held to stay in place. Someone had tried to fashion a clothes line, but had no way to secure anything to it. Who could have thought to bring clothes pins? Once the water was dirty, it was dumped overboard. One of the sailors threw a bucket over the side and then three of them hauled it back up by way of a few ropes. They continued until the tub was nearly full. Then, the next poor soul could begin to dip and wring.

Some people continued to be sick throughout the day. Thank goodness the sky was overcast so those who wanted could stand, sit or even lie down on the deck. The brightness of the sun would not have been welcome, but the fresh air certainly was. Christina recovered as the morning wore on. Barbara gave her sips of water, which she held down, and small amounts of rice with a bit of butter. Christina fell asleep on the deck, curled up next to a coil of rope, which gave her more comfort than she had had in several hours. Barbara covered Christina against the stiff sea breeze with one of the quilts and stood guard so her daughter might be able to sleep for a while, watchful of the clean cover in an effort to keep it that way.

Soon Rufus, Captain North's mastiff, happened along. His duty was to guard the ship from any and all evil, but everyone already knew he was nothing but a big lamb. He sniffed Christina and Barbara for a moment and then settled down for a nap, his muzzle resting on Christina's legs. How calm they both looked, snoozing the afternoon away. Barbara had thought to get that dirty dog away from her daughter, but in truth, Rufus was cleaner than Christina, and, in fact, smelled much better than any of the humans around him.

That day, the passengers received their rations for the rest of the week. They were given dry beans and peas, rice, oats, salt pork, beef and fish, loaves that looked more like large biscuits than bread, and butter. Included was a small amount of tea and sugar. Each day they received ale or beer and enough water to drink and, supposedly, cook with.

Barbara simmered some of the rice for Christina and limited the amount of salt pork she cooked for everyone else. She thought she would cut off the fat portions, but realized little lean would be left. Making a pot of porridge with oats, butter and some rice, her family gingerly took small spoonfuls as they began to feel better.

When night came, they were better prepared for what might come. Barbara had emptied the slop buckets and cleaned them with vinegar. She wished she had brought more of it along, realizing she was going to use it up quickly. Perhaps there was more on the ship she could buy.

The night was hot, the passenger deck even steamier than the night before. The passengers soon learned their environment would become warmer with each passing day. The blankets had not dried and were still up on the deck, but they were hardly needed. Thankfully, Barbara had brought along every blanket and quilt she owned, half of which were still clean. She had been able to wipe down everyone's clothes with the seawater, deciding to let their caps go for the moment. She wished she had had Jacob's lederhosen remade for Ludwig; they were easily cleaned with a single swipe of a cloth.

They finally went to bed, and lay not with their feet, but their heads, hanging over the edge of the bunk to capture what little fresh air passed them by.

That night went much more smoothly than the previous one. They had all eaten much less than the day before and little of the fat. Christina woke up towards morning and lay across her mother's lap on the stool until the sun came up. The others admitted to feeling a bit better than the night before, although everyone, except for Carlie, was sick.

Stephen and Hans had disappeared the night before, curling up in blankets on the deck. That night they fashioned a small tent near the cooking area, lying close together and trying to keep some of the wind off their backs. Unfortunately, Kitty was again unwell.

Barbara grew wiser about which foods in which combinations to cook for her family. Ludwig was the only one who seemed to tolerate the fat in the pork. The girls and Barbara ate mostly rice, peas and beans. The tea was their mainstay, which they steeped again and again until it held no taste at all.

Some days, when the seas were calm, passed with little sickness. Others, when the seas churned and roiled, meant most were intermittently ill throughout the days and nights. They learned to keep the slop buckets to hand and not to wait until the last moment to grab for them.

CHAPTER 27

Deal

After ten days, the coast of England came into view. The passengers and crew would be glad to have the ship docked for a few days so their stomachs and nervous systems could settle.

All were glad to learn they did not have to get off the ship and find a place to stay while they were in Deal. Although staying down on the passenger deck was not welcome for obvious reasons, it was better than taking on the anxiety of looking for lodgings and staying in strange, dirty, inadequate housing.

The women were told rivers of freshwater, not seawater, were available for washing bedding and clothing. Barbara enlisted the help of everyone, even Ludwig, Stephen and Hans, in dragging the mounds of dirty laundry down to a spot on the river. The girls and Barbara hitched up their skirts and waded cautiously into the cold water with an item to wash. They dunked and swished, rubbing it over a rounded, granite stone, which was all they could do given they had no tables or bats to force the water through the cloth. The lye soap they used at home would be useless in a cold river; it needed water heated almost to boiling to dissolve. As the water in the river moved, however, it took along the dirt and grime released from the garments; the constant changing of the water created a better result than simply moving it about in the same dirty seawater as was available to them onboard the ship.

Once the washer had gotten all the dirt and stains out she possibly could, the three men, sockless in the cold water, helped with the task of wringing. It took two to accomplish this task, especially with the heavy woolen blankets. They all wished they had the large posts to use they had back home. A piece of clothing could be wrapped around the post by one person, leaving the other person free for different chores. After the laundry was clean, it was spread out on the grass behind them. Two people would have to stay with the drying laundry to be certain it was not stolen; it was not a terrible job to sit in the sunshine on solid ground and was one of the better-liked boring jobs required of them.

At the end of the day, everything was gathered up and returned to the ship. Those clothes were then changed for the dirty ones they wore, and the process began anew the next day until all their garments and bedding were clean.

When Ludwig and the other men were finished with their laundry duties, they walked down to the harbor. They had brought lengths of twine knotted around small pieces of chopped salt pork. Standing at the edge of one of the smaller bridges, they dropped their lines into the water and pulled out all manner of wiggling crabs that had grabbed onto the bait with their pinchers. Often, they lost their grasp partway up and fell back into the water, but enough were caught to make the activity worthwhile. The men purchased a few hooks, baited them with the fatty pork, and proceeded to catch a large number of sea fish of all kinds. It mattered not when a fish or crab pulled the bait off the line; they had no intention of eating fat while in Deal. They would be feasting on the fresh bounty of the sea instead.

When time permitted, they took bags of netting borrowed from the ship down to the mud flats and looked for spouts of air and sand escaping from the ground. There they would dig, sometimes with their hands, sometimes with their knives, until they reached the clam waiting to be plucked from the sand. Although none of them had ever eaten a clam, they imagined how good these would taste with freshly purchased butter, so much better than the salty, unsavory food they had endured crossing the channel. Once back at the ship, they shared their catch with anyone who wanted some. The Mennonites were especially appreciative.

This scene continued for the next four days they laid over in Deal. By the time they left, their belongings were clean, their bellies were full, and a small supply of seafood was left to eat for the next few days until it spoiled. The passengers faced their trip out into the Atlantic better prepared and more stress-free than they had been coming to England.

The ship *Francis and Elizabeth*, as did all ships flying the flag of Britain, was required to leave from an English port on its way to North America. Representatives of the English Crown inspected the ship, and additional taxes and fees were paid before it could set sail. The Captain and crew had the opportunity to finish provisioning the ship for the long voyage west.

Everyone enjoyed a few days of busy, but peaceful, relaxation. No sickness permeated the ship, although the smell lingered. Just as they were getting used to the calm, the Captain began shouting orders again, and passengers knew they were starting on the final leg of their journey. They were leaving Deal and on their way to America.

CHAPTER 28

Leaving for America

O nce they reached the full openness of the sea, sickness began in earnest. Christina suffered most from the conditions on board, growing thin and pale.

"Momma, could we have some eggs? Only a bite or two. Please, I just want an egg." Christina would plead repeatedly, burrowing her face further into her mother's lap. Ludwig had bought a few eggs for the girls in Deal, but they were devoured on the first day.

"I am sorry, little one," Barbara would reply. "We have no eggs. We have no real bread, or vegetables, or fruit." These were the foods they were all used to and no longer had. How Christina would have loved a few mouthfuls of applesauce.

"We have to make do with what we have." Barbara continued to dole out her cheese, dried apples and bits of ham. They received butter as part of their weekly allotment, but it was growing rancid, and nothing palatable was available to bother putting it on except the rice.

Between their lack of food intake and the increase in sickness, most passengers began to lose weight. Some were plagued by loose bowels while others came down with bloody stools and pain throughout their bellies. The voyagers were growing fearful disease would be the end of all of them.

Once the fever set in, people began to die.

The first was the little Mennonite boy, John, the infant son of Johannes Gnagy. His mother was unable to nurse him, having been stricken with the fever herself. Johannes was advised by the women in his traveling party to make the boy a thin gruel of rice, but it was not enough to sustain him. He quickly died. Whether his death was due to starvation or fever was unknown, but no one really cared. The next day his mother died, leaving her other son, two-year-old Christian, barely alive.

A week or so out to sea, the water calmed, and most everyone began to feel a great deal better. With little wind, however, the ship sat still in the water while the Captain and his sailors trimmed the sails to make the most of the small breezes when they came.

A few more passengers had been taken on in Deal, so the conditions on board had become more crowded than during the channel crossing. As they started down the stairway while the ship was leaving Deal, the air became even more difficult to inhale, and by the time they had reached the bottom, it seemed to have all but disappeared. Ludwig began to wonder if there would be enough for everyone. With the hatches open, some air circulated throughout the area, but they knew with the hatches closed, the air would become stagnant and even more noxious. When the rains came, the hatches were closed and, in some instances, nailed shut.

One might have thought the circulation would improve while the ship was moving, but this was rarely the case. During the times when the ship was calmed, the air took on a quality of rigor mortis, stiff and deathlike, clinging to everyone and everything it touched with long, dirty fingers.

At the beginning of the second week out, the rain began to fall. The first day the seas remained calm, but as the storm grew stronger, the winds began to howl around the ship. As if possessed by an evil spirit, the gale turned into a demon, intent on destroying them all.

The ship *Francis and Elizabeth* tossed its passengers from one side of their bunks to the other, throwing some onto the floor, now sodden with a slippery mess. None of them could keep track of the buckets, which slid around the floor along with everything else, including their possessions stowed under the bunks.

The women and children lay face down on their beds, shrieking and sobbing, certain their lives were coming to an end as the ship
seemed about to break apart into thousands of pieces and sink into
the dark, foaming sea. The men tried to bear the unbearable with
fortitude, but they too were sick and terrified, battling their fear of
feeling the ship falling through the ocean to the rocky bottom.

Barbara was stiff as a board in the middle of their bunk, Carlie
on one side of her and Christina on the other. The act of rubbing a
loved one's back had become a tradition onboard, a way of showing a
sense of caring while giving one's arm something to do. At a particularly bad moment, Barbara felt a little hand, shaking with fear, reach
out and touch her back. Up down, up down, up down.

Barbara was absolutely terrified by the storm. Every fiber of her
being was roasting in the hell of the greatest fear she had ever known.
Her chest was tight, pulled back to rest on her spine by a death grip.
She shook from the inside of her body through to the little hairs on
her skin, slick with a gluey sweat.

She was so afraid they were all going to die. Her beautiful family—the one she had promised Jacob she would take care of—would
be gone. She knew the outcome of the storm was not in her hands,
and if the ship began to take on water, she would simply have to accept her end. The difficult part was accepting the end of her children.

Barbara knew her family was as afraid as she was. How she
wanted to do something to take away their pain. She had always
been able to calm them, take away a small hurt or kiss away the
pain from broken skin. But, there was little she could do now.
However, falling back on a strategy she used when times were difficult, she began to sing, "A mighty fortress is our God…" By the
time she had reached "…But still our ancient foe…" she could hear
little voices and even one unmistakable baritone joining her. She
could swear she heard the voices of the Eckerts blending together
in a strange, shaking unison, following along with the hymn between gasps of despair.

Barbara was now sorry they had ever taken the risk to emigrate over the great water. It held horrors she did not anticipate and could not now tolerate. *Why?* she repeated over and over again. Life back home was terrible as well, but she knew if anyone died there they would do it slowly. Here, they could go from hale to almost dead in an instant.

Ludwig was greatly worried for his family. He knew he had to stay alive so he could take care of them; he was their only source of support, both financial and emotional. What would the four of them do if they arrived in Philadelphia without him? His determination to remain healthy was a struggle, and it took all he had to give. He was concerned his mother was too old to outwit the savageness of this now dangerous journey. The older two of his sisters seemed to be holding their own, but Christina gained strength and then lost it again, like a vine watered by a healing rain and then deprived of everything life-sustaining. He lay beside Thea, stroking her back, singing, and even, to his own surprise, praying.

On the fifth day when the winds seemed to be softening, Ludwig crawled over to his mother on the other side of the bunk.

"Ludwig!" she cried as soon as she felt his presence. "What fools we have been! We should never have left our home. We are going to die. You know it and I know it. It is just a matter of time. And poor Christina. I fear every time I touch her, I will find her dead. Our dear, sweet, little girl."

Ludwig put a comforting arm around his mother. "It is going to be all right," he whispered in her ear. "Calm down; you will scare the children. We are not going to die. This is just one of the storms we have to endure, but all will be well once it is over. You will see. These ships are built to take a lot of wind and water. Hardly any of them sink. Where is your faith, Momma? You are always asking me that question. Why not ask yourself?"

Barbara knew Ludwig was right. Where was her faith? Where was her God? Not sitting on the bottom of the sea waiting for her, but here in the bunk, His arms surrounding all of them. She pictured God in the heavens, just about ready to tell the storm to cease. "Those poor people have had enough." And then it would end.

———————

The fires could not be lit on the deck. The one in the hold was damped down most of the time due to lack of use. Those who felt well enough to move about tried to make a little broth with toasted flour and rice or a cup of tea with a bit of sugar. They tried to clean up what little of the dirty floors they could, but were not able to remedy the smell, pushed through the air by the burning harbingers of death. None of the passengers were sure by this time how many days they had been at sea, and few cared.

On the fifth day of the storm, the sun came out. Most were too weak to move about, but those who could, tried to help those who could not.

Herr and Frau Platscher were found dead of the fever, lying in their bunks. They had probably been dead for several days, but no one had noticed. Their fourteen-year-old son, Michael, was found at death's door, but nursed back to health by his Mennonite neighbors.

When Michael was feeling better, Captain North came to speak with him.

"You know, young man, had the ship passed the halfway mark of the journey, you would have been responsible for the fare of not only yourself, but that of your parents. I am sure you are aware they did not pay their fare before the ship sailed, but hoped to indenture themselves in Philadelphia, and you, as well."

Michael lifted his sore, aching head and nodded it up and down just once.

"Lucky for you, we are far from the midway point on our voyage, so your parents' fares will be forgiven. But you will have to be indentured shortly after we land to pay your part of the debt. I will arrange for a family to take you and pay what is owed the shipping company. You will probably have to work for them for seven years, but if you apply yourself, you may come out of the experience having learned a trade. So perhaps some good will come of all your sorrow."

CHAPTER 29

Underway

B arbara felt weak and shaken up, but managed to get out of the bunk and slowly go about what needed to be done. Before she did anything, however, she went up on deck and made Christina some more broth out of toasted flour. Christina had not fared well during the storm, eating little and vomiting up most of what she did.

Barbara checked quickly on Kitty, lying still among her mass of blankets.

"She has not moved since the storm began," said Adam softly. "Has not eaten or drunk anything, but has not been sick either. She lies here beside me making little noises in her throat." Barbara poured some of the broth into one of their dirty bowls and encouraged Adam to help her sip it.

Ludwig felt helpless in his efforts to care for Christina. He knew she needed fresh, clean water to survive, and there was precious little of that. When it rained, water running off the sails was channeled into casks, but that was meant to be shared with everyone onboard.

As the rain began one warm afternoon, he stripped to his britches and, taking the largest bowl he could find, sat in an out-of-the-way corner of the deck, away from the sails. Holding the bowl over his head, he began to catch the water gently falling from the sky. After an hour or so, he had collected an inch of the precious water. His mother put it in a clean pitcher and begged Christina to take at least a teaspoon of it. This gradually turned into a tablespoon, but that was all she would take at one time.

Christina continued with her listlessness for almost a week after her fever began. Her family was concerned about her health, in fact, her death, if truth be told. She continued with her rants, seeing things that were not there. Asking continually where she was, she yelled repeatedly that she wanted to go home. Barbara held her for hours at a time while the sick girl simply stared at her and said in a quiet, but stern voice, over and over, "I want my momma."

Christina's health seemed to rise and fall as the days drifted by. At one point, she could barely speak, opening her eyes only to be certain someone she loved was looking after her.

Gradually, Christina took little nourishment at all and did not want any of the water offered to her. This concerned Barbara more than anything; Christina would never survive if her body dried out. The humors would become unbalanced and make her child even sicker. How Barbara wished someone on the ship could bleed her, but she could find no one trained to do it. She thought of doing it herself, but decided against it.

Thea and Carlie were lost. Their mother paid them no attention at all except to feed them and ask one or the other to be with her sister while Barbara did other things. Thea had been quite young when their father died, and Carlie just a toddler, so neither of them had had any close experience with death. They knew Christina would go to heaven because she was young, but that was all. Ludwig knew how busy and preoccupied his mother was, and so, spent time every day with the twosome. He tried to make them laugh, but that was not to be. He began to wonder who was making whom sadder.

"Momma," Christina said softly one afternoon. "Am I going to die like Poppa did?"

Barbara was dumbstruck. She had never thought those words would come out of any of her children's mouths. Should Christina be told the truth, or comforted by any means possible? Barbara eventually replied, "No, I do not think so," but had no reason to offer why this statement should be true.

"If I do, will I go to heaven? I know I am naughty some of the time and break God's commandments, but most of the time I try to be good."

Barbara replied, struggling to hold back her tears, "Oh, I am certain you will go to heaven. You are very young, and God wants to take His little children to heaven to be with Him there."

"But I will miss everyone so much. How will I bear it?"

"We will all be along, each in our own time when we are called home."

"But if I die, how will I know I am in heaven?"

"You will recognize it immediately—a lovely, warm place, full of fresh air and sunlight and healthy, well-fed people who, for the most part, have followed God's commandments. Angels will lift you up into God's arms where you will be loved and cherished forever."

"Will Poppa be there? How will he know I am Christina Catharina, his little daughter? He does not know what I look like."

"Oh, my darling, he will know you by your happy face and kind voice, and he will say, right away, 'My dear Christina, I have been waiting for you.' If he has any difficulty, I am certain God will help him. He will introduce you to Carlina and Wilhelm, your older sister and brother, and you will play with them in a golden pond full of silver fishes."

As Barbara continued her story of heaven, Christina's eyes began to softly flutter, and she fell into a deep sleep as her mother's tears fell on her small body. Barbara placed her hand lightly on Christina's chest, feeling for a beating heart. And so they sat together, Christina dreaming of silver fishes while Barbara felt for the life she hoped was still there.

Eventually, Barbara called her other three children to her and gave them a truly sorrowful look.

"Christina is near death," she told them quietly. "So now it is time to say goodbye." They each came and lay beside her, hugging her weightless body as they whispered into her ear how much they loved her.

Christina lay like this for almost a week, rarely waking up, but sometimes muttering about something no one else could understand. Ludwig walked around the deck with his head down while the girls lay together in the corner of the bunk praying for their sister. Barbara asked God over and over to please not take her child, but she said she would understand if He did. She could accept that God needed Christina more than she did.

Tincture of time seemed to be the best remedy. Very slowly, it returned Christina to life and gradually to health. And then one day, Christina woke up and asked for some water and a little rice with butter. Her family knew she was ready to go on with their adventure.

CHAPTER 30

A Troubling Encounter

Thea was growing into a most attractive young woman, and she knew it. Even soon after her birth, villagers noticed she was strikingly beautiful. Thea had seen a few of those new babies, born with purply, puckered faces and pointed heads from long labors, but her mother told her repeatedly how pink and smooth her face and skin had been right after she was born. She had shocks of beautiful dark brown hair, curling into ringlets as it dried before the fire. Even now, her brown eyes looked black at times, filled with an intensity Barbara had never seen in a baby. If Barbara had not known better, she would have said Thea was noble.

Ever since they left Massenbach, Thea's body had continued to develop. Her breasts grew larger and firmer while her hips rounded out and thinned down to her tiny ankles. As the ship left England, she began to bleed, which filled her with apprehension. Barbara explained to Thea that she had become a woman and told her more of the wonders of married life and babies.

Thea did not go without notice among the many single men who surrounded her on the ship. Even before they left Massenbach, Thea had been attracting the attention of the village boys, most of whom were Ludwig's friends. She noticed how she was being treated, and her girlfriends, as well, noticed those male eyes were mostly on Thea and not on themselves. Thea had begun to revel in her new-found role of village beauty, while, at the same time, trying not to gloat or appear vain. Barbara had begun to regret how many times she had commented on her eldest daughter's beauty and began a regular practice of repeating every story she could think of about the sin of vainglory, making certain Thea looked as modest as possible whenever she left their house. She was required to wear her neckerchief, even in very hot weather. She was so striking that Pastor Kimmel had even lectured her a few times about being overly prideful about her person.

Ludwig was extremely protective of Thea. He knew what his friends were thinking about his sister because he was thinking the same thing about theirs. But she was exceptional. Not only was she beautiful on the outside, but on the inside as well. She was known for her kindness and had never been a source of anguish to their mother.

Ludwig became furious whenever he saw Phillip or Johannes or even Stephen looking at her. She moved with such softness, no young man could be blamed for following her with his eyes, except by Ludwig. They were all very careful not to mention her in front of him for fear he would fly into a rage.

Once, he overheard Gustav and Peter talking about her, wondering what she had tucked up under those lovely skirts of hers. Ludwig attacked Peter without warning, growling like an animal as he broke his nose and bloodied an ear. Ludwig was brought before the Village Council for his behavior, but they took pity on him with his solemn promise never to lash out like that again. He only had to serve a few hours in the stocks during the middle of the day when everyone was working.

Peter wore his broken nose as a badge of honor and acted as if he did not mind at all. While Barbara was upset about Ludwig's behavior and his close call with the Council, she was secretly glad Thea had someone to look after her.

Aboard the ship, Ludwig felt even more protective. The Captain told him there were one hundred and forty-nine men on board and seventy-four women and children, along with several babies. One hundred twenty-three of the men were single.

Thea looked much older than fifteen, which complicated perceptions. Ludwig insisted his mother have frequent talks with her, explaining how things were between a man and a woman and how selfish and ill behaved some young men could be. Thea knew she was not to go on the upper deck without her mother or her brother at her elbow. But, she remained hopelessly naive and unthinking. Her experience on the barge with the official in the green jacket had apparently not had much effect on her.

"May I not talk with a young man on the upper deck?" she asked her brother repeatedly. "I talked with young men all the time back home, and nothing happened to me there." While Ludwig fumed and tried to chase as many men away as he could with his cold, piercing stare, Thea continued through her day unaware of what was going on around her.

"If anyone tries to touch you, even on your arm, you must come take my hand," Ludwig told her. This had become his never ending instruction to all his sisters.

As dirty and ugly as their surroundings had become, Thea seemed to always appear fresh and appealing. She had no idea what men were like, especially lonely ones. As much as she resented the preaching and roping in by her mother and brother, she tried to be respectful of their efforts on her behalf and follow their directions. She certainly did not want to disappoint her mother or bring shame on their family.

One Sunday afternoon, Thea went up on deck with Ludwig to enjoy the cool breeze and warm sunshine. She was leaning against the railing when a very nice looking young man came up and started talking to her. She immediately looked for Ludwig, but could not find him anywhere. Her mother was down below telling Christina and some of her friends another Bible story, and, so, did not have her practiced eye on her eldest daughter.

Thea did not want to be rude to the man, that would not be right either, so she smiled her dazzling smile and nodded her head.

"My name is Thea, actually Dorothea. My family and I are from Massenbach." The young man, who was actually thirty-one, over twice her age, introduced himself as Henrich Dressler from Langenselbold.

Thea started to walk along, holding onto the rail, trying to move away from him, but he simply followed her. He moved along beside and then in front of her, eventually turning around and blocking her way. She did not know what to do. Should she turn her back to him and walk the other way? She stopped, leaned against the rail, and began to earnestly scan the deck for Ludwig or anyone else she knew.

"Are you looking for someone?" Henrich asked, flashing her another big smile.

"Only my brother, Ludwig. He is nineteen," she answered. "He was here a minute ago. He is very tall," she added.

"How many in your family, then?" Henrich inquired.

"My mother, and my two sisters. So that makes five of us." By this time, she had decided he was much older than Ludwig and assumed he must be married with children. She relaxed a little. "How many are in your family?" she asked, not knowing what else to say.

"Oh," he laughed. "I am alone. My parents both died of the fever a few years ago and none of my brothers or sisters wanted to come to America. Not a very ambitious lot, I would say."

Now Thea was feeling scared. She wanted to get away from this man, this single man, but she did not know how. Turning slowly and walking in the direction from which she had come, however, gained her nothing. Henrich outmaneuvered her again and was soon blocking her way. Barely moving, he took hold of her slim arms and slid his hands slowly down to hers. She tried to pull them away, but he would not let go.

Where was Ludwig? Several times, he had told her to scream if anyone tried to touch her, but she shrunk from creating a scene or embarrassing Henrich. She tried to push his hand off of hers with her forearms, but he continued to hold onto them while his blue eyes smiled through their thick lashes.

Suddenly, she spied Ludwig and called out to him across the deck. "Ludwig, I am over here!" she called, unable to wave either hand at him. Henrich turned around, saw Ludwig moving steadily toward them, and suddenly dropped Thea's hands.

As soon as Ludwig was beside her, she gripped his arm with both of her hands. "This is my brother, Ludwig," she said. "Ludwig, this is Henrich from Langenselbold."

Ludwig was frowning, feeling Thea's fingers push into the flesh on his arms. "Yes, Langenselbold. The family across from us, Johannes and Angelica Eckert, are from there. Do you know them?" Ludwig questioned, his face becoming heated and red.

With that, Henrich nodded, excused himself, and started across the deck to the other side.

Ludwig grabbed Thea's shoulders, hissing through his teeth, "What were you doing talking with that man? You do not know him, nor do I. Is he married? Is he single? What do you think you are doing?"

Thea felt terrible. "He just started talking to me, then he blocked my way, and grabbed my hands. I looked for you, but you were gone. I was not certain what to do. What should I have done? I did not want to scream."

Ludwig then realized this was all his fault. He had been standing with Thea and Herr Eckert, who wanted to ask him about how the foresail was rigged. They moved off toward the front of the ship together. Ludwig forgot all about his sister, leaving her at the mercy of the single men on deck.

"I am sorry, Thea," he said softly, taking her hands in his. "I wanted to look at the foresail, and I guess I forgot you were there. That will never happen again. I promise."

Thea was glad to know this was not her fault. People were starting to look at them now, and her cheeks were burning at the thought of anyone knowing what had happened.

"We can go down below, now. I imagine Mother has our supper ready," Ludwig said. Mealtime had become an unpopular event, and they grimaced at each other as Ludwig led the way down the stairway.

Just before they reached their bunk area, Thea grabbed the back of Ludwig's arm. "Do you have to tell Momma what happened?" she asked.

He looked as though he might say yes, but after thinking of the worry this would cause his mother, he shook his head and agreed to keep this to himself. And more than anything, they did not want their mother to worry. They both knew she would be disappointed in her behavior, even though Thea had not been in the wrong.

CHAPTER 31

Christina in the Chest

C hristina was bored. The other children on board were restless as well; they had all grown tired of not running or jumping— two of the most forbidden behaviors onboard. And they were very sick of reading the Bible; no one ever had any fun there.

But Christina's plight was worse than the older boys and girls. She could not leave their bunk area alone; one of her family members had to be with her, holding her hand and scanning the environment for hidden dangers. So she could only "go out," as she thought of it, after she begged and pleaded with someone to take her.

Christina had been trying to talk Ludwig into going topside with her, but he wanted a nap and growled at her to go away. She had used all her tried and true strategies for convincing her mother and brother to walk with her; eye fluttering, sighing, sighing again, and even crying seemed to bring the best results. But today no one was responding to any of her ploys. Apparently, she was the only one who had slept the night before with that loud baby crying across the corridor, making such a fuss.

———————

Christina missed Massenbach already. Once her chores were done, the rest of the day had been hers unless Momma had something special for her to do. She knew this would have changed in a year or so when she started school, but for now, she had enjoyed the freedom her sisters envied. She could go anywhere she pleased as long as she did not go near the river. That was verboten.

Most days she would walk out of the back alley, looking over the tops of the fruit trees toward the mountains, craning her neck to see if anyone was working on the grape vines on the steep slopes—pruning, clipping or even picking. Then she would go through the backyards of the village houses until she got to Herr and Frau Gitmann's house. They were always happy to see her and often had a small treat for her—a piece of sliced apple or scraps of warm pretzel, sometimes with butter. After that, she looked for Sophia, hoping they could play together for a while.

Her last stop of the day would be old Widow Neuman and her dog Fritzle. Oh, how she loved Fritzle. They would play fetch with a stick, chase each other around the backyard, or sit quietly under a pine tree while Christina stroked his sleek, dark coat, and he licked her dirty, scraped knees.

When Christina asked her mother for the third time if she could sit at the top of the stairway and been told "No," she gave up. She felt she was in a prison, which in many ways she was.

But escape was not possible; her mother had told her to stay on the bunk with her sisters and not to go anywhere while the rest of the family napped.

Once everyone was asleep, however, Christina decided there could be little harm in walking down the corridor a short way. She grabbed Thea's scarf, and, pulling it over her head, began to creep down the hallway, making herself as small as possible. A woman she did not know walked past her, but Christina lowered her head even more and walked on her tip toes to avoid making any noise.

Once she passed the stairway to the top deck, she decided to keep on going. What could it hurt? She was not on deck, so she could not fall off the ship, and few people were about, so there was little chance of her bothering anyone. After she had gone past quite a few bunks, she saw a flight of stairs which, she reasoned, must go down into the hold below. After looking around to be certain no one was watching, she slowly descended the stairway, glad there was a railing to grab onto.

Once she came to the bottom platform, she stopped and tried to look around in the dim light. Small windows in the walls, right under the ceiling, let in light as well as air, but the huge room before her was only a black void. She gingerly put one foot in front of the other and began to move slowly through the objects scattered in front of her.

All sorts of things filled the room; many chests and casks, all different sizes and shapes. She wondered if there were anything interesting in them. Coiled ropes lay in neat piles, with pieces of sail covering some of the objects she could not see. A large grey cat sat on one of the casks enjoying his lunch, which reminded Christina she was growing hungry.

She thought she would investigate a bit more and maybe open one of the chests. She might even find some treasure.

Off to her right was a chest much like her mother's that had been left with Cousin Johannes. Christina lifted the lid, finding nothing but old rags in the bottom. Next, she tried to open another chest painted a faded red with three initials on the front

She thought the letters might have said "CCF" and giggled to think of herself as a grown woman soon to marry. Then she wondered how it would feel to lie down in the pretty piece of furniture.

She was able to lift the lid a tiny bit, but it was heavy, and slammed shut when she took her hand away. Pushing the top all the way open, she was finally able to hold it steady while she awkwardly climbed inside. But then, she lost hold of the lid, and it slammed shut with a force she was sure had broken the chest into pieces.

Christina used her hands to push open the top, but it was stuck tight. She tried again, with the same result. Putting her feet against the top and pushing with all her might, the lid creaked a bit, but did not budge. She was locked in the box and had no way to get out.

Tears began to trickle down her cheeks, while the chest filled with little sobs. "How am I going to get out of here?" she cried, unable to think of a strategy. When the lid slammed shut, the lock must have jammed, trapping Christina in what could turn out to be her death chamber.

Oh, Momma, what a bad girl I am, she thought. *I should have listened to you and not sneaked down here.*

In a few seconds, Christina realized the direness of her situation. No one would be visiting the hold until they docked in Philadelphia. Rats would be gnawing on her bones when they reached the harbor, and the owner came to claim his property.

She lay there, sometimes calling out, sometimes screaming, sometimes kicking the lid with her feet, but no one heard her. Crying in fits and starts, she eventually fell asleep.

Christina awoke when something landed hard on the top of the box. It certainly was too heavy for a rat; perhaps it had been one of the cats. She had no idea of the day or the time. Had she slept through the night? Or had no more than five minutes passed? She had nothing to serve as a reference. Making all the noise she could, she finally gave up after trying to break the sides of the box with her fists.

The hold was growing cold. The chilly temperature of the water under the ship was beginning to overtake the heat from above. She was very hungry and had to use the privy. The inevitable finally happened, and Christina was forced to face the depths of humiliation. She felt the warm liquid slowly ooze into her skirts and then down the length of her stockings.

At least it is warm, she thought, not knowing the opposite would be true within a short while.

She fell asleep again and was awakened this time by someone moving through the objects in the hold. She put her ear to the side of the chest and listened carefully. Whoever it was, knocked over a metal object onto the floor. She had not heard any heavy foot steps and thought it might be a woman. Then she heard the person bump into one of the chests, tipping it over with a crash.

Christina began to yell again, "Help! Help! I am in the box!"

No one responded, but she did begin to hear something sniffing. A small hole between the lid and the side of the box emitted the sniffs along with a licking sound she did not recognize.

But then she realized it must be Rufus, Captain North's dog. He was very large with short, reddish-brown fur, small, floppy ears and a short, but powerful muzzle on his even larger head.

"Rufus," she began. "It is me, Christina. Do you not remember me? I was sitting on the top deck yesterday, and you came and lay down next to me. I scratched behind your ears." The dog snorted, but that was all the acknowledgement she received.

"Please, Rufus. Go find your master, Captain North. Bite onto his coat and bring him down here so he can find me. Or go and get my mother, or my brother, Ludwig. Make them come down here. You have to!"

But Rufus did not respond and finally sauntered away, looking for a scrap of anything to eat.

Christina wanted to cry again, but all her tears were gone. She lay in the box, utterly defeated, wondering what it would feel like to die here.

She was growing cold. Her damp skirt was cooling her body, beginning to make her shake with chills. She was very uncomfortable and again reviled herself for her foolish behavior.

And then Christina heard a voice, and it was a voice.

"We can try this one," the first sailor said, but was astonished to hear a banging coming from the chest and a small voice calling from within, "Help me! Help me!"

The second sailor whispered, "What do you think that is?"

"Sounds like a person to me, maybe a child?"

They both had the same thought at the same time. They had come down into the hold to find a few items of value they could steal and sell once they got to Philadelphia. They had big plans for the time they would be there. Plenty of rum and plenty of women. George chuckled to himself just thinking about it.

But if they decided to let her out, they would have to take her topside to the Captain, and that would mean less time to hunt. But George had an idea.

"If we are really nice to her and take her back to Captain North, there might be a reward in it for us," he suggested to John, giving him a big wink with his one remaining eye.

"I wonder if this is the little girl everyone has been looking for?"

John rubbed his hands together, grateful in his own way for the golden goose they had so brilliantly discovered.

Together, they yanked and pulled until the lid finally came open, revealing that little girl with the blonde hair everyone had been trying to find.

"Be still, sweetheart," George said with the kindest voice he could muster. "We will not hurt you. What is your name?"

"Christina." She was not sure if she should talk to these men she did not know, but quickly realized they might be the only way to get back to her family.

"Christina Fridberg," she repeated, beginning to cry again as she struggled to get out of her dungeon.

"Now, now, little miss," John said, whistling through the missing tooth in the top of his mouth. "Let us help you."

The two men lifted her up by her arms as gently as they could. George hissed at John, kicking him in the shin as if to say, "Be careful you dumb ox."

Before long, Christina was standing beside the box, hoping the sailors had not noticed her wet skirts.

"Can you take me back to my mother?" she asked as she wiped her nose on her sleeve. "I want to see my mother."

"We will take you back to the Captain," George suggested. "He will know better how to find your mother."

As Christina realized she could never find her way back to her bunk alone, she nodded in agreement, trying to act grateful.

The men each took one of Christina's elbows and escorted her back to the stairway. As soon as Christina saw some light, she felt a great deal better.

They finally reached the top deck and then Captain North's cabin. He was just sitting down with Herr Franken to a dinner of boiled beef and cabbage. But when he saw Christina with the two sailors, he jumped to his feet.

"Are you Christina?" he fairly bellowed.

She nodded, and he could feel his body begin to relax.

He hated it when someone was lost overboard, and that was the reason everyone had given for the girl's disappearance. He hated it because then all the passengers were upset—clinging to their children and each other lest sinister forces were at work and would grab another helpless child, or even adult. Everyone was short with him, constantly insisting he turn the ship around for a pointless attempt to find the person lost to the seas. He was certainly glad this situation had resolved itself favorably.

He grabbed the girl by the hand and dragged her to the Fridbergs' bunk. The two sailors followed, still hoping they might be rewarded by the Captain.

CHAPTER 32

Christina's Return

"Widow Fridberg!" the Captain called as soon as they had descended the stairway. "Widow Fridberg, where are you?"

Barbara was sitting in her usual spot, praying with everything she had that Christina would be found alive. Ludwig had gone up on the deck, but Christina's two sisters were lying down on the top bunk, wondering what would become of them all.

"Momma!" Christina yelled as she reached their bunk. "Momma, I am here!" she called.

Barbara jumped to her feet and met Christina as the little girl threw herself into her mother's arms. Her sisters clambered from their bed, almost falling on top of Christina.

They all embraced in a large ball of gratitude, while Barbara wondered how she would manage to keep her promise to God and never again lose her temper. The sisters wondered the same, how they would not be mean to Christina ever again.

Captain North and the two sailors followed Christina to the happy reunion.

"These two gentlemen found her down in the lower hold, in one of the empty chests," Captain North explained. "She had gotten locked in, and they managed to get the chest open and pull her out."

John and George tried to smile, but were acutely aware this family was one of the poorest of the whole lot. Watching their chances for a reward quickly vanish, they turned and began smiling at the Captain.

"Momma, stop, I cannot breathe. You are squashing me!"

"Oh, my dear, dear girl," Barbara continued to repeat. "You are here. You are here."

Barbara began to look her daughter over. Was she hurt? Had she been molested in some way? "But Christina, look at your hands!" Barbara cried. One could not help but notice her knuckles were badly scraped and bleeding, already becoming the purplish-blue they would remain for most of the next week.

"Evening," Captain North said as he strode away into the coridor. The two sailors decided to follow him hoping he would be better to them than the mother had.

One of the neighbors had already found Ludwig on deck; he descended the stairs three at time and leaped into their bunk area at full speed.

"Christina. What a *schnickelfritz*! Where have you been? We were so worried. We thought you had fallen over the side."

He grabbed her from Barbara, as everyone smiled and laughed while he hugged her tight and spun her around and around.

"Yes," Barbara asked, "how did you get locked in that chest?" She then asked a bit hesitantly, "Did someone put you there?"

Since Christina's return, Barbara had quickly concocted an explanation for herself that someone had grabbed her daughter and locked her in the trunk for nefarious purposes. While she was fearful Christina had fallen overboard, she was also anxious that the little girl had fallen into the hands of an unscrupulous man.

Christina hung her head and replied in a quiet voice, "No, I got in the chest myself." She was thinking of lying, but reckoned she was already in enough trouble with God, and, of course, her mother.

"But how did you get in the hold?" Ludwig asked, frowning.

"I took myself there," Christina answered, trying to lower her head a bit more.

Barbara was dumbstruck. *Had Christina disobeyed her and gone off by herself on purpose?*

At that, Carlie and Thea climbed up into the bed, while Ludwig inched out into the hallway. They knew what was coming.

"Did you deliberately disobey me?" Barbara cried, trying to keep her voice low. "I told you to lie down on the bunk and stay there. Do you remember that?"

Suddenly Christina's world was falling apart. She thought again of lying, but decided that would only add insult to injury.

"Yes, Momma," Christina said, beginning to cry. "I am so sorry, Momma. I will never disobey you again. I promise." But she knew her pleadings were too late.

"You deliberately disobeyed me. Do you know you could have died in that chest? We may have never found you until we reached America. Think of the sorrow you would have caused your family. Think of it!"

With that, she grabbed Christina and, placing the girl over her lap, began spanking her. At first, she spanked through Christina's skirts, but as she became increasingly angry, she pushed the still damp skirts aside and began to spank her bare bottom.

Christina pleaded, "Stop, Momma, please!" as she began to scream and try to fight her way free. She was embarrassed her nakedness was showing and tried repeatedly to pull her skirt down.

"Stop moving!" Barbara yelled. "Be still!"

But Christina continued to wiggle and cry.

"You should be ashamed of yourself. Ashamed! Now everyone will think I do not take proper care of my children. Do you know how embarrassing that is?"

When Barbara could see this wretched girl was not going to obey even this simple command to lie still, she reached for one of the wooden spoons nearby and began spanking her with that. Christina's bottom and the backs of her legs became redder and redder, as they began to swell, and she continued to scream.

And then it was over. Barbara pushed Christina aside and walked into the corridor. She kept walking until she reached the stairway and went up on deck.

She was visibly shaking as she strode to the edge of the ship and then back to the stern. Leaning her head on the railing, she began to cry, big, gasping cries with tears rolling down her swollen cheeks.

I have done it again, she thought. *She deserved a spanking, but not like that. Oh, God, please tell me I did not harm her.* With that, she vomited over the side.

Ludwig picked up Christina and placed her on Kitty and Adam's bed. Thea quickly flew off the upper bunk and lay down by her little sister, putting her arm around her.

"Are you all right, Chrissy?" she whispered into her sister's ear. "Did she hurt you?"

Christina lay on her belly, continuing to whimper.

"Are you hurt?" Thea insisted on knowing.

"Yes, but I will be all right. I was a very wicked girl."

"Yes, you were, but you did not deserve the beating you got. I have never seen her so angry before. But she was so worried something had happened to you. She kept saying, 'I will never forgive myself.' She cried all last night."

Thea pulled up Christina's skirts and began to look for any damage. Her legs were quite red and swollen.

Christina complained, "She hit me on my bones. They hurt."

Thea grabbed one of their large cups and ran up the stairs, returning with it filled with fresh water from one of the tubs near the fires. She grabbed what she thought was a clean rag, wet it with the water and hoped its coolness would have some positive effect.

But Christina began to cry in earnest and tried to swat the rag away with her hand. When Christina told Thea to stop, she did.

"Oh, no," Thea said, now full of remorse. She had not thought the water would be full of salt and make Christina's legs smart even more. Dabbing the skin dry did not help, and Christina whimpered even more. Thea was used to the cool water of the stream back home, which would have been soothing on Christina's legs, but none of that existed here.

Ludwig followed his mother at a distance as he wanted to be certain she was all right. He knew she would be sorry for her behavior as he thought she always was, sorry and embarrassed. Everyone on the ship must have heard both her and Christina screaming and, although this was not an unusual happening onboard, he knew how his mother would respond.

He remembered his father punishing him, but not with his mother's anger. He imagined she would think everyone on the ship was judging her for not keeping her child safe, and they probably were. Barbara wiped her mouth with her sleeve and stood up straight. *Oh God, please, please forgive me,* she cried to herself. *How could I have done this again?* And then with a whimper, *I pray I did not harm her.*

She stood there quietly crying as Ludwig put his hand gently on her shoulder.

Through her sobs she asked if Christina was all right, and Ludwig replied he thought she was, or would be.

"Are you all right?" he asked, trying to modulate the anger in his voice.

Barbara shook her head. He waited for her apology to start taking form, but realized it would never come; it never did.

Ludwig knew his mother's anger appeared when she was afraid, and she certainly had been afraid today. That, coupled with her feeling of embarrassment, must have pushed her over the edge of all that was reasonable. Christina could have died in that chest, and they all knew it.

"Go back down with the others," Barbara told Ludwig. "I want to stay up here until I feel better."

Ludwig shrugged his shoulders as if to say, "Whatever pleases you, Mother," and walked toward the stairway.

Barbara's shame was palpable. It felt like large bunches of some sort of tissue covering her body, hard bunches, like a burl in the crotch of a tree. She still felt embarrassed her shipmates had seen her failings as a mother, but, worst of all, that she had lost herself, her control, her temper, and, perhaps, for a few short moments, her love.

Barbara eventually dragged herself back to the bunk, glad to see everyone had already settled down for the night. She hesitantly reached up to caress the calf of Christina's leg, but Christina reached down and swatted Barbara's hand away, as if it were a fly.

Depleted of tears, Barbara climbed up onto the bunk and found a spot on the other side of Ludwig, as far away from the girls as she could. She was glad Kitty and Adam had not been there for her display. But they, too, were glad Christina had been found. Trying to focus on that, she eventually fell asleep, listening to the oil lamp clanging against the wooden upright.

None of them would ever talk about what happened that night. Least of all, Barbara herself.

CHAPTER 33

Herr Franken

July passed slowly. A few sunny days, then a few cloudy days, then a little rain followed by a small gale here and there. But no storms were as bad as the one they endured during the second week. They slept more than they ever had and told the same stories over and over. Men sat cross-legged whittling on the deck while the women attended to the needs of their children. As they struggled to eat the food they knew they must, they wondered how much longer the journey could last.

Herr Franken was a gentleman, possibly of noble birth, who was a bright light for many voyagers, mostly the children. He had a small berth of his own near the Captain's quarters, and they dined together, obviously friends who enjoyed each other's company. He spoke German, French and English and took great pleasure in speaking English to the sailors who were expecting nothing but German from the passengers.

His clothes were expensive and his person impeccably groomed. No one could understand how he managed this. But best of all, he could read. And he had books. Adam had seen them through the door of his cabin once—a whole big box made of polished walnut full of them.

At the beginning of the voyage, Herr Franken spent nice days on the deck reading, lounging in a chair one of the sailors had carried over for him. He was very friendly, especially to the children. They would sometimes sidle up to him under their parents' watchful eyes and try to understand what he was doing. The only book any of them had ever seen was the Bible, and this object in his lap looked nothing like that.

One day as he sat in his chair, peering through his spectacles, which the children also found strange, he began to read aloud. At first they did not know what he was doing. He was looking at the page and reciting something at the same time. But it did not sound like Bible verses to them. They sat listening to him, entranced.

He explained that words on the page turned into words in his voice, which he could say out loud. But none of these words came from God. It was reading, like the Bible, but it was a different story. It even had pictures, which showed what happened. The children were enthralled and leaned in even closer.

Herr Franken turned the book back to the first page and showed it to them. The picture revealed a thin man with a funny hat on his head that looked like a large, upside-down funnel. He held two long guns and was dressed in a coat made of fur while he sported a long, scraggly beard. The sand beneath his bare feet, or perhaps it was the sky, was strewn with misshapen stars.

"Who is he?" one of the children asked, her eyes widening as she pointed to the book.

"Why, he is Robinson Kreutznaer," Herr Franken laughed, using the protagonist's English given name, just for effect.

"Where is he?" another child ventured.

"He is on a deserted island. He was on a long voyage, but the ship ran into the island and sank. Now, he is stranded."

Christina and her mother were passing by right when Herr Franken was opening to the front page of the book he held, and Christina, who could smell a story a mile away, plunked herself down on the deck, pulling her mother beside her.

"Are there other people on the island?" Christina called from the back of what was now turning into a small crowd.

Herr Franken was amused by the interest of these ragged peasant children, crowding around his feet and soon after them, some of their parents.

"Well," he said, turning the page, "let us read and find out."

With that, he began to read the well-turned pages of his copy of *Robinson Carusoe* by Daniel Defoe, translating it into German as he went along. He had a strong, resounding voice, which could usually be heard over the flapping of the sails and the many other voices and noises on deck.

As he read, he judiciously modified the story so the children, and perhaps some of the adults, would not be frightened. He left out the parts that mentioned Robinson's fear of wild animals, malicious natives, or cannibals. He also skipped over cave-ins, bad storms and the death of any baby animals. When asked what had happened to all the other people on the ship, he fibbed and told them, "They all got in a boat and went home to England."

Herr Franken continued with his storytelling on deck every day the weather was fair. When the deck became too wet or noisy, he went downstairs and they sat around the one table provided for them. Those who wanted to listen learned they had to be at his knee as soon as he began to read, or they would be too far back to hear.

CHAPTER 34

More Conversation

Ludwig and Johannes Eckert had become fast friends; they spent their time comparing their villages of origin and sorting out where they would go and what they would do in America. They found Langenselbold and Massenbach were in the same general area and many of the conditions in each village to be similar. Ludwig explained his reasons for leaving—his family owning no land and, thus, his lack of opportunity and the resources to marry.

Johannes had been a cooper in his own village, but found as time went on, people had less and less money to buy barrels given the lack of resources as the community grew. He had his reservations about traveling with children so young, but he was afraid he would not be able to provide for them if the family stayed. Although he had managed to save some money from his trade and grow some provisions himself, food scarcity was a problem.

He was having trouble buying the hoops for the barrels, which were made by the smiths; they in turn had difficulty buying the charcoal needed for their fires while the charcoal makers could not find enough available wood to make their operations profitable.

Ludwig explained both his father and grandfather had been schoolmasters. He had learned something about butchering meat from his mother's cousin, but could never have made a living with this trade in Massenbach. The village only had meat in the fall when the pigs were slaughtered, and most villagers had the skills to kill and cut up their own small herds. Every housewife in the village knew how to make and smoke hams and sausages, so no living was available there.

He had thought of going to one of the nearby cities to work once he had improved his skills, but he knew he would be at a disadvantage due to the guilds and their influence on the city economy. He was looking for opportunities in his homeland where there were none and had heard about the benefits a move to the New Land might bestow on a family. And so, Johannes leaned on the ship's rail while Ludwig did not, and both questioned, again, if they were doing the right thing by leaving everything they knew.

One evening as the sun started to go down, Henrich Dressler walked by. Johannes knew him from Langenselbold while Ludwig remembered him from the unfortunate situation with Thea. Henrich kept his eyes on the deck while the other two men turned around. None of them acknowledged each other's acquaintance or stopped to shake hands.

"Now there is someone you want to stay clear of," Johannes told Ludwig in a low voice while his face twisted with disgust. "Henrich Dressler. No honor in that man."

Johannes went on to tell him more about their shipmate while Ludwig listened intently. Johannes told him a woman in his town, Philippina Dipple, the eldest daughter of Henrich Dipple, had given birth to a daughter, Elisabetha Catharina Judith, this past May. Philippina was unmarried and had named Henrich Dressler as the father. Her father demanded the Reformed Church elders take action against him, and they summoned him to appear before them.

Ludwig was beginning to understand more about this man and the danger his sister had been in that day. He vowed to speak with her again, although he could not tell her the vileness of the man who had assaulted her. Ludwig asked Johannes what happened next, and Johannes continued.

"The church elders demanded he marry Philippina, and he told them he would. This satisfied her father and the Presbyterium. But, he left Langenselbold that same night and found passage on this very ship. You can imagine how surprised I was to see him."

"At any rate, he left Philippina and their little daughter in even more disgrace than they had been before. Philippina was already twenty-nine and almost past the age to marry. She would have even less of a chance to marry now. Henrich definitely took advantage of her, knowing he would never do right by her. You would think she might have known better. But with her crooked arm and leg from the accident she suffered as a child, she may have thought Henrich would be her only chance." With that, Johannes spit into the ocean in disgust.

Ludwig did not tell Johannes about Thea's encounter with Henrich. He did not want Johannes to think she had been seductive toward Henrich, even at the age of fifteen. He had promised Thea he would not talk with their mother about this, but was beginning to have the idea he should.

A few days following Ludwig's conversation with Johannes, Barbara took him and Thea aside while they were on the deck. "Do either of you have any knowledge of a man called Henrich Dressler?" she asked. "He is a passenger on this ship, from Langenselbold."

Ludwig gulped and attempted to fix his gaze on anything other than his mother's face. "Yes, I believe I have," Ludwig answered, staring at the deck, trying to sound casual and answering before Thea could.

"And what about you, Thea? Have you heard of him?"

Thea looked quickly at Ludwig for any sign of what she should do and decided to lie, even though she knew it was wrong. "I have never heard of him, Mother. How old is he?" she asked, wishing at once she had not brought up the subject.

"He is a man, Thea. A man. Someone you should not be speaking with on deck or anyplace else," her mother glared.

Thea did not know what to do. She kept looking toward Ludwig which he fervently wished she would not. How could her mother have found out about the incident on deck, unless Ludwig told her? And he had said he would not.

"And how did you hear about him, Ludwig? It was not your sister, was it?" his mother questioned.

Ludwig tried to think fast. He knew if she had learned about Henrich from someone else, which apparently she had, both he and Thea could be in for a great deal of trouble.

All of a sudden, Thea burst forth, full of fear and shame that she had not told her mother the truth. "I do know who he is, Mother. I met him on the deck. He talked to me."

"And did you turn around and leave, immediately, as Ludwig and I have told you you must when a strange man approaches you? Or did you just stand there, trying to make yourself more attractive to this man, trying to entice him with your smile?"

Thea was horrified by her mother's accusation, horrified and hurt. "Momma, I tried to leave, but he would not let me. He blocked my way."

And with that, Barbara pulled herself up to her full height and proceeded to slap Thea as hard as she could across the face. "You harlot," she growled. "You harlot. How could you have engaged with this terrible man? Everyone on the ship knows about your shameful behavior. Everyone! How do you suppose we, your family, who you profess to love, feels knowing how you have betrayed us? You have betrayed us all."

Thea reacted to Barbara's blow and fell back into a large coil of rope, her face and her pride stinging with anger.

Ludwig was dumbstruck. How could his mother have hit Thea like that in public, calling her of one of the worse names imaginable? He knew what it meant, but it surprised him his mother did. And Thea certainly did not; at least he hoped so. How could she heap all of this undeserved shame on her daughter?

He did not know what to do or say. But his mother's way of turning every incident into a catastrophe had to stop. They would soon be living in the largest city in North America, not the hole-in-the-wall they had come from. In Philadelphia, he suspected she might be talking with a great many men.

Thea immediately vowed not to cry, and covered her face with her hands as she gulped at the air around her.

"Answer me, you horrible girl. How could you have spoken with him? Did you think you could try to seduce him, an evil man twice your age? And now everyone on the ship knows about your sinful behavior. Sinful! None of us will be able to look at anyone else on the ship now that you have heaped shame on the entire family."

And of course, Thea began to sob. "It was not my fault, Momma. I tried to get away. I did. But he kept grabbing at me."

"And are you lying to me now just as you lied to me when you said you did not know him?"

Ludwig felt obligated to help his sister, knowing what a fearsome creature Henrich was, nevermind the creature his mother was becoming. He wanted to know how his mother had found out about the encounter, but was loathe to ask; it might make the situation worse. He did not have to pull himself up to his full height when he looked down at his mother and said, "How could you treat Thea like this? Do you not understand she was taken advantage of?"

Now it was time for Barbara to be horrified. How could Ludwig speak to her like that? She was his mother and demanded his respect. But as she tried to put his words into perspective the fact that he was a man, and not a little boy any longer, began to creep into her awareness and then bowled her down with its full force. This feeling was something she had always known, something buried within her for as long as she had known what a man was. Ludwig was not her son any longer; he was a man and soon to be the head of their family, if that had not already happened. He was a man, and she was only a woman. Only a woman. Why had she lost her temper like that, like she always did? Perhaps because she was a woman.

Perhaps it was time for her to let go and allow Ludwig to take his rightful place in their family, the one Jacob had placed on her when he died. Perhaps she could let go and allow the man who was her son to take some of the responsibility from her, the responsibility that weighed her down and pressed on her heart. Perhaps it was time. She could not protect her family from the world forever. She was only a woman.

CHAPTER 35

The Fishes

It was the first day of August. They had been at sea for almost a month. The Captain told Ludwig they would have another several weeks, perhaps even a month, until they reached Philadelphia. Ludwig sighed with frustration. He knew the trip usually took about two months, six weeks if the winds were right, but could even be as long as three months. If the ship was blown off course by a storm, it could take even longer.

Ludwig hated to think of what would happen if the voyage lasted longer than expected. He knew they were running low on some of the stores, and many of the perishable food stuffs were barely edible. The smell from the salted pork was becoming more pungent with each cask that was opened.

He tried not to think about the results of running out of food altogether and was loathe to ask the Captain what they would do. He knew there was fresh meat running about the ship on four little legs, but he was not sure if he could successfully butcher anything that small.

The next morning as Johannes and Ludwig were again standing on deck, they saw several sailors on the port side of the ship holding a heavy rope. As the sailors hauled on the line, the two men suddenly saw a large fish jump out of the water alongside the ship. More sailors appeared, and together they were able to wrangle the fish onto the deck where it fought for its life, flipping back and forth from side to side, hurling its body around the deck as if it were trying to jump back into the water.

The fish was enormous. Neither Ludwig nor Johannes had ever seen an animal that big. They thought it must be at least six or seven feet long. While they knew it was not a salmon or trout like they had back home, they had no idea what kind of fish it was. Everyone on deck could hear the sailors shouting at each other in agitated voices and turned to look where the sound was coming from. And then they all moved, as if in a herd, slowly and cautiously, inching toward the scene of the uproar. The children were terrified of the huge fish and tried to walk backwards away from the giant, squiggly mass as the adults moved forward.

Even though Ludwig and Johannes did not know what type of fish it was, the thought occurred to them at the same time. "Can we eat it?" they said, looking hopefully at each other. With that, they were in the front line of the group as it moved forward.

They could then see about seven of the crew, a few holding onto the rope for dear life and the rest trying to stun the fish as they beat on its head with anything to hand—buckets, pieces of wood and even bricks from underneath the coal braziers. At last, it was subdued long enough for one of the sailors to sink a large sword into the flesh just behind its head. Blood squirted everywhere, which brought cheers from the crew and sounds of disgust from the passengers.

Every one of the passengers wondered if they would be given any of that fish to eat once the crew had had their fill. To their delight, another group of sailors started hauling on another line, and a few of the already successful fishermen ran to help. Up came another flopping fish, bigger than the first. The passengers now felt fairly certain the fourteen crew members plus the Captain could not eat all that fish by themselves.

Once the second fish had been bludgeoned successfully and then dispatched with the sword, Captain North appeared, a huge smile on his face. No one knew if he was smiling for himself or for his passengers and crew who had been on the verge of a food riot.

"Well done!" the Captain called at the top of his voice. "Two beautiful blue fin tuna sitting there waiting for us to sail by and hook them. And now they will be our dinner, enough for everyone who wants some."

The passengers breathed a sign of relief, cheering for the fishermen, knowing for sure they would not go to bed hungry that night.

"Any of you passengers who want to help, be my guest," the Captain invited. "We will have to skin and then gut her. We will need men to throw the waste back into the water, help with the cutting up, and scrub and rinse all of the mess off the deck before it dries. Just be careful because the deck will be slippery with all the blood and will get even worse once she is gutted. We do not want anyone sliding into the sea, now, do we?"

One of the sailors farthest away from the Captain yelled, "But if you do, be sure to grab us all another fish, and we will pull you back up!"

Ludwig saw sailors bringing knives and even swords up from below deck. He knew the number doing the cutting was limited to the number of implements, so he turned and ran down onto the passenger deck. He had never butchered a large fish before, but he reckoned it could not be too much different from butchering a pig.

He started pulling everything out from under the bunk until he finally found what he was looking for—his knives. His cousin Johannes had given both to him, one so often sharpened it appeared almost as thin as a needle. But they were both his most-prized possessions. Holding one in each hand, pointing down, he slowly and carefully went back on deck.

When the sailors saw he had not one, but two knives, they made room for him to approach the fish. When another passenger he did not know put out his hand for one of the blades, Ludwig gladly handed it to him.

Passengers and crew worked throughout the day, skinning, cutting, cleaning the fish, and rinsing the deck. Some of the men threw the buckets over the side, filled them with seawater, and pulled them up again. Others manned the large brushes, scrubbing the mess off the deck surface while others in groups of three threw the water from the tubs over the sodden areas.

When the chores were finished, the fish lay in large filets and steaks on the deck, rinsed in fresh seawater until the flesh glistened. The women watched intently, imagining how good that fresh food would taste. They reckoned what was not eaten today could be stored for the next day, perhaps two, down in the cooler part of the hold next to the water.

As the men worked that day, they had the opportunity to talk with their neighbors. Having made another man's acquaintance, they proceeded to chat about where they had come from and where they were going, the usual topic aboard ship.

Ludwig's neighbor was a young man named Jacob. As the two talked, Ludwig learned Jacob was Dutch. He had been born in the Netherlands, but moved with his family to Mainz when he was a boy.

Jacob said his wife had had two stillborn babies and died in childbirth. With no dependents, Jacob wanted to go to America to make a new life for himself. He had recently moved back to Rotterdam because more money could be made working on the docks than in Mainz.

Jacob complained about his father pestering him to move back to Mainz and take over the family business. He imagined Ludwig knew that was what every father wanted—for their sons to take up their vocations.

Ludwig explained his father had been the village schoolmaster, but had died when Ludwig was twelve. He stated he did not believe he had the patience to teach school, and anyway, it would not have been very exciting, nor would it have brought the life he envisioned for himself.

He began to think Jacob's story sounded familiar, but Ludwig could not place him as someone he may have met during the month they spent in Rotterdam. "Perhaps Mainz," he said to himself. And then it came to him.

"Is your surname Hauck, by chance?" he asked Jacob.

Jacob replied, "Well, as a matter of fact it is. Do you know someone named Hauck in Rotterdam?"

"Not in Rotterdam," Ludwig said with a smile. "But I do know some people from Mainz, Marta and Jan to be exact."

Jacob stopped cutting for a moment and asked, "How do you know them?"

Ludwig then told him the tale of their three wonderful days with their new friends, Jacob's parents.

"Really," Jacob replied. "Well now I regret the comments I made about my father, but it is true. On the other hand, he is a wonderful man. He gave me the money so I could book passage on this ship and not have to wait until next year. How many fathers would do that?"

They both laughed, thinking about the coincidence of Ludwig meeting Jacob's parents, and then Jacob booking passage on the ship *Francis and Elizabeth*.

"And your mother," Ludwig interjected. "What a cook! They were both so generous to us. My youngest sister would have stayed with them if given half the chance, I am sure."

One of the sailors came by and told the two that even though they were passengers, they should get on with their chore. If they did not want to work, he was certain he could find two other men to take their places.

The two apologized, smiled at each other one more time, and put their backs into the cleaning up. Ludwig thought he would have to introduce Jacob to his family after supper. What were the chances?

The cook and the Captain decided the fish would be cooked all together in the galley. Cutting it into mess size portions and then firing up every brazier on deck did not make sense. They all knew from experience the only food eaten on the ship that evening would have come from the sea. The cook, in fact, started building up his fires below as soon as the cutting began.

The peg-legged cook stepped forward, his large frame covered by a grey, stained apron made of an ancient piece of sail cloth.

"When the fish is cooked, someone will go round and tell each mess when to come get their food. Just be careful around the fire," he cautioned. "And do not eat too much of it. Your bodies are not used to having any large amount of food at one time."

As soon as the fish was placed on the coals, the delicious smell started to filter up through all the openings in the deck. One woman cried she was so glad to smell something cooking besides salt pork. Some of the children were salivating onto the front of their blouses, but their parents cared little.

Fresh food, fresh, fresh food. Not salted, not dried, not rancid, not covered with a green film. The day before, none of them had known any hope of such a thing happening was possible. Most of them would relate to their grandchildren, as they told the story of their Atlantic crossing, that it was the best surprise they had ever had.

After the men washed up in the seawater, the passengers gradually began to descend down below. They found their eating utensils and gave them an extra cleaning in preparation for the feast. They had no beer to drink, but hoped some water would still be left from what had been collected after the last rain.

The fish tasted even better than it smelled. The ship had never been so quiet during the day as everyone, including the crew, concentrated on their meal. Mothers were seen chewing a mouthful of fish, spitting it out into their hand, and feeding their babies by the pinch-full. They wanted to be certain no bones of any size remained.

The Fridbergs reveled in their feast like everyone else. Kitty was eating small bits of it at a time and announced it tasted good, unlike anything else she had eaten on the ship. Adam was pleased, but kept a careful eye on her to be sure she did not eat too much.

Christina, as usual, was trying to make their present day into some sort of story.

"Was Jonah's whale this big?" she asked. "Was it bigger? How did Jonah get in the whale if it was the same size?"

As she chattered on, everyone else continued to quietly savor the delicious, fresh taste and ignore her questions. Barbara finally told Christina to stop talking and start eating. They would go over the story of Jonah in detail when they were finished with their meal.

Barbara kept a careful eye on Carlie, certain she would over-eat and become sick afterwards. And Carlie knew her mother was watching her.

Why does she always think I will eat too much? she asked herself. Even though there had been little extra food back home, her mother had seemed bent on restricting her access to it. True, she had a little more meat on her than her siblings, but she hardly ate more than they did. She often had the feeling her mother did not like her and could never pass up the chance to be critical.

That night, Ludwig, content with having done a full day's work, dreamed he was swimming through the salty ocean, moving in and out of the water like a flying fish, free from the confines of his past life and heading toward the bounty of the life to come.

CHAPTER 36

Halfway There

Christina had taken it upon herself to keep her family apprised of the adventures of Robinson Kreutznaer. She was the first to sit at Herr Franken's knee every day he read to the children, ready to listen to the story of her bosom friend and hero.

The family were now all going to bed at the same time; lack of light, comfortable sitting space, or enjoyable activity made staying awake into the evening not at all attractive. Christina expounded on Robinson's activities for a while until she fell asleep. After that, the two older girls whispered to each other, imagining what life would be like in Philadelphia. On either side of the three young girls, were two adults, imagining their new lives as well and trying not to worry.

Herr Franken was in the habit of singing gaily to himself, humming really. He even knew tunes, which were not hymns, and so were unfamiliar to the passengers. One tune Christina liked better than all the others was the "Ha-Lay-Lu-La" song. "Ha-Lay-Lu-La, Ha-Lay-Lu-La, Ha-Lay-Lu-La; Ha-Laaaay-Lu-La!" Christina enjoyed singing along with him, as did many of the other children.

She asked him if it was a hymn, and Herr Franken explained it was called an Oratorio, much longer than a hymn with many musical instruments and singers making music together. He had just gone to one of its first performances in Ireland and then raced to Deal to board the *Francis and Elizabeth*.

"I hope you can hear the entire piece for yourself one day. It is the most beautiful music I have ever heard."

"Will I be able to hear it in Philadeflia?"

"No, I do not think so."

"Will I hear it in heaven when I go there?"

Herr Franken allowed as she most definitely would.

Robinson Kreutznaer was making great advances in providing a better home for himself. His first house and storage area had suffered a cave-in, and he had to then labor for two years to make another house. This one was larger, with better outer protection, an inner and outer wall filled between with rubble, not unlike a castle. He made a chair and table where he wrote by the light of a goat fat lamp and prepared, as best he could, for a life alone in a different new land. Ludwig wondered if Robinson longed for the touch of a woman as much as he did.

Life onboard ship began to change. The Fridbergs had made new friends, learning about villages in other German-speaking districts. Passengers compared their living arrangements onboard ship and tried to outdo each other with the sad tales of their now scantier food rations and rotten provisions.

Everyone was bored and discontented, looking for anything to happen that could add some excitement to their lives. Remembering their exciting day of the fishes, they continued to ask the Captain when more might be spotted. He replied the crew would try to catch more when the fish presented themselves.

The Captain encouraged the passengers to keep looking over the rails for any sign of tuna. He knew they would never see any because the fish swam in the deep water. The sailors used a harpoon only after the fish were caught by way of a hook and pulled slowly to the surface. But he knew a long day of balancing on the tilting deck scanning the horizon for fish would keep them busy and out of his hair.

Ludwig made the acquaintance of most of the other men, single and married, on the ship, except for the Mennonites. Through Johannes, he had met the other passengers from Langenselbold. Ludwig was grateful for their little traveling party of three families and two single men, but wished they had set out on their journey, like Johannes, with more people to support each other.

Ludwig met people from places he had never heard of and some he had. As he learned more about the geography of their district, he realized many seemed to come from villages to the north and east of Massenbach.

Closest was Ittlingen. He had been there and knew a few of its residents. Jacob Geiger, a citizen of the village and his wife, Anna Elisabeth, were hoping to go to Montgomery County along with their six children. Besides their young son a little older than Christina, they had five older daughters. Ludwig thought they must be going to Philadelphia to find them all husbands. He was rather taken with the two eldest, although they seemed to want little to do with him. The two younger girls were identical twins, which made Christina giggle whenever she saw them. They had become her two best friends.

Kitty and Adam had gotten to know Philip Schleyhouff and his wife, Catharina. Their two-year-old son, Johan Michael, had captured Kitty's heart. She loved to sit on the deck, talk with her new friend, and hold little Michael on her lap. He was a handsome, lively child, with a thick head of curls and a propensity to chatter. It seemed the single men formed a group and the married men kept close to those with families. The married men talked about plowing and apple trees, while the single men discussed the virtues of the single women onboard. Ludwig was somewhat in between; he was single, but had the responsibilities of a family without being married. He made it very clear, however, he wished to be.

Ludwig knew many, like himself, had left their villages without paying their emigration fees, hoping to evade army service. He supposed it was God's place to judge those who left for whatever reason, and hoped God would not judge him too harshly, even though he had broken his oath to serve Baron von Massenbach. He had to admit he admired Christof Geisel from Eschelbron who had paid the fee to buy himself out of serfdom. It seemed Christof was doing everything the right way.

Many passengers were Lutheran, people with whom both Ludwig and Barbara felt a kinship. A few of the Reformed faith were on board along with, they thought, one Catholic. Differences in their faith, however, seemed to have fallen away; each read his Bible with the same devotion and hope.

The Mennonites made up the largest religious group, coming from different German-speaking districts and even Switzerland. Pastor Kimmel had told Ludwig many Mennonites had left Switzerland because of persecution and even execution, spreading out into different areas of the Holy Roman Empire. It seemed Mennonites did not believe in baptizing their children at birth, which Pastor Kimmel thought was sinful.

Mennonites waited until they were adults to be baptized, having chosen Christ as their Lord and Savior. Ludwig likened this custom to the Lutheran tradition of confirmation at the age of fourteen, but worried what would happen to people who died before they were baptized. Did the Mennonites go to hell as Lutherans did? He thought it was not only sinful, but also imprudent. He felt no ill will toward any of them, but perhaps they were afraid for having been treated so badly in Switzerland, and so stayed to themselves.

Barbara and Ludwig let their guard down a little about the three girls. Thea and Carlie were now allowed to go on deck as long as they stayed together. Christina still had to be with her mother or brother, but did not have to hold their hands unless they were near the rail. Sometimes, Ludwig had to grab Christina if the sea became rough or a sudden wave hit the ship. He still felt nervous about the water and made sure to hang onto the rail with his back to it when he was close to the ship's edge himself.

Michael Platscher was a year younger than Thea. He looked like a boy compared to the young woman Thea was turning into, but he was completely smitten with her. He followed her around like a little puppy, wanting to be by her side, but, at the same time afraid to get too close. Thea could sense his devotion, but was more interested in attention from the older boys.

When she leaned against the rail, he came up to her, not too close, but not too far away. She would smile at him, which would send his poor heart into spasms. Occasionally she spoke to him, usually about the weather or how bad the food was or when they would have fresh fish again. At this, Michael's face would turn beet red, and Thea would suppress the urge to laugh at him.

After a while, she became sick of his continuous presence and so excused herself and walked away. She tried to do it nicely, but sometimes he went as far as to follow after her. Now that Ludwig had given her a longer leash, she wanted to be free to talk with the older boys, but "Not Grown Men," as Ludwig put it.

While she had caught the attention of several "Not Grown Men," somebody in particular had taken her fancy. Standing by the rail seemed to be an invitation for all on board to come closer for conversation, and he often did.

Johan Huber was a year older than Thea. He was a tall, strong, good-looking young man with a healthy countenance, and long, dark, wavy hair, which made Thea's heart flutter at times. He was traveling with the group from Ittlingen.

Johan seemed interested in what Thea had to say, unlike most of the other boys she had met who were interested only in themselves. They talked about how much they missed their motherland and wondered if America would be very different. The couple tried to stand as close to each other as they dared without calling undue attention to themselves. Thea felt a tiny bit sinful, but not enough to stop her behavior.

CHAPTER 37

Complications

K itty had not been feeling well. Her stomach was upset, but it was not the seasick feeling she had had at the beginning of the voyage. Adam was concerned she was not eating enough and tried to give her his share of the food she seemed to like. She looked thinner, which concerned him as well. Because of her pregnancy, she should be growing fatter. He knew little about pregnancy, but did know a woman grew bigger and bigger as her pregnancy progressed.

After she had spent three days lying down and fibbing to Adam she felt a little tired, Kitty confided to Barbara. She had known Frau Fridberg all of her twenty years and felt a sense of trust had developed between them now that she was a grown woman.

Barbara came over to Kitty's bunk and squatted down on her stool, holding onto the edge of the bed as the ship heaved from side to side.

"Kitty," Barbara was hoping Kitty would be truthful with her. "You do not look well. Are you feeling well...or not?"

Kitty replied with hesitation and a tightness growing in her throat. "No, Frau Fridberg, I do not feel well at all. Please do not tell Adam. He has so much on his mind."

"Of course not, dear, not if you do not want me to. Tell me, what is bothering you?"

"Well, my stomach feels queasy most of the time, even on calm days. And my ankles and feet are swollen, even more in the evening. I can deal with those, but the worst part is the headache. It is there in the morning, all day, and all night. It never stops. It throbs and tenses and seems as though it will burn right through my eyes."

"I have some herbs I can give you," Barbara said. "They may calm your stomach and make your headache a little better." Kitty nodded, but quickly stopped when she realized the motion made her pain even worse.

Barbara bent down and reached for her box stored under the bottom bunk. Looking through it, she brought out a few of her precious packets wrapped in small pieces of linen and tied with twine.

"You have not had any bleeding, have you?"

Kitty shook her head.

Barbara ventured, "Or anything else coming from there?"

Kitty shook her head again, trying not to blush. She had never spoken this frankly with anyone, not even her mother. She was extremely naive about her body and the new role it was preparing her for.

In her village, unmarried girls were not welcome at births. They helped to mind the younger children at neighbors or relatives' houses while the mother delivered in front of her kitchen hearth. She had seen one of Herr Miller's sows give birth to a litter of piglets when she was young, so she did know something about the process. She knew it hurt.

Barbara tried to smile, but she was starting to feel the cold press of fear overtaking her. She had known other pregnant women who went off their feed while their ankles got bigger and bigger and their heads hurt more and more.

"Have you felt the baby move?" Barbara asked, trying to sound casual.

"Oh, yes. He moves all over the place all the time. He is going to be a strong, lively one," she smiled with pride.

Barbara was glad to hear that. She tried to push negative thoughts out of her mind, knowing what sometimes happened next.

Barbara got up, walked to the water pitcher and poured out a cup of the brackish liquid.

"Here, dear. Drink some of this. You will feel better."

Kitty sat up the best she could and drank half of the water as she was told. "That is all I want," she said, handing the cup back to Barbara. "Do you know what day it is? I cannot remember. Do we have salted pork or salted fish for our supper tonight?"

"I soaked some beans last night and have been cooking them this afternoon. There is plenty for you and Adam. I put a little bit of salt pork in them, but not much."

Kitty swallowed the bile that had risen in her throat. She hated how salty the provisions were. Salt pork and salt fish followed by more salt pork and salt fish. Everyone was sick of the saltiness, but especially her.

She longed for a nice, lightly smoked sausage steamed in beer like her grandmother used to make. But she knew the sausage she had brought was gone and so was Barbara's. She would have liked an egg, scrambled in her mother's fresh butter with no salt at all. But she knew it would be a long time before she tasted either.

"And rice. Do you think you could eat some of that?"

Kitty nodded and lowered herself back onto the bunk. "I think I will rest until suppertime."

Barbara pulled the quilt up over her and tucked it under her chin. "Yes, dear, just rest."

Barbara got up just as Christina approached Kitty's bunk. She grabbed the girl by the wrist and pulled her away.

"Kitty is going to rest for a while, Christina. See if the Kohler children would like to play that guessing game you like so much. You are so good with them, and I know Gabriel and Lisabeth could use some time for themselves."

Christina smiled at the compliment and turned around, knocking on the post beside the Kohlers' bunk, as she would have knocked on their door at home.

She wanted to ask for some cheese for her supper, but then thought better of it. She felt she deserved a treat given her selfless offer of help.

The next morning was their thirty-seventh day at sea. Most people had conquered their seasickness, but a few had not. Barbara had seen one of the young Mennonite children growing thinner and thinner. The girl was still sick on the rough days, and Barbara had heard she was nothing but skin and bones, wasting away under her thin blanket. Thank God Christina had been able to recover from her fever and seasickness. Barbara made a mental note to include the girl in her prayers, along with Kitty.

The sky was dark the next day, and threatening. Nevertheless, Barbara swept her arm around Kitty's shoulder and steered her toward the deck for some fresh air. She was afraid, though, the cold wind would drive them all back down below. While the air was cool, and the wind was not blowing, they were able to sit on the deck for a while. They chatted together and watched Christina enjoying the story of her now favorite friend.

Kitty told Barbara how sure she was her child was a boy.

"I am definitely fuller on the right side of my belly than my left," Kitty explained. "I was terribly sick the first month or so, and everyone knows that bodes well for a boy. And," she said bending towards Barbara and whispering in her ear, "my right breast is definitely harder than my left."

Barbara was well aware of all the ways for determining whether a woman carried a boy or a girl. She had used them herself, wanting, of course, to have at least one male child. But she did not know if she believed any of it; most of the old wives' tales had rarely applied to her. Supposedly, anything favoring the right side of the body meant it was a boy, and the left side a girl.

"Do you see how high I am carrying him?" Kitty questioned. "It must be a boy."

Barbara smiled and nodded, hoping in her heart Kitty would have a healthy baby, whether it be male or female. The poor woman had endured so much privation during their trip—poor food and water, and air when they were confined below for such long periods of time. With all the sliding around and bumping into things that had gone on, listing this way and that, it would be a miracle if she held that baby in her womb long enough to see it thrive once it was born. Barbara was glad Adam was such an attentive, caring husband; many were not.

The rain began the next day. It poured for five days. They were all restricted, of course, to their berths below deck. They could hear the thunder roaring over the water and hoped any lightning would not find their wet mast pushing up naively from the deck.

Thankfully, the quartermaster handed out cheese on the days they could not cook. The cheese tasted almost palatable when they paired it with a few of the dried apples everyone on the ship had brought. But unfortunately, the apples were all gone.

The water supply was dwindling, and that which remained was tainted. Barbara hoped the rain would slow down some so the sailors could catch it in the sails. They had an ingenious system for collecting it and then directing it into a keg on the deck.

After supper, Barbara and Christina lay in their bunk together while Barbara told another Bible story. The passenger area was too dark to read, even by lamplight. Thea and Carlie mostly lay side by side and giggled, but sometimes they listened to the stories they were hearing for the hundredth time.

The ship rocked forward and backward, side to side, up and down. Sometimes it felt as if it were swirling around in a circle, bobbing up and down in the turbulent sea of trouble. Although most were still afraid of these forces of nature, they were growing used to their feelings of fear overtaking them for long periods of time.

During bad weather the hatches were closed, making the ill-smelling air even worse. That morning, a terrible stench filled the ship, which they had come to know meant another barrel of salt pork had been opened. The putrid smell would linger until the hatches could be reopened.

Every once in a while the ship seemed to bump up against

something in the water. Captain North told a group of women it was only a whale and not to worry. None of them knew for sure if he was telling the truth or not, but the sailors could be seen hiding their heads in their arms while their shoulders shook with laughter.

CHAPTER 38

Resolution

Once the storm had finally passed, Kitty pulled Barbara aside on the deck. "Frau Fridberg," she said with a tear running down her dirty cheek, "I have not felt the baby move since before the storm began. I thought everything might be moving around so much I could not feel him. But he is not moving. He has not kicked or moved his head from side to side. Adam wanted to feel my belly last night, but I told him no. Is something wrong?"

Barbara motioned to Kitty to follow her down below. Kitty lay down on the bunk while Barbara covered her with a quilt, slipping her hand under the old coverlet. She felt over Kitty's belly, up under her ribs and over on both sides, detecting no movement at all. Kitty winced when Barbara pushed tentatively on the right side of her stomach, just under her ribs, and Barbara stopped at once.

Barbara kept her hand where it was for a while, hoping she would feel something move, but the belly was still. What she feared had happened. The baby was dead in Kitty's womb and nothing could be done for it now.

Barbara did not know what to do. Tell Kitty right now? Tell Adam first? Tell them both at the same time? She did not want to tell anyone. The semi-darkness, thankfully, kept Kitty from seeing her face.

At that moment, Christina appeared and wanted to hear the story of Noah again. Barbara took her hand, turned, and both of them started up to the deck. Kitty quickly fell asleep and dreamed of a husky boy with curly, brown hair, growing tall and straight like his father.

When Kitty woke up a little later, she thought she felt some movement in her belly, although more sluggish than before. But, what with the trip up the Neckar, up the Rhine, across the channel and now on their way across the Atlantic Ocean to America, he was entitled to be a little listless. She felt a little dizzy once she was standing up, but overall, more rested and relaxed.

Kitty went to find Adam, hopeful the movement would last until he could feel it himself. She wanted to reassure him the child was fine. Reckoning the baby would be born in about six weeks, she prayed with all her heart he would wait until they reached America to present himself.

Kitty saw Barbara on her way to supper. She pulled Barbara aside to tell her she was feeling the baby move and not to worry. Barbara gave her a wan smile, which she tried to augment with spirited expression in the rest of her face. Again grateful the below decks was dark, she thanked God for the gift of belly gas to girls such as Kitty, and the grace He provided to deal with slow, gathering defeat and disappointment. Barbara knew stillborn babies sometimes moved around in their mother's wombs whenever the mothers themselves moved. It felt like the baby was moving on its own, but it was not.

Several days later, at about sunrise, Barbara heard moaning. Adam appeared and asked Barbara if she could come down to their bunk right then. Something was not right, he told her. She came down the ladder, reached for her shawl, and pulled her box of herbs and medicine out from beneath the bunk.

Kitty was damp with sweat, holding her belly and trying to breathe through what Barbara knew to be labor pains. Barbara went back to her bunk, pulled the soft quilt off Christina, who objected strenuously, and returned to cover Kitty.

"Snuggle up to Carlie," was the only advice she gave to Christina to make up for the intrusion.

"What is the matter, Frau Fridberg?" Adam asked, sitting on

the bunk beside his wife. "Kitty said the baby would not come for at least another six weeks. Will everything be all right?"

Barbara nodded silently, but then decided Adam must know what was happening. She pulled him around the corner and explained the baby had died and Kitty's womb was expelling it. The longer her womb held the dead child, the worse it would be for her, so God was helping her now. Kitty would give birth almost normally, but the baby would be born dead.

She told Adam to find Gabriel and Lisabeth and tell them what was happening. They had weathered two difficult births and one stillborn and would help him accept God's will. He needed to gather some strength for Kitty who was going to need it later on.

"Frau Fridberg," Kitty said as her pain eased, and she tried to sit up. "What is happening? Is this my labor? But it is too early. Will the baby be all right?"

Barbara pulled the covers up around Kitty's shoulders and thought what to do next.

"Yes, your labor has begun," she said, deciding not to tell Kitty the outcome. "I will be right here, and you must take my hand and squeeze it when the pains come."

And come they did, all morning and afternoon. Some kind person had appeared with a large piece of old sail and hung it so Kitty could have a little privacy. The Eckerts packed up a few of their things and told Barbara they were going to stay with some of their Langenselbold friends. Johannes said their children knew everyone and, so, staying in a strange bunk would not upset them.

Lisabeth, Barbara, and a few of the other women they had gotten to know took turns offering their hands and supplying encouragement. A few others brought empty kegs to sit on and made the pretense of trying to knit. The women, as women had done for millennia, tried to keep a chatter going among themselves and with the mother. The more distracted she was, the better.

Barbara was not a midwife, but she had been present at many

births, most with good outcomes. She had kept her eyes and ears open and learned a great deal about the process of giving birth; other women in the village seemed to look to her for help and support. Although Massenbach did have a designated midwife, she could not always be summoned in time to offer any help.

Barbara had had seven babies of her own. She knew more than most *hausfrauen* about labor and delivery, though she certainly would have deferred to anyone onboard the ship who knew more than she. Unfortunately, no trained midwife was making the crossing.

Ludwig, Hans and Gabriel took Adam in tow, taking turns walking him around the deck. They knew what was going to happen. They thanked God for a beautiful, sun-filled day to help Adam and his wife through what would soon prove to be a dark one. Adam alternated between wanting to be with Kitty and wanting to walk as quickly as he could away from his grief. But, he continued to move, as he would also have been unwelcome in the labor room if the birth had taken place in Massenbach.

Thea, who knew about babies and births, tried to explain it all to Christina who chattered away about how much fun a new baby would be on this otherwise unpleasant trip. She thought inwardly the ship was a good place to have a baby because the rocking would keep the baby from crying and waking her up at night.

Kitty's labor continued into the afternoon, and then into the evening. Though she knew the women in her village cried out and even screamed during labor, she tried not to moan, not to weep or make any noise. She felt intensely embarrassed about her predicament in this closely packed ship. But, she truly believed she was a pawn in the hands of the Almighty, doing what had to be done to attain the blissful state of parenthood and fulfill herself as a woman.

Sometimes Kitty laid in the bunk and sometimes squatted on the floor facing her bunk, holding on as if her life depended on it, one woman on either side of her holding her upright. Barbara wished

Kitty had a chair to drape over, even two to help hold her arms up, but of course such usual labor equipment was nowhere to be found.

Barbara had been able to put some extra blankets on the Mullers' bunk, hoping to absorb some of the birth fluids, but with dry blankets at a premium, she tried to conserve them as much as she could. She hoped the girl had the strength of her youth to help her through the next few hours.

By the time the sun went down, Kitty had delivered the baby. Barbara quickly gathered up the little blonde angel in a shawl she had tucked into the bed for that purpose. Kitty knew the baby should start to cry soon and then squawk like a little goat. She had heard that before. But, she heard nothing. And then, she began to sob.

"Why does he not cry? He is supposed to be crying. What is wrong Frau Fridberg, what is wrong?" she sputtered, trying to catch her breath. "Where is Adam? Can he come to me now that everything is over?"

Barbara handed the small bundle to Lisabeth who took it away. Lisabeth began to weep for her dear friend whose heart was surely about to break.

"Kitty," Barbara began. "I am so sorry to tell you, your baby is stillborn."

Kitty was stunned. How could this be possible? She knew this happened sometimes, but not to her. She was a good person who always went to church and prayed thoughtfully throughout the day. And so was Adam. He never took God's name in vain, not even under his breath. They kept all God's commandments. Why was He doing this to her? How could He do this to them?

Adam returned from the deck and sweeping his arms around his wife, burrowed his head in her thick, dark hair and sobbed with her. He did not care if anyone heard him crying; he could not help it. He would ask God later for forgiveness for his lack of acceptance.

CHAPTER 39

A Goodbye

Everyone on the ship knew what had happened. They had known from Kitty's first moan. And, they had known later when they heard a mother's cry and not a baby's. The Mennonites looked the most forlorn.

News traveled quickly. Captain North took out his ship's log and entered in his manicured script on the bottom line of the page, *15 August 1742. Daughter born to Adam Muller and Catharina Stocker, husband and wife. Stillborn.* And when the ink was dry, he closed the book and placed it back on the shelf.

Kitty began to complete her labor, quickly realizing everything was not over. Barbara knew the afterbirth had to be delivered and checked to be sure it had all come away. She hoped she was equal to the task.

Adam was banished back to the top deck where the married men there gave him mostly knowing looks and the single men only blank stares. But, they all said a prayer for the grieving couple.

By morning, Barbara and the other women had cleaned up the bed, someone donating a clean sheet they had hoped to use for themselves. Lisabeth took a small amount of the linen she was saving for a petticoat and started to stitch a bag. She knew she would not need her petticoat to be so full, especially when she was becoming fuller in her own body.

Eventually, Adam climbed into the bunk beside Kitty and held her until they both fell asleep, exhausted and full of pain. He cried for the loss of his first son, his wife's struggle and pain, his paralyzing fear, and the feeling in his breast he had done the wrong thing, selfishly taking her away from all she knew to the New Land. That night, they dreamed only of God in His infinite wisdom.

Barbara and Lisabeth decided to tell the Mullers a small lie and asked God's forgiveness for this very small sin. The Mullers wanted so desperately to have a boy that the two women thought not to tell them the truth. They let Kitty and Adam believe they had had a son, even though they had had a daughter. This might give them some small amount of comfort, which they desperately needed.

The next morning, Lisabeth brought the small bag to Barbara. Lisabeth had stitched "Baby Muller" on it using her best blue thread even though she knew only a few people would see it. She hoped it might make God's search easier, to help Him find the baby girl beneath the wide expanse of the ocean. Somehow, embroidering the bag seemed like the right thing to do.

Putting the sand the captain had given her into the bag and then the little body, Barbara held the bundle while Lisabeth sewed it shut in her small, even stitches, their tears falling in unison on the shapeless linen.

Kitty and Adam woke up to the sudden realization of their loss. They were both upset the baby had not been baptized before it died, but knew nothing could have been done. An unborn baby could not be baptized, nor could a dead one. They prayed together the Almighty would bestow His grace on their little boy, that he would be saved and rest in the arms of the Lord forever.

They began to wonder what he looked like. Did he favor Adam or Kitty, although it was a known fact boys favored their fathers and girls their mothers. Was he blonde like Adam or brown haired like his mother? They talked about asking to see his body, but decided they could bear the loss more easily if they did not. What mattered most to them was that the child knew they loved him, that they would always love him.

Later, Barbara, Lisabeth, Adam and Capt. North stood at the

stern of the ship. Adam would not allow Kitty to be present; he wanted to protect her from any further pain, knowing he could be witness to their grief, enough for both of them. Captain North said a prayer from his well-used Bible, and afterward Barbara leaned carefully over the railing, letting the tiny bundle fall into the dark water and slip beneath the waves.

Kitty and Adam gradually came to terms with their loss. They prayed repeatedly, hoping this would help close their wound and lift their child into the glory of heaven. Kitty's headache and other symptoms quickly abated, making life a little easier for her. Barbara was grateful for Kitty's recovery, knowing she could well have died along with the baby.

CHAPTER 40

Shame

Barbara thought the villagers in Massenbach lived too close together, such that anyone's business was everyone's business. Onboard the ship, however, the living conditions were even worse. Women could be heard screaming at their husbands at all times of the day or night, while men yelled at their wives and punished them with the backs of their hands, or worse. Children were whipped with switches brought along in case they were needed, resulting in screaming children who were yelled at by their parents to be still while they beat them.

Back home, someone in authority would have intervened to keep these more violent behaviors from getting out of hand. The Shaming Mask, pillory or other consequence would have been meted out by the Village Council. The offender would have been harshly punished, keeping a recurrence from happening in the village.

Barbara shuddered as she remembered the use of the Shaming Mask. She was always afraid the Council would sentence her to this punishment for her habit of losing her temper with her children and occasional overuse of the rod, although she never scolded her husband. She knew better than that and she knew Jacob would never have stood for it. He had hit her only once, and she had to admit she deserved it when she told him he had been stupid and ignorant to sell their extra eggs for such a low price. But she greatly regretted it afterward.

The Shaming Mask was only used for extreme breaches of the unwritten village rules. Barbara thought Kitty's mother, Anna Maria, would have been reported to the Council and been made to wear it, but she never was. She yelled at her husband and called him names on a regular basis, always in a loud voice so everyone on that side of the village could hear.

Barbara had only seen the mask used once, and vowed she would never go through that ordeal. Her mother's neighbor, Frau Kleinburger, had behaved even worse than Kitty's mother, gossiping and spreading tales about village inhabitants she knew to be false. She had reported Frau Gopler and Hans Adler to the Council for adulterous behavior and Frau Gopler's near certain pregnancy as a result of their sinful behavior. When the Council called both couples before it, they testified nothing of what Frau Kleinburger said was true. Frau Gopler was not even pregnant. The Council turned the tables on Frau Kleinburger and sentenced her to the Shaming Mask.

Massenbach owned only one mask, which was used for all transgressions, regardless of the charge. It was made of metal, rusted for almost a century, in the shape of a donkey's head with large, curving ears and a short, ugly snout. The mask was a hinged cage that fit over the offender's head and locked around the neck.

Someone from the Council attached a rope to the collar and led Frau Kleinburger around the village in the early evening when everyone would be home. Some people banged on pots while others shouted horrible insults at her. "You have a tongue like a maggot!" or "You will surely rot in hell!" Fresh dung and mud were thrown at her along with the small bits of garbage the village produced. She was even spit upon.

Frau Kleinburger stumbled through the village, pulled here and there on purpose by the Councilman so she would lose her footing. Even through the mask, everyone could see how humiliated and even afraid she was, tears pouring down cheeks, sodden with refuse. Frau Kleinburger was seeing the kind, responsible people of her village turn into demons, releasing years of pent-up anger and frustration. Even her sister, Juliana Hasenfus, joined in, still reeling from the effects of the story Frau Kleinburger had told about her years before. It seemed Juliana had never married and Frau Kleinburger started a rumor Juliana was in love with Herr Schiffer, another woman's husband. So many bad things were said about her after that, it was no wonder she had never been able to find a husband.

By the time Frau Kleinburger was led back to her house, her clothes and hands were covered with all manner of filth. Some of the refuse had been thrown hard enough to move through the openings in the mask, especially the eyes, making her face look like a dung pile with excrement dripping from her nose. Her face stung from the vileness of the filth as her eyes swelled with blinding irritation.

Her husband was sitting at the table in their kitchen with his head in his hands. He fought to hold back tears. How humiliated he felt! She had managed to destroy his good name along with what remained of her own.

Throughout the evening he could be heard upbraiding and criticizing her, calling her all manner of vile names, some of them very cruel. When she tried to speak or defend herself, he corrected her with the switch he had cut expressly for this purpose.

Barbara had difficulty believing how brutal some people could be. The worst thing she had done was throw several handfuls of freshly cracked shells from the eggs she was making for supper, but she picked up the ones that did not stick to Frau Kleinburger's person so they could be fed to her chickens. Frau Kleinburger stopped her behavior for a while, but began again when she could no longer help herself.

CHAPTER 41

The Thief

It was unimaginably boring sitting on the passenger deck with nothing to do. Some days when the sails made too much noise, Herr Franken would read "Robinson" around the one table in the hold. Carlie was not much interested in listening to this; it was only a made-up story that did not amount to anything.

Carlie's most unhappy moments came when she was hungry. This added to both her discomfort and frustration. The food from the mess was supposed to be shared equally, but she felt the portions she received were always smaller than those of the others in her family.

This was not lost on her mother who spent inordinate amounts of time trying to equalize the food everyone consumed. But she had to take into consideration how much of it stayed down, or not. Her greatest fear revolved around Christina, who ate less than anyone and vomited more.

Ludwig, of course, required the most calories, but made a point of seeing his family got what they needed before he did. After Christina's needs were met, then came Thea, followed by Barbara, and lastly Carlie. Then he would take his portion, which was sometimes quite small. The saving grace was taking all of the uneaten food off his family's plates, which filled his belly and added the nourishment his large body demanded. Carlie was the only one who finished the food on her plate. Left to her own devices, she would have gobbled up any leftover scraps, but knew Ludwig needed them more than she.

There was no question the food was somewhere between unappetizing and downright inedible. He thought about gulping down the worms that eased out of the damp hardtack, but could never quite bring himself to do this. He certainly could not chew them into pieces, but wondered if he would feel them wiggling around in his stomach if he did not. In the end, he simply never ate them.

Carlie often begged for the food Barbara had brought along from home. She loved fresh apples, and dried ones even more. They were sweeter. She often thought of sneaking a little of what they had in their box, but knew a repeat of her weakness as they were leaving Massenbach would not serve her well. But she was always hungry and chronically resentful due to thinking she received less than the others.

On the day each mess received their ration, Carlie made a point of going up on deck with her mother, ostensibly to be of help. And her presence was appreciated when it came time to carry their allotment down to the passenger deck.

As she and her mother were picking up their ration one day, Carlie began to look around at the other food. The cheese caught her attention. This was the most well-liked of all of the food considering it was not greasy or slimy or too salty. Taking small bites, she would chew her portion until it turned into a liquid in her mouth and then slowly swallow it. She intended to make the experience last as long as possible.

But on this particular day, the devil she had so long fought had his way with her. She did not know what happened, but before she knew it, she had grabbed a large chunk of the creamy yellow delicacy, turned, and ran down onto the passenger deck, heading for the stern. She knew what she was doing was wrong and would land her in more trouble than she could imagine, but she could not stop herself.

Barbara was aghast. *What on earth did Carlie think she was doing?* They had already received their ration, and Carlie had to know their family was not entitled to more.

Barbara yelled after her, "Carlie, stop! Come back here this instant! Now!" She then realized Carlie had no intention of stopping. Barbara had no option but to run after her wayward daughter and stop her from making this terrible mistake even worse.

The quartermaster saw Carlie out of the corner of his eye, and whirling around, screamed with intensity, "Stop! Thief! Stop her, that girl with the braid! Stop her! She stole the cheese!"

No one within earshot seemed inclined to stop her, so Carlie continued to the very back of the ship. Tripping over a slop bucket in the middle of the corridor, she fell hard on her knee and had to scooch over against the wall near the privy, out of sight.

As her eyes adjusted to the dark, she looked at the piece of delicious cheese, and then back at the light coming through the opening to the deck. She thought about getting up and taking the cheese back to the top deck, but her stomach was not having it. She took one big bite, reveling in its wonderfulness, and then proceeded to consume it as quickly as she could.

As she lay back against the wall, tears flowed slowly down her cheeks. She was beginning to see the reality of what she had done and knew nothing on this earth or sea could set it right. She knew a sort of jail had been built on the ship; two men fighting with knives over a pitcher of ale had been placed there for five days with only hardtack and water to sustain them. At the end of their incarceration, they had each received ten lashes of the cat o' nine tails and been returned to their bunks with bleeding flesh.

Carlie hoped her punishment would not be as harsh, but knew what she had done was just as bad. Would they let her take off her vest and shift before they whipped her? She did not want to ruin her clothing, and Momma would be angry if she did.

The litany began. Thief. Sinner. Ungrateful daughter. Ashamed of yourself! She who had shamed her family beyond imagination. How would any of them be able to hold heir heads up? And it would all be her fault. Sitting there in the stinking, wet sloppiness on the floor, she wanted to die. How could God forgive her this? Never-mind her mother.

She heard footsteps, and a man's voice yelling, "I think she came down here!" He bounded down the hallway. "Here she is!" he cried, grabbing her roughly by the arm and jerking her to her feet.

Carlie continued to sob and tried to get away, but had no success. Her knee hurt terribly. This man was three times her size, big bones or not. Soon other men arrived followed by the Captain and eventually her mother. She covered her face with her apron and continued to cry into it.

"I am sorry," Carlie said softly. "I did not mean to steal anything. It just happened."

"That is what they all say," one of the men remarked.

Barbara pushed her way through the small band of men and eventually reached her sniveling daughter.

"Carlie, what is wrong with you? You should be ashamed of yourself. Give me the cheese right now and, with any of God's grace, the Captain will forgive you."

"I cannot," she replied, holding out her empty hands to show she no longer had it.

"Well, where is it? Where did it go? Did you drop it?"

"No," she said, and, lowering her head even farther down than she thought possible, explained she had eaten it.

Barbara's face turned its usual, shameful red, as she put her hands over her mouth and looked to the heavens upwards of the floor above her.

"I am sorry," Carlie said softly. "I am so sorry."

Captain North was beginning to show his irritation. The circumstances were alarming, but a piece of cheese was hardly the end of the world. But he had never had a child do anything of this import on any of his voyages and was unsure how to proceed.

"Frau Fridberg, take her back to your bunk, and we will decide

what to do with her later. I have a ship to sail here, in case no one
has noticed."

Barbara took her quivering daughter by the shoulders, gripping
a little too harshly to be certain she did not get away. She whispered
into Carlies ear, "Start walking and keep walking until we get to our
bunk. Lower your head to show how ashamed you are of yourself."

By the time Carlie and Barbara returned to the bunk, everyone
on the ship knew what had happened. Carlie's siblings were there
waiting for her, mostly because they did not want to be up on deck
feeling the judgment everyone there was projecting.

Carlie quickly climbed up to their bunk, rolled over to Ludwig's place on the outside, and pulled a blanket over her head. Thea
began whispering with her brother to find out what had happened.
Christina was mostly oblivious to the event, knowing only that
Carlie had been naughty and would probably be switched.

Christina came up to their bunk after lying down with Kitty
and rubbing her feet. She crawled over to Carlie who was now crying softly.

"What did you do?" she asked her older sister in what she
hoped was a kindly tone. "Were you very, very, naughty?"

"Yes, I was naughty. Very naughty. I committed a sin."

Christina's eyes got bigger with each question. "Which one?"

Carlie did not answer, and so Christina began to guess. "Gluttony?"

"Well, in a way."

"Did you take the Lord's name in vain? Were you selfish?"

"Selfishness is not a sin. It is simply not Christian-like."

"Did you dishonor Momma? Did you tell her she was an evil
witch?"

"No, no. All right, if you must know, I stole something."

Christina's eyes widened even more, as she thought through
the list of anything worth stealing on the ship. It came to her; Carlie
must have stolen some food—of course—gluttony. She tried to

imagine Carlie grabbing a handful of salt pork, but that did not seem right to her.

"It was cheese, a big piece of it. And I ate it all. There, now you know everything. Now please go away; my stomach is feeling sick."

The family left Carlie alone for the rest of the day, knowing she probably would not feel like eating supper. They were all fearful of Captain North coming to their bunk and giving Carlie her punishment, most of all Carlie.

And come he did, with a few of his sailors, and Herr Franken to translate in case the situation escalated.

"I have decided to confine you to your bunk for five days. You may have only hardtack and water for your rations. Now that will give you something to think about the next time you try to steal food that belongs to others. And you are to be switched. I am certain you would not want one of the sailors to do it, so we will ask your brother. I assume he is the head of your family now."

Everyone gasped. Food rationed for five days was nothing, but a switching by Ludwig? Ludwig's head shot up as he realized what he was in for.

He had never had to discipline anyone, especially not one of his sisters. His mother had always done that. But if he were going to be head of the family, this would certainly be one of his responsibilities. But how could he ever hit Carlie? He was glad it had not been Christina.

He looked over at his mother who seemed to be agreeing with the Captain. Physical discipline had not been necessary on the voyage so far, and it looked as if this would be Ludwig's first adventure in being a parent. Carlie was sobbing again now; Ludwig wanted to comfort her, but knew instinctively the punisher was never the consoler.

One of the sailors handed him the branch of a willow tree, rugged but bendable.

He then told everyone to leave, as the man of the household should, and told Carlie to come down from the bunk. He wanted to be fair about this. Yes, she needed to be corrected, but not to the point of hurting her.

After climbing down, Carlie put her hands on the board at the foot of the upstairs bunk and braced herself. Ludwig wanted to begin immediately, wanting to have this over with as soon as possible, but something held him back.

He was thinking again of Massenbach and his life there as a boy. His father, of course, was his schoolteacher and, as he thought back about his behavior in school, felt a creeping feeling of embarrassment and regret.

Ludwig did not like school. He knew early on his father wanted him to follow in his footsteps and choose education as his vocation. But Ludwig hated being confined to the schoolroom, especially on nice days; he would much rather have been outside, helping with the harvest or herding the pigs through the woods in the fall. He failed to pay attention and when this became obvious in the classroom, his father was required to hit him across his knuckles with a broad stick as he did the other recalcitrant students.

Ludwig knew how much his father hated hitting him. But Jacob never did it with anger, whether Ludwig was punished at school or in their home.

Several nights a week, when Jacob came to bid his children goodnight as they lay on their pallets, he would say, "Ludwig, it breaks my heart every time I have to hit the back of your hand with the stick. Please try to pay better attention tomorrow." And then the father would kiss the son goodnight and hope for a better day tomorrow.

Ten should be enough, he thought, *but not too hard.* He had never had to split himself between too much and not enough, and this was proving rather disquieting. But he thought ten strokes should suffice. Five would let Carlie believe he did not mean business, and fifteen would be too many.

Carlie bore the beating as best she could, giving out a small cry every time the stick hit her bottom and the tops of her legs through her thin skirt. But more than the pain was the shame. She was mortified. And so was Ludwig. That was the worst punishment of all; knowing she was making her brother, her wonderful, faithful brother, switch her, for everyone on the ship to hear. If she had known this would be her punishment, she would never have taken the cheese, no matter how much she wanted it.

The family was soon back together, Carlie again on her perch of shame on the bunk. No one spoke. They went about getting their evening meal, afterwards listening to Barbara read the evening Bible verses. They were soon in bed, but slept little that night, least of all, Ludwig.

Carlie served her sentence with resignation; bread and water, that was all. Her knee hurt terribly, but she told no one. Both of her legs had always been a subject of concern with her family; they bowed outward in a most unattractive fashion. Of course, her mother constantly commented on her large bones, but she did have large wrists and ankles as well. Her chest protruded in an odd way; Barbara told her these issues would remedy themselves with time, but Carlie did not believe her. She had seen people in the village with these same characteristics—large wrists and ankles, and an odd bulge of their breast bone.

Throughout those five days, Christina and Thea took turns lying next to the villain, rubbing her back, singing her songs, and telling her stories. The tried and true Fridberg way of dealing with anything unpleasant persisted. Barbara sat on her stool, trying to find a place in her heart to forgive her wayward daughter. She was not successful at first, but pressed on until she finally was. Ludwig spent his time on deck, certain no one would dare to outwardly heap shame on him. After all, he was the man who had corrected this unfortunate girl, his own sister, just as a father would have done. He expected, in fact, to receive a bit more respect because of it. After her sentence had been served, the family, without any discussion of it, climbed the stairway together and tried to put the "cheese theft" behind them.

More Decisions

B arbara had been grateful for the curtain put up during Kitty's delivery, but someone had come and taken it down so it could be reused during another birth or prolonged death. Neither she, nor her family, nor anyone else, had a place providing for any privacy.

Although two latrines were located at the stern, people often used the buckets on the floor when they could not get there in time. She tried to keep everything clean in their area, although the floor proved the most difficult. She was running low on vinegar and once it was gone, she would have nothing else to use but seawater. But, at least that had salt in it.

While it was next to impossible to keep everyone's bodies clean, Barbara concentrated, with some success, on their hands and faces. Every couple of weeks, she would have them change into their other sets of clothes and then take the dirty ones up on deck. When she washed clothes at home, she did so in the cold water of the river, but at least she had her bat to force the water through the cloth. She owned a wash tub, but never had any wood to burn beneath it.

As with everything else that was "washed" on board, Barbara would dunk it as vigorously as she could, wring it out, and put it somewhere to dry, hoping even the dark fabrics would bleach in the sun. Clotheslines had come into communal use once someone began to whittle clothespins from some of the kindling. The airing out and bleaching by the sun on the deck may have done more for the clothes than anything else.

Despite her fear of going hungry and the unfortunate incident with the cheese, Carlie appeared to have weathered the journey better than anyone. She maintained her appetite despite the vile conditions and did not appear to have lost any weight. Her mother's hope that Carlie would grow into her body had not yet happened, however. Her knee continued to hurt, sometimes causing her to limp. But no one had commented on it yet.

Carlie managed to keep her long brown hair, worn in a single braid down her back, freer of lice than any of the others. Thea quipped Carlie was too contrary for any lice to stay around, which resulted in a week's long quarrel between the two of them. Carlie's feelings were easily hurt, and she did not take at all well to teasing. Ludwig had tormented her by saying if she started sleeping on the outside of the bunk instead of him, she could keep the lice away from everyone else. Another week's long quarrel.

While Christina's chipper little personality continued to grow, her body did not. Massenbachers were used to having thin children, but Christina looked ill and probably was. As was with all the passengers, hope was held that soon they would all have good food to eat in abundant supply.

Thea was coming into her own as an adult and had become her mother's helpmate. Despite her thinness, her beauty was flourishing. She had more than one incident of having to fend off more interested men, but had learned to do it with a certain grace so no one was offended

Everyone on board was in a foul mood. People were tired, dirty, and sick of the conditions they had been living under. Anyone who did not begin the voyage with swollen, bleeding gums had them now. Their bodies had been ravaged.

Some of the provisions were gone, while others had deteriorated badly. Even the worms in the hardtack were becoming listless. The sugar was completely gone as was the brandy. While the rice looked like it would last the rest of the voyage, the beans were getting low in the casks. Rations for each mess had been greatly reduced. Most people did not notice this for they had begun to eat only until the feeling of hunger was gone, and then they stopped.

Passengers, crew and even the Captain were chronically thirsty. Poor Rufus walked around the deck panting from the heat, looking for something that would slake his thirst. Thankfully, he knew not to drink saltwater, but he could be found after a rain licking the puddles on deck, something the humans onboard had seriously considered. The water had gone bad after only a few weeks, but they continued to drink it out of fear their thirst would kill them. A cup of cool, clear water was what they needed most.

The Fridbergs were not the only family in turmoil. One of the Mennonite men had died miles back, and so the group looked even more forlorn than before. Children besides Christina had become even thinner and their parents continued to worry. The thought that they had made a grave error in judgement by choosing to cross the Atlantic was pervasive. And Barbara was no different.

Ludwig, on the other hand, never lost his faith in their dream and remained positive this journey would lead them to opportunities they had never imagined. He had gotten to know several men on the ship, some quite well, and hoped their relationships would continue to grow even after their arrival in America.

Kitty had not been well since the birth, as they called it. Not the stillbirth, not the death, not the catastrophe. She and Adam had, together, brought a child into this world who, they chose to believe, had drawn at least one breath. No one told them their child had been a girl and not a boy, and while it was a sin to lie, all concerned felt this insignificant fib would give the Mullers some hope for the future. But Kitty was so sad. Her face never brightened; she never laughed or even smiled. Adam knew once they got to Philadelphia she would turn around and become her old self again, but for the present, it was rough going.

Adam had decided taking his young wife into the wilderness

would not do. He and Ludwig talked at length about joining forces to master life in their new city; Adam knew he could learn a host of skills quickly. Philadelphia was surely a city of growth, and anyone with a good back and lots of ambition could make a life for himself. And then, Kitty would have the benefit of a family; the Fridbergs loved her like a sister.

Barbara fared worse than any of the adults. She felt so old, full of painful joints and a fatigue so pervasive she thought it would never pass. Three of her teeth had fallen out on the voyage, and the ones left bled constantly.

What bothered her most was that they did not know what they were going to. Yes, in general she knew they were beginning a new life full of all the pablum a booking agent could spew. But once landed in the city with the ship and its few advantages gone back to England, they would be on their own. True, the thirteen of them would pool their assets and alternate their supports, but who really knew what they were in for. Another horrible boarding house for God only knew how long? Food almost as bad as that onboard the ship? Filth worse than they had ever known? But then Barbara would hear God's voice urging her on, and she would put the next foot in front of the other.

CHAPTER 43

Almost There

One afternoon, Christina came down the stairway calling for her mother. "Momma, Momma, you cannot believe it!" she yelled. "Herr Kreutznaer has a friend. Finally, his own friend!" Herr Franken had again passed over the parts of the story about wars, death, and cannibalism, and produced a bosom friend for poor, lonely Robinson. "His name is Friday!" she finished, proud she had been the first child to make the announcement.

Just about everyone on board was following the tale, whether hearing it from Herr Franken himself, or listening to others, mostly the children. They discussed the finer points of the story, none of them knowing he would soon be saved by a passing ship and returned to his home in England.

Herr Franken waited until they were nearing the coast of America before he ended the story. He did not want Robinson to have the comfort of reaching home while these poor wretches continued to suffer. He was acutely aware his life on board ship had many amenities theirs did not. At times, he felt a bit guilty, but justified the benefits of his status by unselfishly reading to them to make their days a little brighter.

On the first day of the voyage, Ludwig had found a post and recorded the passing of each day by cutting a notch in it with his knife. (When he heard Herr Kreutznaer had done the same on his island, he felt a manly pride in having thought of it first.) He had just cut the seventieth mark when he heard Thea yelling to him.

"Ludwig, come up on deck. Hurry! Come up now. We are almost there!" Others around him heard her as well and pushed past each other to the bottom of the stairway in a frenzy.

The Captain had seen the signs of land for several days. Driftwood and other debris began appearing in the water, while every once in a while a bird would fly by and land on one of the booms. Clouds of mist collected more than it had out to sea. No one could see the bottom of the sea yet, but he knew the water was becoming shallower as the ship pressed onward.

The Captain and his crew knew from experience not to tell the passengers they were nearing the end of their voyage. They knew if they did, passengers would pepper them with questions about how long, when, or why not now. Sometimes, as had happened during the voyage already, wind would carry the ship in a direction away from its intended course. That could add time to the journey, something the passengers were loathe to experience.

But then one day, that unmistakable sight of land in the distance appeared. The cat was out of the bag. What the passengers were seeing were islands at the mouth of the Delaware River, not Philadelphia a hundred miles downstream, and what they thought was the end to their misery. But all those passengers trapped for almost ten weeks on what felt like a boat to hell, assumed they would be stepping onto the wharf in Philadelphia within no longer than an hour.

Captain North finally spoke to those assembled on the deck. The date was 19 September 1742. The immigrants quickly quieted when they saw him standing on the bridge. Thank goodness the day was sunny and not too cool.

"We are approaching the islands at the mouth of the Delaware River," he began. Most people were weak from their many hardships, but all tried to stand even if they had to hold onto something or someone. Soon a cheer, at first quiet, but then growing louder and more vigorous, arose from the passengers. A few of the crew joined in.

The Captain said he would offer a prayer and those who were able knelt. He read a short passage from the Bible, "But they that wait upon the Lord shall renew their strength; they shall mount up with wings as eagles; They shall run and not be weary; They shall walk and not faint." He continued, "Oh God, thank you for bringing us over the ocean, to the safety of a new land. We praise your name and ask your forgiveness for any sins we may have committed along the way. Amen."

With that, the passengers cheered again. Those too weak to get out of their bunks and climb the stairs to the deck, lay back as they heard the voices of their fellow voyagers and knew arrival was at hand. They had survived.

The crew of the ship *Francis and Elizabeth* dropped anchor. Another cheer as it splashed through the surface of the water, another as it was felt to hit the bottom of the river. They had survived.

The day was beginning to grow dark now, as the sailor in charge made his rounds, adding more fuel to the braziers. He knew from experience appetites on board would be better now that the ship had stopped moving, even if the food itself was hardly edible. He fervently hoped the masters would not buy up years' old food to provision the ship he sailed on next; it made everything else so difficult to manage.

Captain North went on, "Tomorrow morning we will begin sailing up the Delaware. It will take a day or two, perhaps even three, depending on the tides and winds. When we dock in Philadelphia, everyone must stay on the ship. No one may leave until they have settled their account with me or my assistant.

"A doctor will come aboard and anyone sick will be examined. Those suffering with a contagious disease must stay on the ship until they are cured of it. And if you are ill, do not try to hide; they will find you.

"Men sixteen years or older must go to the Court House to swear allegiance to King George II. You will all have to sign a statement to this effect. But do not worry; if you are not able to write, simply make your mark and the scribe will write your name for you."

Everyone tried to take in what he was saying, but it was truly the first time in months they had had to think about anything so important.

He continued, "As I said, no one may leave until they have settled their account. Those of you who owe money, will be indentured to a kind master, who will take you for his own servant for a set period of time. He will pay your debt in exchange for your labor. If you are not indentured, you will return to Rotterdam when the ship embarks for Europe. You will, of course, still be accountable for your fare westward and your provisions traveling eastward. And remember, if any of your family members died after the midway point of our voyage, you will still be responsible for their passage."

Those who knew they would be indentured hung their heads in shame and fear, having known either before they left Rotterdam or as their money ran out on board what their fate and that of their family members would be. Barbara knew she and Ludwig had enough to pay for the few things they had purchased on board. She had twice bought vinegar, some medicine when Christina was sick, and extra brandy when she needed to keep up her strength. She had asked every time how much the provisions cost, but never received an answer.

The Captain went on, "The corporation will continue to provide you with food and drink until you leave the ship. I know provisions were not adequate during the final days of the voyage, but you will now receive fresh water, fresh bread, and perhaps even some fresh fruit. I have already heard the apple crop was much better than usual this year. Organizations in Philadelphia, which help German-speaking newcomers may bring some provisions as well.

"Once you have paid up, been cleared medically, and denounced the Kings of Prussia, you must leave the ship. If you need a boarding house, do not ask me or any of the crew where they are because we do not know. There may be people on the docks who speak German and have come to help you."

Barbara started down the steps, part of the slowly flowing mass of hungry women about to prepare one of the last meals on the ship. Barbara had soaked peas, cooked rice, and had the last bit of her cheese she had hidden away for their supper. She had seen the small boat, dispatched before the anchor was even dropped, which had been sent, she was told, to bring back several casks of fresh water. How grateful she was that she and her family would be tasting it before they lay down to sleep for the night.

Everyone was excited. It was over. The lucky ones had survived. They were all weak and in some cases quite ill, but they were still alive. Barbara said her own prayer that the widow she was, her man-son, beautiful daughter, growing daughter, and impish daughter had arrived safe, if not completely sound. They all slept, cuddled up next to one another, waiting to meet their new world for the first time.

CHAPTER 44

21 September 1742

Christina awoke at dawn. She quickly pulled on her clothes, dispensed with the ladder, and tossed herself over the side of the bunk, easily missing Adam's belly as she passed. She knew it was forbidden, but she went up the stairs and onto the deck by herself. She could not imagine how she would get into too much trouble given the ship was not actually moving.

Christina looked over the railing, able to see so much more than yesterday with no other people about. She could see land, trees, many boats and even some people on shore, up early like herself.

She was so glad Herr Kreutznaer had been rescued and returned to his home in England, and she felt somewhat the same. She had not been rescued, but she had been taken safely to her home, her new one, as it were.

Other people began to appear on deck, some she had gotten to know and others who had remained strangers. She said good morning to her friends, Christiana and Anna Catharina, the Geiger twins, marveling again at how God could make an exact copy of anything whenever He wanted.

When women her mother's age saw her, they began to look for Barbara, knowing she must be close by. When they found she was not, they spread a collective mantle of safety around the girl. They did not scold, but gave her that look of "What are you doing here alone?" No child her age was allowed on deck by herself. She did not know it, but the ship's passengers had early become like the village back home; everyone worked together to keep all of the children safe, the best they could, at any rate. It was not always perfect.

Ludwig was then at her elbow, picking her up in a bear hug, jumping up and down a few times, and then returning her feet to the deck. She giggled as she always did.

"You are not supposed to be up here by yourself," he said, trying to sound authoritative. "Momma will have your hide."

Christina, always ready for an emergency, said, "She does not have to know I came up here alone, does she?"

Ludwig thought again of the sadness he felt knowing his father had never met Christina. He could not help but wonder what his father would have thought of all this—leaving home, crossing the ocean, and becoming English citizens instead of Prussian peasants. He was sure his father would be pleased.

Within forty-eight hours, the ship made its way down the Delaware River and berthed at one of the busy docks on the east side of the city. Most of the passengers stood on deck so they could see Philadelphia appear through the mist. The Fridbergs were among them and held hands as it approached. They would not be able to leave the ship until the next day, but took in as much as they could of the busy wharf and what little there was of a colonial skyline. When they heard a clock somewhere chime five, they reluctantly filed down the stairs as Barbara started to cook what they all hoped would be their last supper on the ship.

The following morning, passengers awoke to sailors walking around the passenger deck calling, "Men sixteen and over, up on deck!" Ludwig, Gabriel and Adam quickly pulled on their britches, grabbed something to eat, and hurried toward the upper deck. Every man knew today was the day he would become a citizen of Great Britain.

They lined up in no particular order, but Ludwig pulled Gabriel and Stephen in front of him. He could see Hans and Adam a few men back and signaled them to join him and the others. But the

Captain appeared and shouted, "Stay in line! We will march into the city and back in the same order."

The line of boys and men proceeded down the gangplank and took their first steps into the life they had been awaiting for so long. It was a fair walk to the Philadelphia Court House, but the Captain did not march them very fast knowing many were sick and most were in poor physical condition. Some of the men who were seriously ill had been left behind, but the Captain would take care of them later in the day.

All of them were astounded by what they saw. They had seen Rotterdam, with its spectacle of diverse people and business of the day unfolding, but it compared not at all with what was in front of them. Even more people, with more bizarre or fashionable costumes, in frantic motion. The men did not think it possible, but it was louder, dirtier, shabbier, and smellier than the Dutch city they had left behind. It was overwhelming, but they immediately loved it. Ludwig took himself by the shoulders, gave himself a shake, and vowed to move forward with his life despite the confusion and panic overtaking him.

They soon approached the Court House, a stately edifice with even more people milling about it. The line of men climbed the stairs on the outside of the building, filed in, and, before long, an official with an interpreter quieted them down and proceeded to explain the process. He would read the Declaration of Allegiance to their new sovereign, King George II of Great Britain. The interpreter would repeat the declaration in three parts in German, and they would then repeat what he had said. After that, they would file past the scribes sitting at the long tables who would show them where to sign their names as new citizens of England. Hans was the only one of Ludwig's friends who could not sign his name, so Ludwig kept a sharp eye out to be sure one of the scribes helped him.

Ludwig approached the list of names in front of the clerks. This man had just finished putting a point on the well-used quill and handed it to Ludwig. Ludwig looked at the piece of rag paper, wondering how he would sign his name. *Was he Ludwig or Jacob, or perhaps both of them?* He wanted to retain his German heritage at all cost, but knew he would need to Anglicize himself if he expected to make a living in Philadelphia. If he had to depend on Germans for his living, he was sure he and his family would spend a good deal of time hungry. Jacob seemed more English to him than Ludwig and so that is what he wrote. Jacob Fridberg. He felt a bolt of pride surge through him, which he hoped was not going to make a tear appear at the corner of his eye. He smiled, put the quill down, and stepped quickly behind Stephen. The other two were smiling as much as he was.

Before long, the line had marched back to the ship. Some of the few single women had already settled their accounts and were ushering their families down the gangplank. One was leaning against the railing as Ludwig went by, sobbing as she clutched her young son. He reckoned she could not pay her passage, and the people she thought might help her had not come yet. There was certainly time, he told himself, but she was obviously terrified at the prospect of having her son purchased by a family different from the one who chose her.

Ludwig hurried along, wanting to settle up with the Captain as soon as possible. He knew they had some money left and thought it would cover all they had purchased onboard. He would feel better once they had left the ship.

Barbara met Ludwig on the passenger deck at the bottom of the stairway, clutching their funds in an old handkerchief. They climbed back onto the deck to where the line to see the Captain had formed.

The better part of an hour later, they were breathing more easily. Their expenses were less than they had thought. Now they could gather the girls and finally put the ship *Francis and Elizabeth* behind them. The eight Massenbach adults had agreed they would go into the city together, remain together, and find a place to stay. They were counting on finding a boarding house but had heard some immi-grants had to spend their first nights sleeping on the streets because there were no rooms to be had. It was said Germans with kind hearts often met the ships and offered their brothers and sisters assistance. They hoped this would happen for them.

CHAPTER 45

Disembarking

The last thing Adam had to do was retrieve Kitty's chest from the storage area. Hans went down with him, and when they eventually located it, Adam sat down on the floor and put his head in his hands.

"Oh, my God," Hans said. "This is terrible." Kitty's chest was pushed up against a few stray barrels of putrid water, which had leaked all over one one side of the chest. They could both see the lid had been cracked in three places by someone trying to force the lock open. Adam finally got up, placed the three pieces of blue-green painted wood on top of each other and looked into the trunk. He could easily see it contained less than half of what had been in it when they boarded the ship. Adam had taken a few things out of it, but not many. He could not make out what had been taken, but he was certain Kitty would. Adam hoped the thieves had not taken the clock her grandfather had made; it meant almost as much to her as the chest. He rummaged around a bit, but did not see anything that looked like the wooden timepiece.

"Do not worry, Adam," Hans said. "Tell Kitty I will be able to fix it so the damage will hardly show."

"On we go, then," Adam said. "I will carry the wet end, and you can take the other. I will be glad when this is done with."

Kitty was even more upset to see the chest come out of storage than she had been to see it go in. Her husband and Hans set it down in an out-of-the-way place, and she began to assess the damage. The clock was gone. All of the linens she had spent her teenage years hemming, were mostly gone and the ones left had been stained by the filthy water. It hardly seemed worth it to carry it off the ship, but Adam was not about to suggest that. They were able to use some of the empty space to carry their other belongings and almost all of Hans'. Adam and Kitty had thought they would have to wait on the dock while the others went to find housing, but now it would not be necessary. Adam and Hans could carry it between them without much difficulty

After they were all together on deck and the Mullers had relayed their sad tale about the chest, they started down to the docks, waving goodbye here and there to their shipboard friends. "Perhaps we will meet again," was heard as they parted.

The girls and women were as astounded by the Philadelphia docks as their men had been. The three mothers held onto their children while the five men tried to make a protective ring around the group. They moved cautiously, led by Ludwig because he was the tallest. Hans and Adam followed behind with the chest as a barrier to any trouble.

They listened for their German language. They heard what they thought was German, but for some reason, could not understand it. They knew that different forms of the language were spoken in different areas, and such had been the case on the ship. Ludwig called it a dialect.

The group wandered along the dock, trying to avoid being run into or over. Carriages and carts were everywhere. They made note of a few food stalls they could return to if need be, but wanted to press on until they found a place to stay for the night. Noon was fast approaching.

The men spread out, asking everyone who looked like they might be German where they could find a boarding house. They were ignored, side stepped and laughed at. After an hour of this, they became wholly discouraged. They had been told Philadelphia was a friendly city, but did not now believe it. A couple of people were willing to give them directions to one house, but when they got there it was full, with no chance of any room in the near future.

But luck was finally with them. Gabriel heard language he understood and stopped two men so he could talk with them. Ludwig quickly joined in.

"Excuse me," Gabriel started, "we are newly arrived from the State of Wurttemberg and are looking for a place to stay with our families. Do you know of such a place?"

The taller man, probably the father, doffed his hat and welcomed them to Philadelphia. He explained he and his son had come from Alsbach aboard the snow *William and Mary* in 1738.

The younger man, who appeared to be about eighteen, said, "I was only fourteen, but now Philadelphia is my home, too."

The two newcomers sighed with relief at having met someone who might be able to help them. The men seemed agreeable and friendly, even though Ludwig knew he and Gabriel were dirty, travel worn, and looked like good-for-nothings.

Gabriel continued, "We are looking for a boarding house. Do you think we might find one? We are three families and two single men, thirteen of us in all."

The father, who had introduced himself as Herr Tolener, asked his son if he thought the family staying with the Merners was still there or had moved on to Lancaster County. The son said he was not sure, but they could find out. It was only a short walk.

CHAPTER 46

A New Home

The small gaggle of new British citizens followed the Toleners a short way until they came to a large, four-story house located on the southeast corner of Walnut and Fourth Streets. The house was a pristine white, with manicured gardens, and a large stable they could see in back of the house.

Herr Tolener told them to wait in the street while he went inside. After a short while another man joined him, a Herr Merner who was obviously German as well.

Herr Tolener told them there was room for them to stay in Herr Merner's shed. He used it for storage for his import business, but there was nothing in it now. He was waiting for another shipment, which would arrive toward the end of next month. The shed was unheated, of course, but the weather had not yet turned cold and they seemed to have brought plenty of blankets with them. There was a pump in the courtyard, and they could help themselves to all the water they needed. If they wanted meals included, Mistress Merner would be happy to oblige.

Stephen and Ludwig turned back to the other adults, explained the situation, and they agreed the price was more than fair. In fact, it was practically nothing. They all breathed a sigh of relief. Just an hour before they had not known where they would lay their heads for the night.

Gustav Merner introduced himself and said they were welcome to stay in the shed, but no longer than a few weeks. His said his wife did not like him to rent it, especially to immigrants, and here he whispered, "Even though she and I and our two children were in the same situation you are in ten years ago." He led them around to the back of the house where a large, one-story, frame building took up most of the yard. He unlocked the door and led them in.

"It is not much, but it sits on piers so the floor is not too damp. I see you have pallets, so you can spread them out on the floor and make yourselves at home."

The shed was quite large, much longer than wide. Along two of the walls were several tiers of shelves, and on the back, a large south-facing window, which would let in a good deal of light. A door stood in the middle of the east wall, and they thought it most likely went to the outside. Large boards together with saw horses were piled on the floor under the window. Herr Merner told them he used them to make tables so he could store some of the more fragile goods from his business.

He went on to say he had a store down on Water Street where he sold a variety of small wares—combs, hats, knives, all sorts of things he imported from London and Bristol. He also had various fabrics and trimmings, all of which were sold, he added, at very reasonable prices.

The shed housed all the merchandise that would not fit in the store. When most of it was gone, he sold the inexpensive things to the hucksters and put the nicer items in the basement of his house. He was always afraid of someone breaking in and stealing the stock out of the shed. Nothing was ever stored in the basement of his store, however; it was close to the wharves and full of rats. Mistress Merner did not like rats and would not have her husband going down into the shop basement for any reason.

"You know the price," he said. "I would let you stay here for nothing, but the mistress says we cannot be giving outright charity to immigrants. They might get it into their heads they can live the rest of their lives and never work." He stopped here and rolled his eyes as he smiled mischievously. "We can feed you, too, morning and night. Would you like that?"

After Ludwig and several of the others nodded, he clapped his hands and said, "Splendid, then. It is settled. I will bring out a couple of lanterns when it starts to get dark. The privy is over behind the stable."

Ludwig and the others started pulling out their pocketbooks, but Mr. Merner said, "No need for that now. We can settle up tomorrow."

After he left, the group quietly stood there, even the children. Even Christina. They had a safe place to sleep, food to eat, and the floor—for the first time in ten weeks and three days—was not moving. They were exhausted and dirty, but happy and feeling full of hope.

The men set up a table near the door. They also found over a dozen small, empty barrels they could upend and sit on around the table.

Barbara suddenly began to cry. She sat down on one of the small barrels and covered her face with the end of her apron.

"What is the matter, Frau Fridberg?" Lisabeth Kohler asked with concern. Ludwig heard this and came over to his mother, pulling a barrel up beside her.

"I suppose I am only tired. Tired and relieved," she said as the adults circled around her.

"Yes, but we are in America, and we are all grateful for our great good luck in finding Herr Merner and a place to live. At least for a few weeks." Everyone agreed.

"Come," Hans said carrying another barrel to the table. "We can finish unpacking, and then we can all wash up by that glorious pump that has fresh water in it.

"Fridbergs," Hans said, "you take that corner, and the Kohlers can have the other. Adam, you and Kitty can stay along the wall there, and Stephen and I will sleep by the door in case anyone tries to come in."

"And what are you going to do?" Gabriel teased. "Wrestle them to the floor and tie them up? Or invite them in for a good night's sleep?" After making an assortment of faces at Gabriel, Hans invited them all to get busy.

Everyone spread out. They had been packed together for so long, they could not resist the opportunity to sleep so their bodies did not actually touch. There was at least a foot between each pallet so their "bedroom" took up most of the shed. Stephen and Hans brought in Kitty's chest from outside and found, after putting the top somewhat back together, they could use it as a sideboard.

By this time, Christina was sitting in a circle in the middle of the floor playing a game with the the two Kohler girls. Barbara was so happy with her little daughter. She vowed Christina would certainly be the first to have children. Lisabeth was happy, too.

The weary immigrants pulled out their eating implements and took them out to the pump to give them a good scrub. No one had any food left, except for Barbara who still had some olive oil. Kitty found the vinegar she knew she still had, putting it on top of her chest with a genuine smile.

After what seemed like only an hour or so, Herr Merner opened the door and came through holding three lanterns. He lit them and placed two on wrought-iron hooks on either side of the room and the third one on the table. "Oh, good," he said. "You found the casks. I forgot to mention them." As he turned to leave he said, "Betsy should be out soon with your supper."

When the table was set, Gabriel asked everyone, even the children, to stand. He wanted to say a prayer.

"We have not been to church in months," he began, "have not even seen a Pastor. But...I know we have all prayed, sometimes silently and sometimes not. ('Like when we thought the ship was going to sink,' Carlie said in a low voice.) But let us bow our heads, and I will say a prayer, and then anyone else who wants to can speak."

For the next while they thanked God, over and over, for bringing them to America, all of them safe and sound. They told what they were grateful for, and how they could not have made the trip without their faith. At the end, Christina said, "Thank you, God, for getting us off that tippy boat."

Suddenly, the door shot open and a young girl entered carrying a large pot full of something hot. Barbara rushed over and helped her bring it to the table. She assumed this must be Betsy.

She must be a servant, Barbara thought. *Here we are, in America, being waited on by a servant.*

She turned around and began dishing out the hot, luscious smelling stew. The thirteen new citizens of Philadelphia settled into a meal they had not had in months.

Not for the faint of heart, Barbara thought. *Not for the weak. But for the faithful. Those who waited upon the Lord and waited for the good things in life to come.* It was then she realized she would not have to die to feel comfortable and truly loved by God. It could happen right here, right now, in their New Land.

Family of
Johan Jacob Fridberg

JOHAN JACOB FRIDBERG
Born: 13 May 1701, State of Württemberg, Holy Roman Empire
Occupation: Schoolmaster
Died: 18 Mar 1735
Father: Andreas Fridberg
Mother: Anna Elisabetha Muller

WIFE: MARIA BARBARA NELLINGER
Baptized: 12 Jun 1701, Massenbach, Württemberg, H.R.E
Married: 24 Nov 1722, Massenbach, Württemberg, H.R.E
Buried: 24 Nov 1790, St. Michael's Lutheran Ch., Philadelphia, PA
Father: Johan Jacob Nellinger
Mother: Maria Sybilla

CHILD 1: LUDWIG JACOB FRIDBERG
Baptized: 25 Sep 1723, Massenbach, Württemberg, H.R.E.
Buried: 16 Nov 1781, St. Michael's Lutheran Ch., Philadelphia, PA
Occupation: 1756 Butcher

CHILD 2: BERNHARDINA DOROTHEA FRIDBERG
Baptized: 9 Jan 1727, Massenbach, Württemberg, H.R.E.
Buried: 23 Sep 1784, German Lutheran Burial Gr., Philadelphia, PA

CHILD 3: JULIANA CATHARINA FRIDBERG
Baptized: 24 May 1728, Massenbach, Württemberg, H.R.E.
No record of her exists after 1742 in either Massenbach or Philadelphia

CHILD 4: CARLINA JULIANA FRIDBERG

Baptized: 2 Nov 1729, Massenbach, Württemberg, H.R.E.

Buried: 22 Mar 1730, Massenbach, Württemberg, H.R.E.

CHILD 5: JOHAN WILHELM FRIDBERG

Baptized: 25 Apr 1732, Massenbach, Württemberg, H.R.E.

Buried: 25 Apr 1732, Massenbach, Württemberg, H.R.E.

CHILD 6: CARLINA FRIDBERG

Baptized: 4 Nov 1732, Massenbach, Württemberg, H.R.E.

Buried: Philadelphia, PA

CHILD 7: CHRISTINA CATHARINA FRIDBERG

Baptized: 26 Jun 1735, Massenbach, Württemberg, H.R.E.

Buried: Philadelphia, PA

Acknowledgements

I would like to say thank you to everyone who encouraged me in this endeavor. Those who showed faith in my abilities and skills have been my partners in creating this story, which I have wanted to tell for so long.

The staff at the Winslow Public Library deserves much of the credit. I did not step one foot outside of Maine to access the books I needed for any of the research I did. They tapped the Maine InterLibrary Loan system as well as WorldCat to find the information I needed to tell this story. Their suggestions for where and how to proceed were invaluable.

I would also like to thank those who read the early version of the book and provided me with helpful suggestions. They are: Claire Prontnicki, Jeffrey Short (fellow Fridberg ancestor), Marcel Duhamel, Annabeth Rynders, and Megan Landry (medical consultant). Most helpful was Ellie Duhamel who encouraged me and helped me sort through how to put this part with the other and hang which adornment on which piece of infrastructure. I only wish she were still here to see the final product.

And last of all, I would like to thank my teachers—all those in college courses, adult eduction classes, community classes, and workshops who taught me the basics and the fine points of effective writing and encouraged me to use them. Rod Labbe and Kim Sedlock are the most recent of these mentors.

I would also like to give a shoutout to the Universe, which day after day gently rained its goodness onto my keyboard and then went off to make us a nice cup of tea.

Reading List

Ancestry.com. *Massenbach Church Book*, Lehi, Utah, 2022

Burgert, Annette Kunselman. *Eighteenth Century Emigrants, Volume 1: The Northern Kraichgau*, Breinigsville, PA, 1983

Fogleman, Aaron S. *Hopeful Journeys: German Immigration, Settlement, and Political Culture in Colonial America, 1717-1775*, Philadelphia, PA, 1996

Scheer, Teva J. *Our Daily Bread: German Village Life, 1500-1850,* North Saandich, BC, 2010

Wokeck, Marianne S. *Trade in Strangers: The Beginnings of Mass Migration to North America*, University Park, PA, 1999